Brutally Honest:
Discovering a God You Can Trust With Your Deepest Wounds and Darkest Desires

A Contemporary Parable Based on Psalm 109

By Paul Coneff and Lindsey Gendke

Jesus spoke all these things to the crowd in parables; he did not say anything to them without using a parable. (Matt. 13:34, NIV)

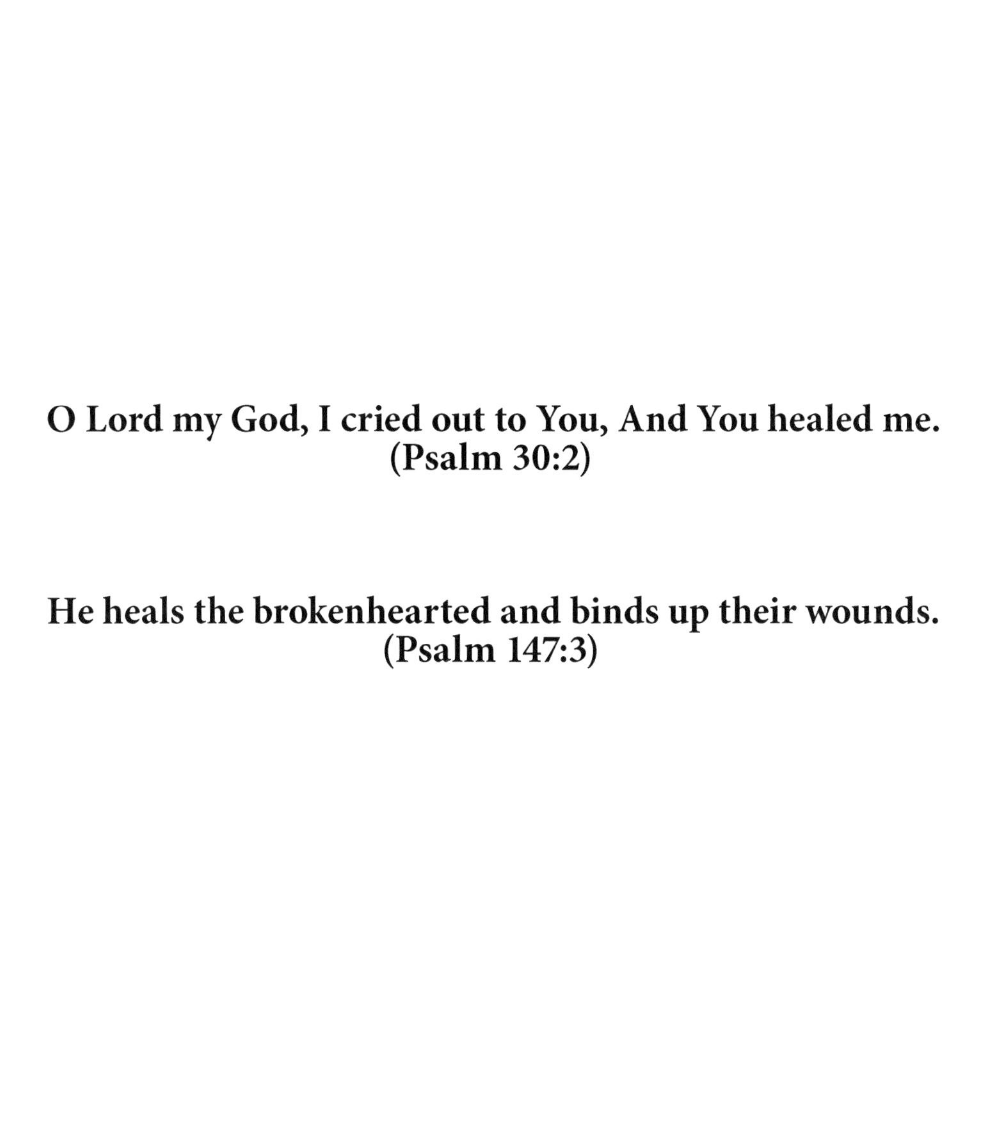

O Lord my God, I cried out to You, And You healed me.
(Psalm 30:2)

He heals the brokenhearted and binds up their wounds.
(Psalm 147:3)

LithoTech
Berrien Springs, MI
Credits:
Images of the fruit tree and Christ carrying His cross:
Designed by Cristina Coneff

Image of the heart on the cross: Designed by Jed Lewis

Front and back cover design by Cristina Coneff

Cover image: AdobeStock_183320926

It is the authors' sole discretion to capitalize every reference to Jesus (He, Him, His, etc.) throughout the book to honor Him as our Lord and Savior.

Disclaimer: Everyone struggles with feelings of anger, frustration, fear, grief, etc. While the information, Scriptures, and prayers in this book are intended to address those feelings in the context of discipleship, they are *not* intended to be a substitute for any treatment by medical or mental health professionals.

Dedication

This book is dedicated to our "Abba" Father. Many see Him as the "bad cop" who is against us, while Jesus is the "good cop" who is for us.

My prayer is that we will discover the freedom to:

- Trust in God's faithfulness to **us** when we have been deceived, betrayed, rejected, abused, controlled etc. *(which is the opposite of trusting someone who has violated our trust)*

- Trust that our Father's heart is big enough, compassionate enough and strong enough to see, hear, and heal our deepest wounds *behind* our darkest desires in a **process** of healing and freedom *(which is the opposite of offering a quick-fix approach that will not work)*

- Trust that His **process** of seeing us, hearing us, and walking with us in *daily, on-going* conversations will lead to deeper healing and freedom in our own hearts – and sharing His heart of compassion with others

STRAIGHT 2 THE HEART'S TRAINING MINISTRY IS DESIGNED FOR THE LOCAL CHURCH

This book shares Straight 2 the Heart's prayer and discipleship process through a combination of Scriptural study and fictional characters in the story. It is *not* a training manual. Training opportunities and other resources are offered through our ministry website, www.hiddenhalf.org.

Professional counseling needs to be offered by someone with professional training. Professional counseling is also different from the discipleship process shared in this book.

Straight 2 the Heart's discipleship process has been specifically designed to be used in the church environment by non-professionals, even as many professionals are using our resources with their clients.

We have intentionally designed the discipleship process to create safety for the person receiving prayer. This includes preventing church members from sharing "solutions/judgments" such as "you just need to have more faith," "just believe," "just try harder," "if you were really surrendered . . . " etc. (Please count the number of "Christian clichés" in this skit showing how the person "listening" fails to hear the heart of the person sharing her pain and loss: [Youtube] God Never Said That: Promo 2 - LifeChurch.tv)

Instead we emphasize the power of listening to and honoring the person's story first and foremost. Next we offer to pray with the person at God's throne of grace to receive the faith, strength, hope, and victory that Jesus has already gained for them through His suffering, death, and resurrection.

It is also important to understand that we are not offering "quick fixes" *(or diagnosing problems, offering unsolicited advice, or making judgments)*, because we understand that the journey of healing and freedom in Christ is an ongoing process. That said, the power of connecting our stories of suffering with Jesus' story of suffering in prayer and discipleship definitely offers real anchor points of hope and change in the journey of healing and freedom (Col. 2:6-7; 1 Cor. 15:31; Gal. 2:20).

* This is a book sharing scriptures and stories with examples of praying Jesus' story into a person's story. We keep praying and discipling the person so he or she can move into ministry, with a testimony, in their community as they experience the *whole* gospel for the *whole* person so it can go to the *whole* world.

* **And again, this book is not a training manual.** Training is a "hands-on" experience where a mentor trains you to pray with someone multiple times. And then you move from the role of facilitating prayer for someone to being trained to mentor someone else to pray with others.

Just as Jesus spent quality time *with* His disciples in person (3.5 years + 40 days after His resurrection + having them pray for 10 days), this kind of "hands-on" training cannot take place through a book or manual.

Contents

Authors' Note

Twenty-five years ago, a professor in my master's program, Dr. Calvin Thomsen, commented on a paper I wrote about Psalm 109. He said, "This is a fresh look at Psalm 109... you should consider developing it into a book." While it is probably too late to get extra credit in his class, I have finally followed through on his suggestion with my cowriter Lindsey Gendke, a quarter of a century later.

It is written in the form of a fictional story with characters we have created to help us see:

1. How we can move from *knowing* Bible truth intellectually to *applying* Bible truth personally.
2. How we often struggle to be honest with ourselves, with God, and with others.
3. How we can receive healing and freedom in Christ as we learn to trust God with our deepest wounds and darkest thoughts—wounds and thoughts He already knows about.

So while the truths from God's Word are real, the characters are not real, they are fictional, and they do not represent any individuals. All of our own stories are unique in many ways, even as the themes may overlap with those in this book, or the stories of other real individuals.

We have also condensed key lessons about the process of prayer and discipleship into this story so you can "see" what it looks like—even as discipleship is a process that takes place over time in the context of Christ-centered, caring relationships.

Our prayer is that you will:

1. Let the truths of God's Word and HIS-story speak into your own story.
2. Connect your story with Jesus' story in a way that moves you into ministry, with a testimony, in your community.

FOREWORD

I first learned of Paul Coneff in 1990 when he began using music from a production I'd worked on to help heal survivors of sexual abuse. From the beginning it was clear to me that he had a heart for sharing the love and compassion of Jesus Christ with people suffering from deep pain and trauma wounds.

But it was not until we sat down for dinner one evening when he was visiting Nashville that I fully understood his unique way of presenting the suffering of Christ that is consistently supported by the events recorded in scripture.

When he explained to me that Jesus had been broken in every way that we are broken I was finally able to see the hidden half of the Gospel that you will learn about in these pages.

In speaking with Lindsey Gendke I've discovered her heart for helping people find connections and share their stories, moving past clichés to the deeper truths that God has for all of us. This kind of honesty, which may be uncomfortable at first, is the necessary work of healing our hurts.

The title of this book completely captures the spirit of Psalm 109. It is a Psalm where David is brutally honest, speaking out of a place of deep pain. Only a God big enough to deal with this kind of honesty is big enough to worship. That's the God you will meet in these pages.

It is a rare calling to walk with others in their pain. Coneff and Gendke do that here, offering guidance and support for the healing journey. Along the way you'll find new ways to think about prayer, and a deeper understanding of forgiveness. In the process you'll discover the path to a healthier relationship with our marvelous Creator God and to healthier relationships with others.

As you read may you find the hope of Christ and be set free to walk in the light of His love.

—Steve Siler, May 2019

Steve is the President of *"Music For the Soul" and the author of The Praise and Worship Devotional and Music for the Soul, Healing for the Heart: Lessons from a Life in Song.*

Chapter 1
What Makes You Angry?

Sondra's Story

"What makes you angry?" The question reached the kitchen table where Sondra slumped, head in hands, poring over newly arrived divorce papers. Her two girls, four-year-old Autumn and six-year-old Alice, sprawled on the rug below her, coloring. The two girls were miniature versions of their mother: wavy auburn hair, green eyes, and dimples when they smiled. But none of them smiled much these days.

"C'mon, everyone. What makes you angry?" The question came again from the living room, muted by the kitchen's closed double doors, from Gary, a tall, slender guy who was leading the Bible study.

Lost in her thoughts, Sondra didn't heed the question, but let it hang in the air. She had let her parents know, clearly, that she would not be joining them for the Bible study tonight. For two weeks, she had been hiding out in their home, and she wasn't yet ready to be seen.

Gary's slate blue eyes scanned the small group before him. Tim and Elizabeth, the middle-aged parents of Sondra, sat on the couch opposite him. Jeff and Sheila, a couple in their early forties, sat on two folding chairs to his left. And Zach and Caitlyn, the pastor of their church and his wife, sat on a loveseat on his right. Gary waited for a response from the group.

On the other side of the door Sondra paused from her papers and raised her eyebrows. *Really?* Was she hearing this right? Was God toying with her?

"Did we all come to this meeting today with happy hearts and perfect lives? Anybody blow up at a family member while trying to get here today? Anyone see something on the news that makes your blood boil? Anyone got coworkers that tick you off?"

The group members chuckled, but no one said a thing.

What makes me angry? Ha. Where do I begin? Sondra blinked back tears. *How about being here today, for one. How about living with my parents again for the first time since I was twenty-one? How about being suddenly single and broke?*

At thirty-one, with a bachelor's degree, two beautiful daughters, and a beautiful face herself, Sondra was supposed to be in the prime of her life. For the six years of her marriage, she'd had to regularly flash her wedding ring to fend off men. But now, the one man who should have stood by her was gone. Cory had left a couple months ago, saying he just couldn't commit to one woman for the rest of his life.

Sondra shook her head, dark curls brushing her shoulders, as if to clear her thoughts.

"Talk to me, guys," Gary tried again. "I know we're Christians who aren't supposed to 'get angry,' but you can be honest." Gary paused, but still, no one spoke.

"Okay, let's try coming at it from a different angle. I was attending a conference for pastors and I jokingly asked the registrar if there were any presentations on how to strangle church members and not go to prison. Without blinking an eye, she said, 'No, but if there is one, please let me know, I definitely want to attend.'"

Gary laughed, as did everyone else.

"So, I know we have anger in the church. Now, let me ask again: What really makes you angry?"

"My wife taking too long to get ready!" a male voice offered.

"My husband not asking directions when we get lost!" a female voice added.

Laughter erupted.

Despite herself, Sondra rose from her chair and tiptoed to the double doors. Those two voices sounded familiar. She peered through the crack, trying to glimpse the owners of the voices.

She caught their profiles immediately, and she drew in her breath and pulled away from the door. It was Zach and Caitlyn! High school sweethearts. Her friends from academy. She hadn't talked to them in about a dozen years, since high school graduation. *Great. Fun reunion that'll be, comparing life stories.* Sondra hoped to delay that reunion for as long as possible.

"What else makes you angry?" Gary asked.

"Dishonest politicians," Tim offered.

"As if there are any honest ones!" a deep and commanding voice responded.

Sondra leaned forward once again to look, this time, on the other side of the room. The voice belonged to a man around age forty with sandy blond hair and laughing eyes. Sondra squinted. Was that Jeff? It had to be. Sitting beside him was Sheila, his wife. Sondra had served punch at their wedding when she was fifteen. But how Jeff had changed!

Sondra remembered Jeff being slightly overweight and very ordinary during her teens, when she'd attended church with her parents. Now, years since last seeing him, he'd shed the excess weight and sculpted his muscles.

He'd traded slumped posture for strong, broad shoulders. He looked like someone she would have dated during her college days. She found it hard to look away, and didn't realize that she had actually pushed the door open a crack and was staring, one-eyed, at Jeff.

"That's good, guys," Gary chuckled. "Taxes, politicians. No argument there." He paused. "Anything else make you angry?" His voice softened. "How about things hitting a little closer to home? Do we have any problems in our church, in our families, that we like to pretend aren't there?" At these words, Sondra gazed to the middle of the room, where Gary sat straight across from her in a folding chair. Tall and slender, with thinning blond hair but a full smile, he looked to be about her dad's age.

"Child abuse."

"Racism."

"Sexism."

"Someone who cheats on his wife and leaves his family struggling to survive financially." Those words came from Tim, her father, whose back was to Sondra and who didn't know she was listening.

At this last answer, Sondra startled, bumping the door with a small thud.

She gulped and whirled back, the swinging door folding her into the safety of the kitchen, but not before Gary's eyes met hers.

"Those are great responses," Gary said. "All of those can make us angry inside and lead to bitterness." He shifted in his chair, considering the woman behind the door. Tim and Elizabeth had shared just a little about their daughter's pending divorce, and how they hoped she would eventually join their Bible study. *Lord, please speak to her tonight*, he prayed silently. *Please let her hear this message and begin to feel some hope.*

Roots of Anger

Gary looked away from the door and gazed at Tim and Elizabeth, who sat directly in front of him. "Did you realize that anger is a secondary emotion?" he continued. "We feel angry because we feel threatened somehow, or we've lost control, or because we've been hurt. There is a root there, and it goes deeper than anger."

He paused, and Sondra did too. She stood frozen, too scared to peek through the crack again, but unable to step away.

"Let me ask you a question. Why would we choose to use anger to protect ourselves? How does anger make anything better? How does it make us *feel* better?"

In the silence that followed the question, Sondra slipped to the table and grabbed a kitchen chair. She set it down gingerly near the double doors and sat facing her girls.

Alice looked up with delight. "Mommy, are you watching us?" She wasn't used to her mother's full attention these days.

"Shhh, yes, I'm watching," Sondra whispered, leaning forward, arms on thighs. "I'm watching you color those pretty pictures. Can you draw me a picture of a unicorn? And Autumn, can you draw me a picture of a princess and her castle?" She hoped that unicorns and princesses would divert her girls long enough for her to listen to what Gary had to say.

When no one answered him, Gary said, "Let me rephrase the question. What's *good* about anger? Is there a good kind of anger and a bad kind of anger? Is there a type of anger that can actually, *legitimately*, protect us?"

"Sure, like when an adult realizes a child is being abused and takes action to stop it." That came from Zach.

"Great answer. There are times when anger is helpful; it activates a response where action needs to be taken, and it leads to a positive outcome. But what about other types of anger? Can we be so angry that it infects our lives, and the lives of others, until we destroy relationships with others, with ourselves, and even with God?"

Sondra clenched her jaw. It was like he was talking directly to her.

"How do we know the difference between good and bad anger? And how do we heal from the bad kind?" Gary got quiet, as if he had all the time in the world, as if there really were an answer to his question.

Sondra snorted. She leaned back in her chair and crossed her arms over her chest. Was this man, Gary, suggesting that it was even *possible* to get over the betrayal she'd suffered, and the anger she faced as a result? *Just try,* she mentally dared Gary. *Just try to tell me to get over my anger.*

"Over the next few weeks, we're going to look at how Scripture addresses anger in a real way. But tonight, I want to lay some groundwork for our topic, to show how the Bible is relevant to where we are right now, no matter whether we struggle with anger, fear, panic, worry, anxiety, addiction, you name it."

Chapter 2
The Hidden Half of the Gospel

Jesus' Story

"I'm bored, Mommy." Autumn looked up from her coloring book.

Sondra sighed for the millionth time in the past two weeks. "Here." She fumbled her iPhone out of her pocket. "You can play your princess game on Mommy's phone."

In the past, she would have tried harder to entertain her daughters. But since Cory's crushing announcement, she could hardly muster energy to keep everyone clothed and fed. While she resented having to stay at her parents' house, she was grateful for their support. She knew she was letting her girls down, sleeping late, hiding under three showers a day, pretending to look for work while surfing on the Internet—but with her mom at home with the girls, she could afford to check out a little. She just couldn't deal with the full responsibilities of being a mother right now.

With Autumn thoroughly engaged on the phone, Sondra crumpled again into the hard back of the kitchen chair to continue listening to Gary.

A Gospel for Those Who Have Been Sinned Against?

"Typically, we hear that the gospel of Jesus is three things:

1. He died
2. He rose from the dead
3. He gave us forgiveness of our sins.

"And that's great and completely true…*as far as it goes.* But what does that gospel offer us when we are living with pain and lies from abuse? From betrayal or rejection by a spouse? How can that gospel heal us from addictions we just can't break? How does that gospel help us when we keep blowing up in anger, no matter how hard we try not to? How does that gospel help us forgive people, like our parents, or a spouse, who have caused us pain and suffering?

"In other words, how does the gospel that Jesus died to forgive my sins help me when I was the one *sinned against?* How does a gospel of forgiveness for my sins help me when I am hurting?"

Sondra stared blankly at her hands. No one in the living room spoke.

"Don't know how the traditional gospel helps in those situations? I didn't know either. And it frustrated me when church members or my pastor told me to 'lay it down at the cross.'

"It frustrated me to hear about the 'new life' that Christians were supposed to get when they accepted Christ. Did Christ's promise of new life only apply to certain things in life? Did it mean we could be free of drinking, for instance, but we couldn't be free from anger? Did Christ come to offer us partial freedom, or did He come to give us full freedom?"

Sondra knew the answer to that. Her parents had quoted her the verses just recently. "Get rid of all bitterness, rage, and anger…forgiving each other as God in Christ forgave you" (Eph. 4:31–32). Those words echoed in her mind, and they made her even angrier. Just how was she supposed to put off those emotions that came as naturally as breathing?

"Jesus came to offer us *total* freedom and restoration. And He did it by including more in the gospel than we usually talk about."

The Hidden Half of the Gospel

In the living room, Gary leaned in, locking eyes around the group. "There is a 'Hidden Half' of the gospel that is clearly supported in the Bible, but often overlooked by Christians."

Tim cocked his head. "What do you mean by the 'Hidden Half' of the gospel?"

"In a nutshell, it's the suffering of Jesus," Gary responded, "and what that suffering means for our suffering."

"Okay, Tim said. "I'm interested. Tell me more. What does the suffering of Jesus mean for our suffering?"

Sondra's ears perked up. *Good question.*

"Well, perhaps the best way to say it is to use Jesus' own words. Jesus said, over and over again, as did His disciples and other Bible writers, that He came to *suffer*, die, and rise from the dead for our sins. He didn't just die for our sins, but He also died for our suffering.[1] Hebrews tells us He suffered 'in every way' we suffer so He could be our merciful and faithful high priest and offer us help in our time of need. That right there is the basic pillar of Straight 2 the Heart: Jesus suffered so He can understand us, relate to us, and heal us, when we are suffering."

"Okay," said Tim. "That sounds good.

> Because He Himself suffered when He was tempted, He is able to help those who are being tempted. (Heb. 2:18, NIV)

---

[1] See these Scriptures for more on the suffering of Jesus: Luke 9:22; 22:15; 24:24–27, 44–46; Acts 3:18, 24; 17:2–3; 26:22–23; Heb. 2:9–10, 17–18; 4:14–16; 5:7–9; 13:12; 1 Pet. 1:11; 2:21, 23; 3:18; 4:1, 13

"Hold on," Elizabeth jumped in. "I'm intrigued, Gary. So, to add to Tim's question, why is your ministry called Straight 2 the Heart?"

Straight 2 the Heart Discipleship Ministry

"Basically," Gary answered, "everything we do at Straight 2 the Heart is meant to get to the heart of the matter, so to speak. It's meant to address issues that we are struggling with *right now*—sensitive issues that, sometimes, our churches don't know how to address in light of the cross. We talk about 'laying our burdens at the cross,' but what does that really look like in the nitty gritty details?

"Well, our goal in all that we do is to connect two hearts at the cross—the heart of our 'Wounded Healer' with the heart of His wounded son or daughter—in a way that is Biblical, personal, and practical. With discipleship groups that pray together and support one another, we can:

a. Move from information about the gospel
b. To application of the gospel
c. So that it leads to transformation in our lives."

Tim nodded. "Sounds good."

"Now," Gary clarified, "Our Bible study here tonight is setting up the *information* piece about Jesus' suffering...and as we progress in our study on anger, I will encourage you to *apply* the information in your own lives through some 'homework.' But ideally, when I work with churches, doing a Bible study or a series of talks, people will benefit the *most* from these teachings if they go on to form small groups."

"Which I'm hoping to do in our own church, after this Bible study..." Zach said, smiling. "But we'll talk about that later. Go on, Gary. You were saying Jesus suffered to help us with whatever sensitive issues we are dealing with..."

"Yes, that's right. Our prayer and discipleship groups are a place where it's safe to bring our deepest wounds and darkest desires—because that's what Jesus wants us to do. He suffered in the most severe ways so He could help us with anything we are going through, whether it's anger, depression, relational issues, or anything at all."

A God Who Understands

"I'm going to list off some experiences, and I want you to tell me: Who are these words describing?

Abandoned	Mocked
Betrayed	Beaten
Abused	Bruised
Tempted	Unjustly treated
Rejected	Unfairly accused

"Okay, that's the list. So, who are these words describing?"

At the exact same moment, Tim said "us," and Elizabeth said "Jesus."

Gary nodded. "It's all there in the Bible, in all four gospels, but also in Isaiah 53, a chapter that predicted Christ's suffering. Isaiah 53 is the one chapter from the Old Testament that is quoted more often than any other in the New Testament. That reminds me."

Gary pointed to his Bible and looked around the group.

"If you get a chance, please read Isaiah 53 before our next meeting. This is a prophecy about what Christ went through for us, and I want you to be thinking about it."

> Isaiah 53 stands as the second-most quoted Old Testament chapter in the New Testament authors—second only to Psalm 110. However, if New Testament allusions are included, Isaiah 53 far outdistances every other Old Testament passage.[2]

He put down his Bible and looked again at the group. "We are abandoned, Jesus was too. We get betrayed, Jesus was too. We are abused. Jesus was abused. We are mocked and beaten, and so was Jesus. We are tempted to numb our pain, and tempted to get angry with our abusers, and so was Jesus."

---

[2] Jonathan Lunde, Following Jesus, The Servant King: A Biblical Theology of Covenantal Discipleship (Grand Rapids, MI: Zondervan Academic, 2010), p. 70.

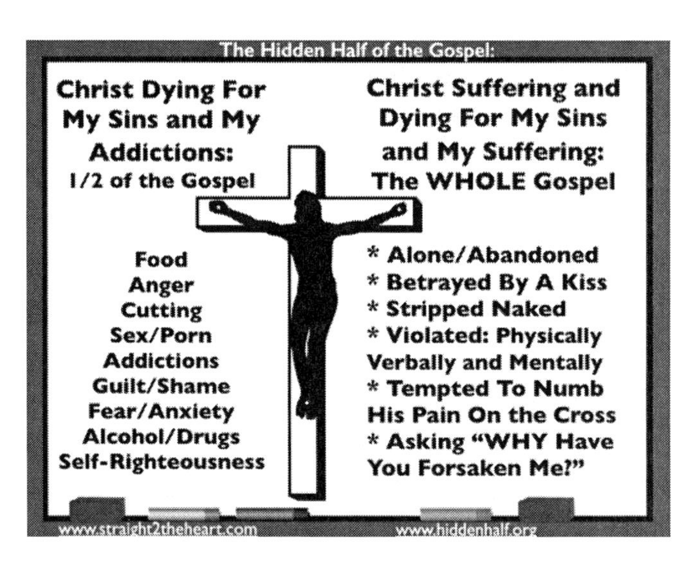

Gary paused again. "Do you think *this* Jesus who suffered can understand us? Do you think He has something to offer us in the midst of our pain and temptations? Pastor Zach knows what I'm talking about."

Gary looked at Zach, who nodded.

"Zach was at the men's retreat three summers ago where I helped present the principles of Straight 2 the Heart's prayer and discipleship ministry. He has a pretty awesome testimony of how the Suffering Messiah changed his life. Pastor, why don't you jump in here?"

Really? Sondra thought. The Zach she had known ten years ago was problem-free. He came from a good family, as far as she knew, he had a clean record in high school, and he found a great Christian woman in Caitlyn. After high school, the two had headed off to a Christian college to do bigger and better Christian things. After college, they were married and became partners in ministry. *They did things the right way*, she thought. *Unlike me.*

How she regretted even dating Cory now. Cory, the good-looking older guy with a Mustang. Cool, non-Christian Cory, who had noticed Sondra waiting tables at the local diner and left a single red rose and a phone number along with his tip.

Now, ten years and two kids later, she was here, hiding, single and ashamed behind her parents' double doors. She felt shut out not just from the society of her old friends, but shut out from God. And so angry! At Cory. At God. At herself.

My life has been such a mistake! I was so stupid! Sondra thought now, head in hands.

She was brought back to the present by Zach's voice.

"Well, I know it might be hard to believe, because you have all known me as your happy, easy-going pastor for the last two years, but I used to be a very angry person. Caitlyn can tell you."

Sondra's ears perked up. When Caitlyn said nothing, Sondra took a chance, stood slowly, and again peered out the doors.

Caitlyn was staring at Zach, eyebrows raised. "You didn't tell me you'd be sharing about this," she said under her breath. "You really want me to tell them?"

Zach held Caitlyn's gaze for a moment, but Sondra couldn't see his face. Then he turned abruptly to the group. "I shouldn't have put Caitlyn on the spot. Let me just suffice it to say that I grew up in a tough home with lots of anger and abuse—I know you guys didn't know that either—and I carried that anger, plus some other baggage, into our marriage. I was able to cover it up from Caitlyn while we were dating, but once we tied the knot, it started to come out, and it was ugly.

"Are you okay with me sharing this?" Zach had turned again to his wife.

The look on her face was hard to decipher. Was she scared, or relieved? Sondra held her breath.

"I'm fine," Caitlyn said quietly, sincerely. "I just didn't know you wanted to share all of this."

"Not all of it." Zack turned back to the group. "That would be too much for our first night. I guess I could sum it up by saying that, after Caitlyn and I left for Seminary in our mid-twenties, while I was completing my studies, we got to the brink of divorce. I was making choices and behaving in a way that no woman should have to put up with."

He looked tenderly at Caitlyn. She was sitting up straight now and gripping his hand, a show of support. Her features had softened, a brave smile warming her face.

"I'm so fortunate that God intervened. After that summer men's retreat with Gary, Straight 2 the Heart's discipleship ministry came to campus, allowing me to hear the message a second time. By then I was ready to reach out and ask for help. The professor prayed with me and another friend of mine, and discipled us on a weekly basis so we could continue praying together on our own. I started to identify with Jesus, how He was tempted to protect Himself with anger and tempted to numb His pain, and I was able to let Him deal with, and heal, my heart. Caitlyn started to see the changes about halfway through the prayer sessions, until she said I was a completely different person."

"Straight 2 the Heart saved our marriage," Caitlyn agreed, turning to the others.

"Well, *Jesus* ultimately saved our marriage," Zach said. "But Straight 2 the Heart led me back to Jesus in a way that finally, *really* made a difference in my life. Before that, I was sincerely seeking to be a Christian, getting my pastor's training. I was hoping that studying the Bible and preaching and teaching it would somehow sink in and fix the horrible person I was. But it wasn't working. Nothing worked, until I prayed with Straight 2 the Heart." Zach paused. "Right, Caitlyn?"

"Right." She beamed at him, and the image of the two of them filled Sondra with both wonder and bitterness. She wondered at what her friends had just shared. What was the full story? How had Zach covered up such an apparently sinful life? And what did he mean that Jesus could actually, *really* make a difference? The picture of their happy marriage reminded her of the life she had wanted for Cory and herself. A picture that was now shattered.

"Well, time is getting away from us," Zach spoke up. "Anybody interested in finding out more about what Gary and I have shared?"

Heads nodded. Sondra backed away from the door, tiptoeing around crayons, forgetting her chair.

Zach continued. "You're in luck. As you know, Gary has offered to run a Bible study group for three weeks on anger so we can see for ourselves how God's Word speaks into our daily struggles in a way that relates to us. And we are grateful for you and Elizabeth offering to host it in your home."

Sondra's head swung back to the closed doors. *Seriously? Three more weeks?* Her parents hadn't told her this Bible study would be ongoing. She'd thought it was a one-time thing.

She pictured the entire church filing into parents' living room, watching her life unravel piece by piece.

Pastor Zach continued to talk about meeting details. Meanwhile, Sondra heard coats shuffling and Bibles closing. Things were wrapping up.

Must get out of here, Sondra thought, shooing her girls out of the kitchen. She knew she would have to face Zach and Caitlyn at some point, but not today. She just didn't know how she would talk to them without crying. A sweeping glance caught her divorce papers, and she snatched them from the table. "Let's go," she urged Autumn and Alice. "I've got fruit snacks in our room for you."

****

A few minutes later, the guests had left and Elizabeth headed for the kitchen.

Thud. One of the doors met with an unexpected bump, and Elizabeth's head barely escaped as it swung back her way.

"Oof!" Elizabeth uttered, her shoulder taking the blow.

"Are you okay?" Tim called from across the living room. He was putting folding chairs back in the closet.

Gingerly, Elizabeth slid the opposite door open and craned her neck into the kitchen. That's when she saw the abandoned chair by the door and crayons on the floor.

"Tim, come look at this!"

In a moment, she felt her husband's warm breath on her neck.

He whistled. "Looks like the scene of a drive-by Bible study."

"Yeah," Elizabeth mused, wide-eyed.

"So." Tim turned to his wife. "Do you think Gary's talk got to her?"

"It must've." Elizabeth nodded. "As Gary was talking tonight, I couldn't stop thinking about her. I think this could really help her."

"I know," Tim added. "And I was thinking of forcing her to come next week by reminding her that we're providing room, board, and child care."

"You wouldn't!" Elizabeth guffawed.

"Oh, I would." Tim nodded solemnly.

"Tim! She's not twelve!"

Tim coughed and said under his breath, "Acts like it sometimes."

Elizabeth didn't argue.

"But..." Tim continued, "I think what we have here is evidence that I don't have to force her to do anything. God is already working on her." He picked up the chair and walked it back to the table. "You just watch." He set the chair back where it belonged as Elizabeth stooped to gather crayons. "She'll be here next week."

"I hope you're right." Elizabeth crossed the kitchen and turned on the faucet to do her nightly dishes. Under her breath she prayed, *God, thanks for getting my little girl to Bible study tonight. Please bring her back next week.*

Your Turn: Read Isaiah 53

Who has believed our message and to whom has the arm of the Lord been revealed?

2 He grew up before Him like a tender shoot, and like a root out of dry ground. He had no beauty or majesty to attract us to Him, nothing in His appearance that we should desire Him.

3 He was despised and rejected by mankind, a man of suffering, and familiar with pain. Like one from whom people hide their faces He was despised, and we held Him in low esteem.

4 Surely He took up our pain and bore our suffering, yet we considered Him punished by God, stricken by Him, and afflicted.

5 But He was pierced for our transgressions, He was crushed for our iniquities; the punishment that brought us peace was on Him, and by His wounds we are healed.

6 We all, like sheep, have gone astray, each of us has turned to our own way; and the Lord has laid on Him the iniquity of us all.

7 He was oppressed and afflicted, yet He did not open his mouth; He was led like a lamb to the slaughter, and as a sheep before its shearers is silent, so He did not open His mouth.

8 By oppression and judgment He was taken away. Yet who of His generation protested? For He was cut off from the land of the living; for the transgression of my people He was punished.

9 He was assigned a grave with the wicked, and with the rich in His death, though He had done no violence, nor was any deceit in His mouth.

10 Yet it was the Lord's will to crush Him and cause Him to suffer, and though the Lord makes His Life an offering for sin, He will see his offspring and prolong His days, and the will of the Lord will prosper in His hand.

11 After He has suffered, He will see the light of life and be satisfied; by His knowledge my righteous servant will justify many, and He will bear their iniquities.

12 Therefore I will give Him a portion among the great, and He will divide the spoils with the strong, because He poured out His life unto death, and was numbered with the transgressors. For He bore the sin of many, and made intercession for the transgressors. (NIV)

For Further Study

Read *The Hidden Half of the Gospel: How His Suffering Can Heal Yours* by Paul Coneff and Lindsey Gendke. This book, based on the principles of Straight 2 the Heart ministry, tells the story of how Jesus suffered to identify with *us* in our suffering.

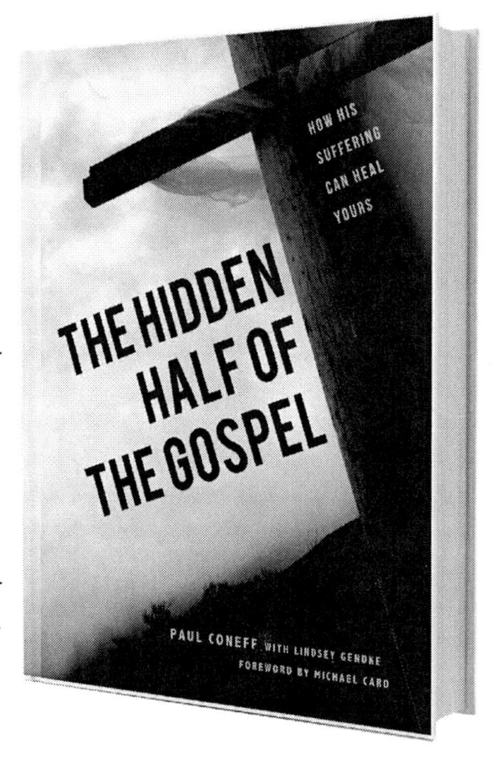

Walk with Jesus through Gethsemane to Calvary along with a group of real individuals who found Jesus to be a "very present help" in the midst of their own suffering and went on to share his love and grace with others. Stories include recovery from depression, abandonment, betrayal, shame and guilt, physical and sexual abuse, pornography and cocaine addictions, and rejection.

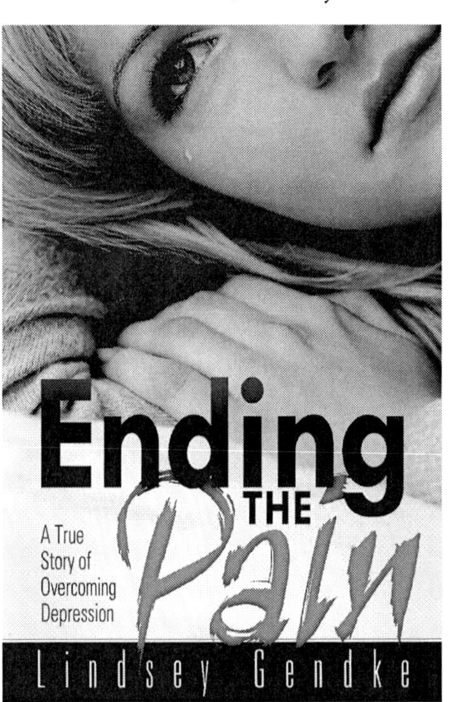

You can also read author Lindsey Gendke's story of moving from despair to hope in her memoir, *Ending the Pain: A True Story of Overcoming Depression*. Read how God not only saved Lindsey from suicide, but also answered the deepest desires of her heart and moved her into a ministry offering living hope to others.

Chapter 3
God's Timing

Sondra's Story

One week later on Monday night Elizabeth sat on the couch, in the same place she had sat last week, and Sondra was nowhere to be seen. Jeff and Sheila had just arrived and were taking their places on the folding chairs to her right. Tim was showing Zach in.

Elizabeth checked her watch again. Six-forty-nine. They were supposed to start at seven.

"Hey everyone!" Zach announced, slipping off his winter coat. "Caitlyn texted me from work to say some friend needed a favor… or something like that—but she said she'll join us as soon as she can."

Elizabeth leaned over to Tim, who had just plopped down beside her. "Are you sure you haven't heard from Sondra all day?" she hissed.

Tim raised his eyebrows, unfazed. "Nope. Last I heard was same as you heard. She left this morning to 'job hunt'." He placed air quotes around "job hunt."

Elizabeth crumpled back into the couch. She had invited her daughter to this Bible study last week and reminded her again this morning, but both times Sondra had just shrugged and said nothing. She hadn't said much about anything all week, in fact, sleeping in late every day and letting Elizabeth get the girls off to school. It was only after her parents left for work that Sondra appeared. And on the days Elizabeth didn't work her nurse's shift, Sondra ditched the house as soon as she could. Sondra clearly didn't feel like talking, and for once in their relationship, Elizabeth wasn't forcing her. She had learned that pushing Sondra didn't work.

Since Cory had picked up the girls three nights ago, Tim and Elizabeth had seen and heard from Sondra even less. She *said* she was job hunting today, but with Sondra staying out until midnight the last three nights, Elizabeth knew that wasn't *all* she was doing.

"Should we get started?" Tim asked the group, and Elizabeth's head swung to glare at her husband. Did he have to act so nonchalant about this?

Right then a tap sounded at the door.

"That'll be Caitlyn," Zach said, rising for the door.

"Here, let me." Jeff, sitting closest to the entrance, rose and opened the door with one fluid movement.

"Hey Cait…" Jeff did a double take. "You're not Caitlyn!"

Everyone craned their necks to see who it was.

"Sondra!" Elizabeth breathed. Framed in the doorway was her little girl, rosy-cheeked, windblown, and beautiful as ever in a fitted black coat, felt gloves, and designer boots. She looked dressed for a night out, but instead, here she was, at Bible study.

"You made it." Elizabeth squeezed Tim's hand. He glanced at her as if to say, "See? Told you so."

"Sorry I'm late," Sondra mumbled, suddenly self-conscious. She half-turned and motioned beyond the door. "Come in, quick, and warm up."

Next it was Caitlyn bustling through the doorway, then a last gust of frigid February air before Jeff pulled the door closed. In the confusion of coats and scarves and gloves coming off, Jeff was able to drink in the dark-haired beauty before him virtually unnoticed. It was a vision that would have caught any adult male's eye, but especially the eye of someone who remembered her as an awkward teenager.

"Wow Sondra, long time no see!" he said.

"I know." Sondra blushed and looked down.

"Yes, it's great to see you," his wife, Sheila, added.

Everyone knew Sondra had been staying at her parents' home for the last few weeks, but until now, no one had mentioned her name in the large group.

"Were you able to help your friend?" Zach asked Caitlyn, as she sat down next to him.

"Well, yes…" she grinned, and then turned to motion to Sondra, who blushed. "Sondra here needed a ride."

"Oh?" Elizabeth's eyes drifted to her daughter.

"My car broke down." Sondra shrugged, annoyed by her mother's apparent curiosity.

"Oh no!"

"Yeah, I guess it was God's timing," Caitlyn said to Elizabeth.

By now, everyone else was looking on, so she turned to address the group. "I had just sent a friend request to Sondra on Facebook. I said I was going to your house," she motioned to Elizabeth, "and Sondra accepted my request and told me she was sitting at the library without a ride."

"Really?" Elizabeth could hardly contain her pleasure.

Sondra looked away to hide her rolling eyes. She did not add that Bible study had not been her intended destination that night. In reality, she had intended to finish her job hunting and then go out drinking, as she had done the past few nights…but then her car hadn't started. She didn't tell her mother, and she hadn't told Caitlyn, about the pang of conviction she'd felt at the engine's choked rumble, and finally her angry prayer, zinged at God like a rock:

God, are You kidding me? Really? Now? Are You trying to tell me something? God, You better give me something here, some sign that You're still up there and You care!

She'd marched back into the library then, reopened her laptop, and logged into Facebook. And there was Caitlyn's friend request. Waiting for her answer.

"What timing," Elizabeth marveled.

"Yeah," Sondra wilted, unable to disagree. The timing was pretty hard to ignore. And then Gary's Bible study on anger. It seemed pretty clear that God wanted her here, that He wanted to help her somehow.

Okay, God, she prayed inwardly. *You did a pretty good job getting my attention tonight. I don't know what You want from me next, but I guess I'll keep my eyes open.*

Right beside her, Elizabeth was saying her own prayer: *God, thank You! You used a broken-down car to drive my girl to Bible study tonight! Your timing is perfect!*

Out loud she said to her daughter, "So is your car still at the library?"

"Oh shoot! Yes!" Sondra's head snapped up. "That reminds me. I've got a job interview for tomorrow morning at Benjamin Franklin Elementary School. But we're supposed to get some freezing rain tomorrow. I doubt if I can get my car towed and fixed before then."

Sheila had been listening from across the room and now she stepped closer to join the conversation.

"Sorry, did you say you have an interview at Ben Franklin?"

"Yeah, that's right."

"Well Jeff does his rounds over in that part of town in the mornings. He's usually just driving around at that time, right, Jeff?"

"Huh?" Jeff looked up from a conversation with Gary.

"I was just saying you do rounds over in the west side of town in the mornings. Sondra needs a ride tomorrow morning to Ben Franklin. I'll be stuck at work, but I thought maybe you could take her." She looked expectantly at Jeff.

"Oh!" Jeff's eyes lit with understanding. "Sure!" he turned to Sondra. "You just let me know what time you need me to pick you up, and I'll make sure you get a police escort to your job." He grinned at the damsel in distress in front of him, enjoying the thought of his new rescue mission.

"But there might be bad weather..." Sondra said.

"No problem," Jeff shrugged. "Even if it's freezing rain, that's no problem; police officers don't get days off for bad weather!"

Sondra exhaled gratefully. "Thank you, Jeff. That would help me out so much."

"And thanks for the ride here, Caitlyn," she said, turning to her old, yet new friend. "I guess things are working out, in some ways," she said softly, more to herself than anyone else.

Chapter 4
The Angriest Prayer in the Bible: Part 1

A Study on Psalm 109:1–16

"Well, please carry on," Sondra gestured to the group. "I know you probably already started." Without making eye contact with Elizabeth, she sat beside her mother on the couch, Zach and Caitlyn on her left.

"Actually, we were just about to start," Gary assured her, "so your timing was perfect. Nice to meet you, Sondra, by the way! I'm Gary." Gary leaned over the coffee table between them and extended his hand.

"Nice to meet you too," Sondra replied, shaking his hand.

"Hear that?" Tim whispered in Elizabeth's ear. "God's timing is perfect!"

"Zach, why don't you begin with a word of prayer?" Gary asked.

"Sure."

Everyone bowed their heads as Zach prayed: "God, Thank You for bringing us all here safely. We give this time together to You. As we read Your Word, help it to speak to the different challenges we face in our lives, and draw our hearts closer to Your heart. Amen."

"Thanks, Zach." Gary looked at the group. "Let's jump right into our topic of anger with a Psalm that is known as the most hostile of all the Psalms. It is Psalm 109, and it is so *angry*, so hostile, that it was the only Psalm never used in Jewish worship." Gary raised his eyebrows and grinned a little. "Are you ready to see what an angry King David sounds like?"

The group nodded and murmured affirmatives.

"Okay then." Gary opened the worn Bible on his lap. "Let's tackle Psalm 109, verses 1 through 16, tonight."

Elizabeth pulled an extra Bible from the coffee table and slipped it into Sondra's hands, grateful it was going to be used tonight.

"I want us to take turns reading a couple verses out loud. I'll start by reading verses 1 through 5," Gary said.

Do not keep silent, O God of my praise!
2 For the mouth of the wicked and the mouth of the deceitful have opened against me; They have spoken against me with a lying tongue.
3 They have also surrounded me with words of hatred, and fought against me without a cause.
4 In return for my love they are my accusers, but I give myself to prayer.
5 Thus they have rewarded me evil for good, and hatred for my love. (Psalm 109:1–5)

Why Is David Angry?

Gary put down his Bible and looked up. "Why is David asking God not to be silent?"

Jeff studied the verse for a moment before speaking. "Well, clearly David is under attack. It says wicked people are lying and talking smack about him and…" he rechecked the verses. "They are fighting against him, undermining his leadership. And David wants revenge!"

Sondra kept her eyes fixed on her Bible, as if rereading the verses. In reality, the words swam before her. *What must everyone think of me?* she couldn't help wondering.

"Right, good," Gary said. "Anything else there? Any indication as to who is doing this to David?"

"Well," Sheila said, "David says he loves them."

"Yes, good. So, if David loves these people, are they his friends, or are they his foes? And what difference does it make?"

Now Zach spoke. "If David loves them, that must mean they are friends. It means he has some history with them. He must have some good memories with them, but now, apparently, something has drastically changed. They've turned against him."

"They've betrayed him," Caitlyn added.

"Good, guys," Gary said. "Obviously, it always hurts when someone attacks us. But what hurts more: being betrayed by an enemy, or by someone close to us?"

"Someone close to us," almost everyone said. But Gary noticed that Sondra kept silent.

"Yes," said Gary. "David's been betrayed by a friend. Unfortunately, betrayal is often a painful part of leadership. Dan Allender, in his powerful book on leadership, *Leading With A Limp (p. 31),* puts it like this: 'If you lead, you will eventually serve with Judas or Peter . . . . It is like looking at ten people who serve on a committee with you and wondering, Who will take my words and soak them in kerosene and attempt to burn down my reputation?'"

Zach nodded with knowing. "I can relate to that. I'm a young pastor, but already I've learned that I can't make everyone happy. Dealing with disgruntled church members, and their hurtful words, is a real concern for pastors. I can feel some of David's pain, there."

"Yes," Gary said. "So we can start to understand why David is really angry."

Gary shifted in his seat. "Now, here's a transition: he says he is giving himself over to prayer in verse 4." He paused briefly to let that sink in. "Is turning to God to pray a good response?"

Tim nodded. "The best!"

"That really shows maturity," Elizabeth added. "Most people in that situation would not pray as a first response."

"No kidding," Jeff chortled. "I know I wouldn't!"

"You're right," Gary said. "Jeff, would you read the next verse, please, and everyone take turns reading two verses after that. Also, as we read through verses 6–16, let's ask ourselves one simple question: Would we want David praying for us?"

Key Question: Would We Want David Praying for Us?

Jeff took a moment to find his place in his Bible and then read in a strong voice:

> 6 Set a wicked man over him, and let an accuser stand at his right hand
> (Psalm 109:6)

Sheila picked up where her husband left off:

> 7 When he is judged, let him be found guilty, and let his prayer become sin.
> 8 Let his days be few, and let another take his office.
> (Psalm 109:7–8)

Tim read the next two verses, and as Tim read, Gary looked around to see the response. Most were staring intently at their Bibles, but Jeff soon started to chuckle.

9 Let his children be fatherless, and his wife a widow.
10 Let his children continually be vagabonds, and beg; Let them seek their bread also from their desolate places.
(Psalm 109:9–10)

"Wow." Tim finished his verses and turned to look at his wife and daughter. "He doesn't stop! He goes after the whole family! Gary, I already know I don't want David praying for me…well, maybe if the wife makes me mad!

"Care to continue?" he nudged Elizabeth.

She frowned at her husband. "Watch it, buddy. The wife may be a widow, but the man here is dead!" Then Elizabeth looked down calmly and continued.

11 Let the creditor seize all that he has, and let strangers plunder his labor.
12 Let there be none to extend mercy to him, Nor let there be any to favor his fatherless children. (Psalm 109:11–12)

Elizabeth shook her head and turned to Sondra, who picked up in a surprisingly strong voice:

13 Let his posterity (future family members) be cut off and in the generation following let their name be blotted Out.
14 Let the iniquity/sin of his fathers be remembered before the Lord, and let not the sin of his mother be blotted out.
(Psalm 109:13–14)

Finally, Zach and Caitlyn read the last two verses.

15 Let them be continually before the Lord, That He may cut off the memory of them before the earth;
16 Because he did not remember to show mercy, But persecuted the poor and needy man, That he might even slay the broken in heart. (Psalm 109:15–16)

Gary let a space of silence fill the room after those final words.

Zach had been through the Bible study before and waited with Gary in amusement for a collective reaction. Jeff and Tim were chuckling. Sheila's eyebrows arched in confusion. Caitlyn and Elizabeth looked at Gary expectantly. And Sondra, finally, for the first time, looked up and caught his gaze. Her eyes, once aimless and cloudy, now stared deep and fierce.

Gary held her gaze for just a moment before he blinked and said, "Okay, so what does everyone think? Remember, this is David, who was known to be a 'man after God's own heart.' What are some words to describe how he's feeling here?"

"He's really ticked off!" Jeff said. "Or can I use a more colorful word?" Sheila gave him a hard elbow. "Jeff!" she hissed. "No, you cannot!"

"Well, it's true," Sondra piped up, with no humor whatsoever. "I can think of some colorful words that describe David's feelings as well."

"He is definitely upset," Zach agreed, with an encouraging smile.

"He wants revenge—in a big way. David wants this man, his wife, and his whole family to suffer as much as possible…in *every way* possible!"

Gary's eyes twinkled at the lively discussion. "Are there any other words that come to mind?" he asked.

"Maybe 'raging' or 'livid,'" said Tim. "David is raging mad."

"Definitely right, to all those descriptions." Gary rose and approached a whiteboard he had set up near his chair. "Let's write down 'anger' here, just to sum things up, knowing that *rage, revenge, hate,* and *the desire to see someone else suffer* are all very much a part of it. What else do you notice? What are some specific ways David is handling his anger? Even when he's 'in prayer'?"

David's Form of "Anger Management"

Sheila glanced around the group and, when no one spoke, said, "His words here are just terrible. I can hardly believe they're in the Bible! There's no way to justify this level of hostility to another person."

"I see your point, Sheila," Elizabeth said. "It's kind of scary how hateful he sounds in this chapter. It says he wants his enemy's wife to be a widow, and their children to be fatherless." She glared at Tim. Tim put up his hands in mock defense.

Caitlyn piped up. "It also says he wants the widow and children to live in poverty, having their home destroyed and all they own taken away. He wants them to be reduced to begging—and for no one to give them any pity or kindness."

Gary nodded. "Good. Good discussion, guys. And if all that were not enough, David wants entire generations of this man's family, from *before* and after, to be completely cut off and forgotten by the world. You can't get much more thorough than that!" Gary sat back down before asking, "Thoughts, anyone?"

Zach leaned forward. "My first thought is *how ironic* David's words are. Just think of it: he's complaining to God because this man *didn't have mercy on him*...and yet, David is asking God *not to have any mercy on the man!*"

"That's true, Zach," Tim jumped in. "In a way, David has become just as vengeful as his enemy."

Gary nodded. "Interesting, isn't it? Can you see how anger blinds us?"

"Definitely," Elizabeth mused.

"Any other thoughts or comments?" Gary asked.

"What does he mean by having generations cut off?" Sondra asked. "Especially the generations that came before this man?"

"Good question. Let's look back at verses 13–15 again. Phrases like, 'Let his descendants be cut off, their names blotted out from the next generation,' 'May the iniquity of his fathers be remembered before the Lord,' 'cut off the memory of them from the earth,' and so on.

"In Hebrew culture, his words all mean variations of the same thing. David is asking God to make sure this family is lost forever, in every possible way. He wants God never to forgive them, never save them, and never redeem them. And he wants all human record of them to be erased, so that they have no worldly connections and no heritage or history to be remembered."

"Wow," Sondra said.

"Yeah." Gary smiled wryly. "Basically, David wants the other guy—and his whole family— to suffer, so that he knows what kind of pain David is in."

There was an awkward silence after that, so Gary continued: "It creates an interesting dynamic when we've suffered, but then want to inflict suffering. Actually, Dan Allender put it really well in his book *The Healing Path.*" Gary looked down at his notes and read the following quote:

> We want relief from our pain. We want someone to care [for us] and comfort us, but we also want justice, vengeance. The dark desire to make our betrayer pay places us in the *strange position of being both victim and abuser.* (Dan Allender, *The Healing Path,* p. 64, emphasis added)

Sondra looked down at her hands. *I know how that feels.* Images of slashing Cory's tires or setting fire to his house flitted through her mind. She would never say it here, but her desire for revenge was about as potent as King David's.

Summary of Psalm 109:1–16

Gary cleared his throat. "Let's go back over some of the verses we've discussed tonight. Jeff, why don't you summarize verses 2 and 3 for us? Then Sheila, if you could do the same for verses 4 and 5, and Tim, verse 8, from what we read today? As you summarize, I'll write down your responses so we can review what we've learned about the man, about David's prayer for the man, and where Jesus can identify with David in this painful experience."

Jeff looked down at his Bible. "From verses 2 and 3, we see that this man and others made false accusations against David. They've lied about him for no reason."

"Thanks, Jeff," Gary said, writing down "false accusations, lying" on the board. "Sheila? What do your verses say?"

"These men were friends of David's, but then they turned on him, returning evil for good and hatred for friendship. And they want to take advantage of some situation where he is broken hearted, so they slay him or kill him."

Gary nodded solemnly. "In other words, betrayal at many different levels—from people David trusted." Sondra winced as Gary wrote "betrayal" on the board. "Alright, Tim. You're next. What does verse 8 tell us about this man?"

"Well, we know David definitely wants this guy to die. It also sounds like he has some sort of official leadership position."

"Good." Gary wrote "leader/official position" on the board.

(see summary in column 1 on the next page)

What we know about this man and his family:	What David wants God to do to this man: (and family)	What Jesus has gone through to identify with David and us:
1. Wicked, deceitful 2. Making false accusations and lying 3. Betrayal/hatred from someone David trusts and loves 4. Leader/official position with no mercy – seeking to slay/kill David when he is broken hearted		

"And yes, David does want to see this man die because of all he's done." Gary paused from writing to address the group.

"Actually, it's interesting to note that Psalm 109:8 is a fulfillment of prophecy, and is quoted in Acts 1:20, as part of Jesus suffering to identify with us. Just thought I'd throw that in."

> For it is written in the book of Psalms: "Let his dwelling place be desolate, and no one live in it;" and, "Let another take His office." (Acts 1:20)

"Can we look at the verses again? What else does David want God to do to the man and his family?" Gary paused as the group reread the verses and called out answers. He wrote down the following in the second column: *(see summary in column 2 on the next page)*

What we know about this man and his family:	What David wants God to do to this man: (and family)	What Jesus has gone through to identify with David and us:
1. Wicked, deceitful	1. Judge him in court	
2. Making false accusations and lying	2. Make his prayer sin	
3. Betrayal/hatred from someone David trusts and loves	3. Man dies–his family become beggars	
4. Leader/official position with no mercy – seeking to slay/kill David when he is broken hearted	4. Have no mercy for him or his family–with all the generations before and after him being lost forever	

"As we look at this list, can we all agree that David's words and desires here are not good? That it's not good to essentially tell God that He should grab a few of the lightning bolts He has lying around and use this man and his wife and children for target practice?"

That brought out a few smiles and laughs.

"Right," said Zach. "Not good at all. I think I'll pass on having David pray for me, at least when he's angry at me."

"So, what are we to make of David's words here?" Gary prodded.

"Well, it's hard to know," Sheila said. "Like I said earlier, it's hard to justify David's words, no matter what the other guy did. I mean, does God want us to pray this way when we're angry?" She looked genuinely perplexed.

Does God Want Me to Respond Like David When I Am Angry?

The group mulled it over for a moment, and then Jeff said, "Could this be an example of the Old Testament 'eye-for-an-eye' theology of wanting justice? I agree that David's words are kind of sociopathic, but it sounds like he has some really good reasons to ask for revenge. So…I don't know…maybe this is telling us that sometimes it's okay to *pray* for justice?"

"Hmm, there is definitely an element of Old Testament theology in this psalm," Gary mused. He turned to the rest of the group. "It's true, many people operated on that 'eye-for-an-eye' mentality back then. But the man is *lying* about David. Is that the same as generations before and after being lost and cut off from salvation? No. It is way beyond an 'eye-for-an-eye' principle. But it raises the main question you guys have been driving at: If David's harsh prayer is inspired by the Holy Spirit and it was okay for *him* to respond this way *to God back then,* how should *we* respond when we are wronged and *we* want revenge?"

Jeff grinned and shrugged. "I suppose wielding my police badge and pointing my gun isn't the answer you're looking for?"

Gary smiled at the joke, as did others, but he kept quiet...as did everyone else.

Finally, Sondra sighed and said, "I really don't know. It feels natural to want to hurt someone back." After a long pause, she added, "But in my head, I know that's wrong. David's words seem wrong to me, especially since they're in a prayer!"

"David's words are not what most Christians would expect to read in Scripture," Gary agreed. "Let's go back to the point we all agreed on: David's words are not good. So let's look at it another way: what is good about David's anger?"

Chapter 5
The Angriest Prayer in the Bible: Part 2

A Study on Psalm 109:1–16

What Is Good about David's Prayer?

"Well, at least he's praying," Caitlyn ventured. "And I guess that's a good thing. He's talking to God—and he's being brutally honest about what he wants."

"Right," Zach agreed. "And he's not actually going out and *doing* all those things to this man and his family. That's a positive!"

"Excellent! That's exactly the point here: David is being honest with God. David is not perfect, but he is authentic—something that, sadly, a lot of Christians struggle with."

Jeff whistled and shook his head. "I never would have thought about the fact that David is being honest with God here. If I heard someone making these threats, I'd just think 'get a restraining order!' He sounds out of control."

Gary nodded in acknowledgement of Jeff's words. "What does it mean to you to think about David being so open and honest with God? If David actually prayed this prayer, and if God thought it was worth showcasing in the Bible, what might that say about God's character?"

What Does Psalm 109 Say about God's Character?

Tim spoke now. "In many ways, this prayer is very unexpected and challenging. But it is kind of freeing to realize that David's God is a God who can handle such honesty—and that He is still the same today. He's not a fragile God, shocked into falling off His throne because of David's brutal honesty and his desire for revenge. Besides, when it comes right down to it, God already knows our deepest, darkest thoughts and feelings."

"That's true, Tim," said Gary. He turned to Zach now. "Zach, would you please read Psalm 139:1–6, to support what Tim has just said? And then go ahead and tell us what it means to you."

Lord, You have examined me and know all about me.
2 You know when I sit down and when I get up. You know my thoughts before I think them.
3 You know where I go and where I lie down. You know everything I do.
4 Lord, even before I say a word, You already know it.
5 You are all around me–in front and in back–and have put Your hand on me.
6 Your knowledge is amazing to me; it is more than I can understand (Psalm 139:1–6, NCV)

Zach looked up from his Bible. "David is saying that God knows all my thoughts and my words before I even say them. If I can share those freely and honestly with Him, then I have a God with big shoulders. He can handle anything I lay on Him."

Gary leaned forward with a smile. "That's a great way to put it, Zach. It's as if God is saying, 'Now we can have a real conversation.'" He sat up straight now and lowered his voice.

"However, it's been my experience that many Christians don't feel like they can share their darker thoughts, feelings, and desires with God. Or with each other, for that matter."

He looked around the group. "Anybody here ever paste on a smile at church when you really felt horrible on the inside?"

"Oh, definitely," Caitlyn nodded.

Sondra snorted. "Forget playing church," she said, barely audible. "I just stopped going."

Elizabeth flashed her daughter a brave smile. Others nodded sympathetically.

Zach said, "You're not alone. I think a lot of people do that. In fact, I *know* a lot of people do that."

Sondra nodded, head down.

"You guys are spot on," Gary concurred. "So often when we're angry, we just shut down. And that means, instead of growing closer to God, we are actually separating ourselves from the only One who can bring us healing and peace."

Sondra busied herself with warming her cold hands. Zach's and Gary's words penetrated her heart somehow. *That's how I feel,* she thought. *I feel separated from God.* She placed her hands under her legs, continuing to mull over the discussion, and then a simple, yet profound thought came to her: *I thought I felt separated because God left me alone...but am I the one keeping us apart?*

Why Brutal Honesty?

"Let's take this honesty theme a bit further," Gary said. "We've established that the good thing about this Psalm is David's honesty. Now, let's personalize this in the context of our *own* anger. Why is it important to be honest with God and with others when we're angry, or hurting, or dealing with *any* emotional problems?"

"I can speak to that," Zach said. "Think of it like this: if we had a flesh wound or a physical disease, what would happen if we just covered it up and never treated the infection?"

"It would just continue to fester and get worse," Sondra answered.

"Exactly. Like I shared last time, I had a rough childhood that left a lot of scars, and until I talked to God and others about them, I could never heal from them. I could look good on the outside, but Caitlyn knows it was just an act."

"Why didn't you talk about it, Zach?" Gary prompted.

"Because I didn't think it was safe or acceptable, especially as a pastor. I mean, most of the pastors *I* know stick to telling *other* people's stories. Right, guys?" Zach looked at the group. "Has that been your experience, too?" Almost everyone nodded.

Gary spoke. "I think you're right. Pastors typically don't like to air their dirty laundry, but I would add that many Christians don't, either." Gary stroked his chin thoughtfully. "So, what would you say it takes for a person to share his or her darkest thoughts, feelings, and desires with others?"

Zach gazed at the ceiling, considering. "For myself, it took an open invitation from other men who were in ministry with me, men who were in a similar situation in life. But even then, it wasn't easy."

"Which is understandable." Gary raised his eyebrows. "Pastors have to be careful about what they share."

Zach nodded. "Yes, we do have to be careful. But at the same time, if pastors, or people in ministry, have deep issues, it's our responsibility to get help for our problems *somewhere*. If we deny that we need healing ourselves, then we will severely cripple our ability to help others."

"That's a great point," Gary said. "It's important to *get help* somewhere, and share our stories *somewhere*, for so many reasons… one being the spread of the gospel. The apostle Paul tells us that the gospel story could not be shared without sharing our own stories (1 Thess. 2:8)."

Tim crossed his arms and cocked his head. "How's that?"

"Well, when we share what God has done in our lives, it brings the gospel close to home. How can we tell others how Jesus' suffering heals our suffering, unless we share our stories?"

"Ah. Good point," Tim agreed.

"Another thing," Zach added. "When we share our stories, we not only heal individually and spread the gospel, but we also create a healthier climate at church. When we create safety within the church to share our stories without giving advice, without trying to 'fix' each other, we can have real community."

"That's true," Gary concurred. "When we talk about brutal honesty, we're talking about lots of things that impact the church. But it all starts with the individual." Gary leaned forward and lowered his voice, to punctuate his next words:

"Many people cannot begin the journey of healing, or even the walk of faith, until they have told their story to someone else. For many people, their greatest need is to have someone hear and honor their losses. Before they can grow in the Christian walk, they need to talk about their being sinned against and hurt. Telling people to 'just have more faith,' 'put the past in the past,' 'you just need to forgive and forget,' 'just be positive and think happy thoughts,' and so on, does a lot of damage. In fact, these clichés tend to add more pain, and often drive people away from God, and away from the church. People who hear these clichés often feel judged and believe church is not a safe place. So they don't talk about their pain; they cover it up."

Gary looked down at his notes. "I like how Dan Allender expands on this temptation to deny our problems and our pain. If you don't mind, I'd like to read another quote from him." Gary picked up the page and read:

> The first great enemy to lasting change is the propensity to turn our eyes away from the wound and pretend things are fine. The work of restoration cannot begin until a problem is fully faced...
>
> There is a natural reluctance to face problems. Christians seem to despise reality. We tend to be squeamish when looking at the destructive effects of sin. It is unpleasant to face the consequences of sin–our own and others.
>
> The journey involves bringing our wounded heart before God, a heart that is full of rage, overwhelmed with doubt, bloodied but un-broken, rebellious, stained and lonely. It does not seem possible that anyone can handle, let alone embrace, our wounded and sinful heart.
>
> *But the path involves the risk of putting into words the conditions of our inner being and placing those words before God for His response.* [3]

---

[3] Dan Allender, *The Wounded Heart: Hope for Adult Victims of Sexual Abuse* (Colorado Springs: NavPress), pp. 14, 19, emphasis added.

Sondra inhaled a long, thoughtful breath. She liked what Gary was saying, and she could relate to David's prayer. As she thought of sharing her pain with someone else, she also felt a small bit of her burden lifting. At the same time, she still felt that she had to try and be more than who she was, to show others what she thought they wanted to see in her. She wondered, *What would it look like to have a safe place to speak openly and honestly?*

"Let's move on to a different point now so we can fill in the third column," Gary said. "We can all probably relate to covering up something at church, because when we're supposed to be Christians who 'have it all together,' it feels risky to show that we're flawed human beings. So, let's talk about who we should share our pain with. I'm sure you know where I'm going with this." Gary smiled.

Elizabeth smiled back. "Jesus," she supplied.

"Jesus. That's right," Gary repeated.

First, Tell Jesus

"When we met last week, we talked about how Jesus was made like us in *every way* and suffered temptation in *all* points just like us. We also touched on some experiences Jesus went through, like abandonment, betrayal, abuse, rejection, and temptation. If you did your homework and read through Isaiah 53, you saw this theme pretty clearly. We learned that because He suffered these temptations, He was able to become the great High Priest who can empathize with us in our weaknesses, allowing us to go boldly to the throne of grace.

"Now, let's apply this to Psalm 109. How can Jesus identify with David being lied about and betrayed in Psalm 109? Can He identify with the temptation to wish harm on others who have hurt Him?" Gary picked up his marker, preparing to write the group's responses on the chart.

How Did Jesus Identify with David?

Jeff responded quickly. "Absolutely. The Pharisees and other religious leaders were always lying about Jesus."

"Judas betrayed Him, after having been a follower and friend of Jesus throughout His ministry," Zach said.

"And Peter lied about Jesus during the trials," added Caitlyn. "He denied knowing Jesus three times, and the third time with cursing."

(see summary in column 3 on the next page)

What we know about this man and his family:	What David wants God to do to this man: (and family)	What Jesus has gone through to identify with David *and* us:
1. Wicked, deceitful 2. Making false accusations and lying 3. Betrayal/hatred from someone David trusts and loves 4. Leader/official position with no mercy – seeking to slay/kill David when he is broken hearted	1. Judge him in court 2. Make his prayer sin 3. Man dies–his family become beggars 4. Have no mercy for him or his family–with all the generations before and after him being lost forever	1. Religious leaders lying about Him 2. Judas betraying Jesus 3. Peter denying Jesus 3x, cursing Him the 3rd time 4. *Tempted* to not have mercy on those hurting Him–*Tempted* to curse them (wish ill on them)

Gary nodded, writing down the responses. "It's easy to find many places where Jesus would have been tempted to respond like David did after he was wronged. And Jesus can still identify with us today when we are hurt by our loved ones.

"Also, since you mentioned cursing, Caitlyn, let me say one quick thing about that. When we see cursing in the Bible, it doesn't mean using foul language; it means wishing ill on others. David is definitely wishing ill on the man and his family."

Gary glanced at the clock on the wall. "And I think we'll have to stop here for the night. But before we close with prayer, I want to ask each of you to be thinking about Psalm 109:1–16 this week week, especially these two important questions:

- What kind of God is able to handle all our thoughts, feelings, and desires, no matter how strong or ugly they may be?

- How is David trusting in God's faithfulness to heal him first, instead of trying rebuild his relationship with the man who has betrayed his trust – with no sign of changing his words and actions?

And remember, we're not just talking about feelings of anger and revenge, like what David wrote about. We can also share fear, panic, anxiety, shame, grief, and guilt with God. It's important because it can help us to know that we are heard, or as David Augsberger has said, 'Being heard is so close to being loved that for the average person they are almost indistinguishable.'"

> Being heard is so close to being loved that for the average person they are almost indistinguishable.[4]

"And now, for your homework assignment for the week…"

Gary pulled a handful of papers out from beneath his Bible and passed them around.

"It's pretty simple, but I went ahead and wrote it out for you to take with you. And you don't have to worry, it's all-voluntary. There won't be a test and you will not be receiving a grade. I just want us to continue increasing our awareness of the negative thoughts behind our negative feelings, and negative desires. Then ask God, *What are my negative thoughts?* And *What negative experiences did Jesus go through so He could be tempted to believe the same negative thoughts I have?*

"I am also including a sample prayer this week that you can rewrite in your own words.

"We'll go over these questions some more when we get together next week, including:

(1) How all of this impacts our picture of God and His character, and

(2) What difficulties we create for God and ourselves when we are unable to be honest with Him."

"Tim, would you like to have closing prayer for us?" Gary asked.

"Sure." Tim bowed his head. "Dear God, thank You for this powerful prayer of David's and how it shows us that You are a God who wants us to be completely honest with You. You already know everything that's in our hearts and minds, and You can handle even our deepest and darkest thoughts, feelings, and desires.

"Thank You for allowing Jesus to be lied about, betrayed by a friend, denied by Peter, and attacked by the religious and political leaders so He could identify with the pain and heartache in our lives. Thank You for walking with us each day this week and helping us to grow into a more honest and trusting relationship with You. In Jesus' name, amen."

---

[4] David Augsberger, *Caring Enough to Hear and Be Heard* (Baker Pub Group, 1982), p. 12.

"So," Gary looked up. "Everyone liking this so far?"

"It's great," Elizabeth said, aware of Sondra's heavy breathing beside her.

"I'm so glad you came," Caitlyn said, turning to Sondra. "Although, I'm sorry your car broke down."

"Ugh," Sondra shrugged. "I guess I was supposed to be here tonight."

"I think so," Caitlyn agreed, their car conversation fresh in her mind. On the ride here, Sondra had given her the basic details of her divorce.

Caitlyn lowered her voice. "Keep in touch. If you want to hang out before next week, please call me. You have my number now. And I'm always willing to listen."

"Thanks," Sondra said. "Maybe I'll be ready to share more soon. Actually," she raised her eyebrows. "I want to hear more about what Zach shared tonight."

Caitlyn nudged Zach with her elbow. "You hear that, honey? You opened the door on our story."

Zach smiled. "I guess I did, didn't I? We probably don't have time right now, but I'll tell you what. If you come back next week, I'll tell the story. Deal?"

Sondra nodded and smiled, too. "Deal." Somehow, reuniting with her old friends made her feel not so alone. And the invitation to consider trusting in God's faithfulness to heal her anger and pain in her heart *first* was growing on her. Naming all the harm Cory created when he betrayed her and their daughters would not be easy, and it was better than living with it inside of her heart. Maybe, just maybe, things were beginning to look up.

Your Turn – Part 1: Review Psalm 109:1–16

What it looks like when David begins to trust *in* God's faithfulness to him:

- **Instead of** giving into the strong temptation to trust in his anger and desire for revenge – as a form of "self" protection and control (false idols that leave us empty) from the pain of the officer who is betraying him
- **Instead of** trying to trust or forgive the officer who is betraying him
- **Instead of** trying to change/control the officer who is betraying him

Do not keep silent,
O God of my praise!
2 For the mouth of the wicked and the mouth of the deceitful have opened against me; They have spoken against me with a lying tongue.
3 They have also surrounded me with words of hatred, and fought against me without a cause.
4 In return for my love they are my accusers, but I give myself to prayer.
5 Thus they have rewarded me evil for good, and hatred for my love.
6 Set a wicked man over him, and let an accuser stand at his right hand.
7 When he is judged, let him be found guilty, and let his prayer become sin.
8 Let his days be few, and let another take his office.
9 Let his children be fatherless, and his wife a widow.
10 Let his children continually be vagabonds, and beg; let them seek their bread also from their desolate places.
11 Let the creditor seize all that he has, and let strangers plunder his labor.
12 Let there be none to extend mercy to him, nor let there be any to favor his fatherless children.
13 Let his posterity *[generations in the future]* be cut off, and in the generation following let their name be blotted out.
14 Let the iniquity of his fathers be remembered before the Lord *[generations in the past]*, and let not the sin of his mother be blotted out.
15 Let them be continually before the Lord, that He may cut off the memory of them from the earth;
16 Because he did not remember to show mercy, but persecuted the poor and needy man, that he might even slay the broken in heart.

Your Turn – Part 2: Applying What You've Learned

What are 2–3 thoughts I have about myself when I have been hurt by others, and/or when I am feeling angry, sad, afraid?	What are 2–3 experiences Jesus went through so He could be tempted with my negative thoughts?
❑ I'm alone/abandoned ❑ Why God? ❑ I'm different ❑ No one under-stands me ❑ I'm not good enough ❑ I'm not deserving ❑ I'm rejected ❑ I'm not wanted ❑ I'm bad/dirty ❑ I can't speak up, have needs, be seen or be safe ❑ I have to perform and try harder ❑ Be in control ❑ I'm a failure ❑ I can't trust/get close to anyone ❑ I'm powerless, helpless, weak, hopeless, useless ❑ I'm not worthy ❑ I can't be forgiven ❑ Can't be accepted ❑ I'm not important ❑ I'm not loved ❑ I don't belong *Self-will Lies*: ❑ I have to trust in my own strength or wisdom ❑ I am good enough ❑ I have no needs in my life ❑ I have to be the center of attention all the time ❑ See how spiritual I am ❑ See how superior I am ❑ I am better than others ❑ My past is in the past (denial) ❑ My security is in being right, knowing more than others, and (or) trusting in religious activities ❑ Other ____________________ ❑ Other ____________________ ❑ Other ____________________	❑ Born to an unwed mother ❑ No father ❑ Had a step-father ❑ Refugee in Egypt ❑ Tempted in the desert after 40 days ❑ Rejected by loved ones ❑ Struggling to surrender His will to God's will ❑ Alone/abandoned by those closest to Him ❑ Betrayed by a kiss, sold for the price of a slave ❑ Stripped naked, physically, verbally and mentally abused by Satan, the Priests, Pilate, Herod ❑ Shamed, humiliated and embarrassed ❑ By men in power over Him who should have been protecting Him and supporting Him ❑ **TEMPTED** to numb His pain when His situation seemed to be hopeless and useless ❑ Had difficulty breathing ❑ Crying out "My God, My God, **WHY** have You forsaken Me?" ❑ Being un-fairly, unjustly accused, arrested, tried, convicted and murdered ❑ **TEMPTED** to take all of His abuse personally ❑ Suffering and dying for my sin, shame, guilt, regret ❑ A Man of grief and sorrows ❑ Other ________________________ ❑ Other ________________________

Your Turn – Part 3: Sample Prayer

**It is important to rewrite this prayer in your own words.*

The more details you include, the more personal and meaningful your prayer will be.

Dear God, Thank You for knowing my whole story, including all the ways I struggle to be honest about my negative thoughts with myself and with You.

Thank You for thinking about my story and having Jesus fulfill prophecy, going through negative experiences in His ministry with family, with friends, and with religious leaders when He: (*I write in 2-3 experiences I checked off in the right-hand column on page 50, in this part of the prayer*)

____

____

____

Thank You for His example in prayer, choosing to be open and honest with You in Gethsemane and again at Calvary when He was tempted with the same kind of negative thoughts I have, that I am: (*I write in the thoughts I checked off in the left-hand column on page 50, in this part of the prayer*)

____

____

____

____

Thank You for taking everything connected to my false identity—with all of my negative experiences, negative thoughts, feelings, and desires—to death on the cross, *in* Christ (2 Cor. 5:19).

I also confess that You raised Jesus from the dead to heal me and set me free to receive my truest, deepest identity as Your son or daughter so I can share with You openly and honestly as often as I need to. In Jesus' name, Amen.

Your Turn – Part 4: Reflection Questions

Please read the five options below and check the one that accurately describes how Jesus responded to temptation during His deepest, darkest moments in Gethsemane and as He was hanging on the cross at Calvary:

Section I: How did Jesus deal with His temptations to believe negative thoughts?

"Jesus answered and said to them, "Most assuredly, I say to you, the Son can do nothing of Himself, but what He sees the Father do."(John 5:19, NKJV)

❑ **1.** Did Jesus push down His temptations to believe negative thoughts in the garden and on the cross? (The "down boy/down bad thought" approach that emphasizes my need to do all the work – in my own strength)

❑ **2.** Did Jesus try to talk Himself out of Satan's temptations to believe negative thoughts in the garden and on the cross?

❑ **3.** Did Jesus try to talk Himself into believing that God loved Him, telling Himself the truth that God wanted the best for Him, that God had not forsaken Him on the cross and that God, His Father, had accepted Him?

❑ **4.** Did Jesus try harder to obey God, try harder to trust in His own behavior, His own performance – in His own strength and try to talk Himself into, and convince Himself that God loved Him and that God accepted Him?

❑ **5.** Did Jesus talk to God about all the negative thoughts Satan was tempting Him with, *immediately, openly, honestly, and continually*, in the garden, and again when He in the garden of Gethsemane? And when He was hanging on the cross?

* Only one option is based on real faith, real trust, real love, real hope, real honesty, and real righteousness by faith IF Freedom =

A deeper and deeper *daily* dependence on Christ.

Section II: Reflection Questions

"Take every thought captive to the obedience of Christ." (2 Cor. 10:5, KJV)

1. What difference does my answer make in my understanding of God and prayer?
2. What difference would it make if I could share with God as openly and honestly as Jesus did in Gethsemane and Calvary and King David does in Psalm 109?
3. Do I take my negative thoughts, feelings, and desires to God like David does, and like Jesus does, sharing them openly, honestly, and repeatedly with God?
4. Do I ask God where Jesus was tempted, in principle, in a similar way?
5. Do I tend to deny my thoughts, stuffing them down or trying to turn them off, and trusting in the "out of sight, out of mind" approach? Or do I try the "talking myself out of them" approach?
6. Do I tend to dwell on them, rehearsing the experience in my mind and/or with others, over and over again?
7. Do the negative people and experiences in my life draw me closer to God or push me farther away from Him?
8. How does David's prayer help me to find freedom from the pressure to try and be more than who I am when I see how:

    a. His prayer is filled with words of brutal honesty, sharing his deepest wounds and darkest desires?

    b. His prayer reveals a deep trust in a God who is big enough, strong enough, and loving enough to handle *my* deepest wounds and darkest desires?

Chapter 6
Marriage on the Rocks
Jeff and Sheila's Story

"So, what did you think of the Bible study tonight?" Sheila asked Jeff as they buckled into the car and pulled out of the driveway.

"Hmmm?" Jeff mumbled, fiddling with the radio.

Sheila curled her fingernails into her palms so she would not snap at Jeff. She was trying not to react out loud when he ignored her, as he often did these days. Whether it was a physical barrier, like a door or a computer screen, or just noise, it seemed he was always putting something between them.

Sheila swallowed her annoyance and tried again. "What did you think of the study tonight? I saw you talking to Gary. What did you guys talk about?"

Jeff fiddled for another moment, finally resting on a sports news channel. "Oh. I just told him he was doing a good job. I thanked him for the Bible study." He turned up the volume a couple notches.

"Oh." Sheila swallowed, wincing at the blaring sportscast.

When Jeff didn't go on, she picked up the papers Gary had given her. "I was looking at these reflection questions Gary sent home with us. I don't know if you saw them, but I thought they were pretty interesting."

No answer.

Sheila pretended not to notice his indifference. "Here's a good question." She picked one at random and read: "'Do I take my negative thoughts, feelings, and desires to God like David does, and like Jesus does, sharing them openly, honestly, and repeatedly with God?'"

She looked at her husband's profile and only waited a moment before forging on. "That's such a good point. I didn't like what we were reading at first, but I see what Gary is saying. If we aren't honest with God, then our negative thoughts are going to poison our lives."

While Sheila studied him, Jeff fixed his eyes on the road ahead, saying nothing. Like so many other times, Sheila felt the sting of rejection. Each time he put this distance between them, it hurt.

"Hey, Jeff. Earth to Jeff!" She tried to keep her tone light, but her anger was hard to mask. "I asked you a question, Jeff. Should I expect an answer tonight? Or maybe you want to put me on your 'to-do-list' for tomorrow? Should I have my secretary call yours so *she* can find a time to fit me in?" She knew she had gone too far, but she couldn't stop herself.

"What, Sheila?!" Jeff suddenly exploded. "What do you want from me? I went to the Bible study, just like you wanted. I could've stayed home and watched Monday night football, but instead I went to this *thing* with you, okay? Isn't that enough for you? Geez."

Sheila crossed her arms tight, to hold herself back from spewing more venom.

"It's not a *thing*, Jeff," she whispered. "It's a study on anger. A problem, if you haven't noticed, that we seem to have in our marriage."

"No kidding." Jeff stared straight ahead, knuckles whitening from clenching the steering wheel. More silence.

She looked at him incredulously. *How can he have so little to say to me?*

She remembered early in their marriage when they both regularly exploded at each other. After the wedding, it didn't take long to find out that they both had tempers, and it didn't take much to set them off. In their twenties, it seemed like they fought all the time over one thing or another, whether who got to choose supper or whose parents to spend the holidays with. They went round and round, hurling insults until they'd exhausted their ammo or someone stormed off. Jeff had been known to kick and punch in the heat of the moment—thankfully, never Sheila—but he had punched several holes in their walls and smashed at least a half dozen dishes.

Sometimes she almost wished he would punch or kick *her*, so she could point to the bruises and *prove* the abuse she felt. In recent years, in which he tended to avoid fighting altogether, she found that her emotions blazed higher and longer than when she actually vented them to Jeff. Being insulted was exasperating, but being ignored was infuriating.

And these days, it seemed like he ignored her all the time.

She wasn't sure what had tripped the switch, but about six months ago, Jeff had just stopped engaging with her. Now they were forty-one, busy with their careers, busy parenting their thirteen-year-old son, and she busy with church activities. Early on the busyness was a habit she had adopted to avoid fighting with Jeff; now it was a habit she maintained to numb the ache of an empty marriage.

But it was becoming so empty. The distance between Jeff and herself had become a gulf that only grew. As time went on, she knew how to reach him less and less. Where she could once count on getting his attention with angry words, she could count on nothing these days.

Now when she nagged him, he withheld even his anger, reverting to silent treatment instead, and she almost couldn't stand it.

That's why, when this Bible study on anger had appeared on their church calendar, she knew they had to go. The topic was certainly on point for their marriage; plus, it gave them a rare activity together. A "desperate date night," she had said to her mother, but not to Jeff. She'd asked Zach to invite Jeff, to beg him to go so he wouldn't be the only younger couple there next to Tim and Elizabeth.

As they neared home, she threw out one last zinger.

"I was just asking a question, Jeff. At least you could have the courtesy to answer me."

And suddenly, he took her bait.

"No, Sheila. You weren't just asking a question. You were putting me down, like you are so good at doing. You were disrespecting me, like you do all the time when I don't give you the answer you want. But as for the question you asked me, here's what I think:

"Maybe *you* should ask *yourself* that question. Do *you* 'take *your* negative thoughts and feelings to God like David does and' . . . what were the words? . . . 'Are *you* open and honest with God?' Huh, Sheila? I don't know if you bring your 'negative thoughts' to God, Sheila, but you certainly bring your garbage to *me*."

He gave a bitter laugh. "Maybe you should try talking to God, first, Sheila. And get the heck off *my* back." They had arrived home, and Jeff had pulled the car into the garage. With a violent turn of his wrist, he killed the engine and jerked the keys from the ignition.

Stunned into silence and frozen to her seat, Sheila watched Jeff throw the driver's side door open, step out, and slam the door shut. In a moment he disappeared into the house.

Chapter 7
A Stormy Ride
Jeff and Sondra's Story

On Tuesday morning Jeff woke to a gray sky and a menacing forecast. When he took his trash to the curb, he discovered that the downy softsnow from the day before now crunched underfoot. When he turned on the kitchen TV, the weatherman predicted freezing rain throughout the day and single digit temperatures by nightfall; he told viewers to stay home if at all possible.

"You still want a ride this morning?" Jeff texted Sondra.

"Yes please," pinged her reply almost as soon as he texted. And then a follow up message a few seconds later: "As long as it's not going out of your way. I can't afford to miss an opportunity; I really need a job! (But only if you're already driving this way!)"

He grinned at the length of the text and its careful punctuation. "That's a woman for you," he muttered, leaning his forearms on the kitchen counter to reread the message and send a quick "thumbs up" icon.

"Are you talking about me?" Sheila approached from behind, and he jumped a little.

"Oh, hey. It's you." They hadn't spoken since their argument the night before.

"Yeah, it's just me." Her voice had lost the sting from the night before and now came out flat. Sheila filled her electric kettle with water and turned it on. *Sorry to disappoint you; were you wanting someone else?* she thought, a small throbbing in her heart. She didn't look at Jeff, but busied herself with unloading the dishwasher while her water heated.

He watched her for just a moment before he remembered to reply. "I was just setting up the ride with Sondra." *At least* one *woman will appreciate me today,* he thought.

"Oh," was all Sheila said.

He thought back to how mornings after fights with Sheila used to be different. They were tense, like now, but it used to be that one of them would apologize to the other. In the past, it was usually Jeff apologizing, because Jeff always took things further, punching and kicking things in their home.

"I'm sorry, Sheila." He used to say. "You deserve better. Can you forgive me?" And she always forgave him, because she knew she wasn't perfect, either.

But now they rarely apologized. The tension hung in their home like a familiar companion, like a pet odor they'd grown used to.

Should I apologize this morning? Jeff wondered, pouring himself a cup of coffee. He hadn't apologized in a long time, because he hadn't blown up for a long time. Last night had been a slip-up.

But I really don't think I did anything wrong. I didn't go looking for a fight. She was the one egging me on.

He thought back to what he'd said to her about taking her ugliness to God instead of to him, and he didn't regret his words. Maybe he regretted the anger with which he'd spoken them, but the words were true.

His thoughts were interrupted by another ping: "I'll be ready in forty-five minutes," texted Sondra.

"Sounds good," he texted back, wishing communication with his wife could be so basic. He picked up the TV remote and sank onto a kitchen stool. *If she wants to, she can apologize. If she doesn't, then that's one more conversation I get to avoid.* He fixed his eyes on the TV screen until, out of the corner of his eye, he saw Sheila leave the room.

****

Sondra was waiting for him by the window. As soon as Jeff drove up, she bounced out of the house and down the walkway to his police cruiser. He unbuckled his seatbelt, leaned over, and pushed the passenger side door open. "Welcome to your police escort; I hope you enjoy the ride!"

She smiled and plopped onto the seat. "Hey, thanks again, Jeff. I really appreciate it."

"No problem, m'lady." He re-buckled his seatbelt and turned to look at her before shifting into gear. "Now, are we on time, or do you need me to turn on my lights and sirens? We can go to this interview in style, if you'd like."

"Gee, thanks," Sondra grinned. "But that's not really the first impression I want to make."

He laughed. "Good point. We'll go the boring way, then."

"Thanks, Officer."

There was a brief pause while Jeff looked both ways and maneuvered onto the icy road. From the corner of her eye, Sondra studied his profile, the solemn, hard jaw. He seemed much more serious here than he had at Bible study. She'd seen him play the joker just last night, but as she squinted through sideways eyes, she noted a certain depth in his brown eyes and strong chin that she hadn't seen before.

Soon the pensive profile evaporated. Jeff turned and asked, "So, how've you been?"

Sondra let out a hollow laugh. "Ha. That's a good question. Are you sure you want to know?" The candid answer surprised even her.

Jeff's eyes widened innocently. "Sure. Why wouldn't I want to know? You're a girl I used to know back in the day . . . boy, it's been awhile, hasn't it? Back in the day when we went to church together. Who doesn't like to find out what past acquaintances are doing with their lives?"

Sondra exhaled. "Well, I guess you've noticed I haven't been going to church much."

"I didn't say *that*. I said I hadn't seen you at *our* church for a long time."

"Well, you would have been right if you'd said the other, too. I haven't been to *any* church much since you last saw me."

Jeff waited for her to go on, but she didn't. "Okay," he prodded. "So what? No judgement here. I'm just a guy making conversation. So, what else is going on? You're back in town now . . . " he trailed. "You made it to a Bible study . . . " he trailed again, then tried, "You're looking very old and grown up now, compared to when you left for college."

"Gee, thanks!"

"I mean that in a good way!"

She studied his profile again, and decided he was sincere. "Well, thanks." She softened. After a deliberative moment, she added, "I guess you probably heard about my divorce."

"Yeah." He glanced at her briefly. "You know how word gets out." He looked back at the road. "I'm really sorry about that." After a pause he added, "You mind if I ask what happened? I mean, I hope you don't mind me saying it, but I think a guy would have to be pretty stupid to walk away from you."

She blushed and looked down at her lap. "No, I don't mind. It's nice to hear someone say that."

"You're welcome." They had exited Tim and Elizabeth's subdivision, weaved through some backstreets onto one of the city highways, and now Jeff was turning on his right-hand blinker for the I-64 onramp, which led over the bridge into the west side of the city. Sondra estimated a ten-minute drive from here to her interview.

"There's not really time to tell the whole story."

"Hey, I don't need a dissertation. A nutshell works for me. If you want to tell me. Or if you don't, I get it, too." But as Jeff said the words, he realized he really wanted to know. What *would* cause a guy to leave a girl like Sondra? She was not only beautiful, but also quick-witted and fun to talk to. He couldn't help himself and asked, "Did you leave *him*?"

He slowed the car as they merged with traffic onto the ramp. He maintained this slower speed until a half mile onto I-64, where a car had spun out on the shoulder of the road. Now traffic slowed even more, as drivers craned their necks to see the incident.

"Do you have to respond to that?" Sondra asked.

"Nah," the police station is just two minutes away. I'll radio it in real fast. Don't want you to be late for your interview."

Sondra peered out her window and thought about her response, while Jeff radioed the dispatcher. The sky was so gray today. And it seemed to be growing darker. The drizzle was turning to heavy, rapid rain on the windshield.

What happened between me and Cory? It was a question she'd been asking herself nonstop for the past few months . . . and one she still didn't have a good answer for.

"Done." Jeff said, replacing the radio in its place on the console. He stared straight forward, remaining conspicuously quiet.

Sondra took a deep breath. She wondered if talking about Cory would make her cry.

"To answer your last question, no, *I* didn't leave Cory." She clasped her cold hands together and re-clasped them several times, before she realized what she was doing and simply sat on them. "He decided he couldn't commit just to me, and he told me so. Basically, he told me to call my parents and let them know I was coming with the kids, because he was moving into a condo with a woman who *makes him happy*, and I wouldn't be able to afford the house payments by myself."

"Wow," Jeff whistled, eyes darkening. "What a jerk!"

"Yeah. Looking back, I can't believe I didn't see this coming, but I guess I was just blind to the signs. I *didn't want to see it*, but he was planning this for awhile." She took a shuddery breath. "I said something to him one day a few months ago, like 'I'm not that happy anymore in this marriage,' and he just took that and ran with it." She blinked and a couple tears dropped from her eyes. She whisked them off her cheeks. "The next day was when he told me he wasn't happy either, and said he was leaving." Her voice wobbled, yet her words came out perfectly measured and clear. "He left that week and said I had two months to get out of our house."

Jeff frowned. So much there to respond to. But they were nearing the bridge and her destination. He chose one of the easier questions he could ask. "Why didn't you fight to get the house? I sure would've. You deserve at least that much."

Sondra cleared her throat and smoothed her hair. “Oh, you better believe I was going to. But then I decided if he was going to be so nasty, basically pushing us out of his life, I wanted to get myself and the girls as far away from him as I could. I didn’t want the reminders in that house. You know … how when someone dies it’s hard to see their old stuff, and smell their old smells, and things? I just didn’t want to be around any of it.”

“That makes sense.” He nodded and slowly drove the last stretch of highway before they would reach the bridge. The arches were just barely visible in the distance, but he noticed it was taking a long time for the whole bridge to come into view. *Why is the traffic piling up so much here?* He wondered before he realized Sondra was talking again.

“So I’m giving up the house, but fighting in court to get my share of our assets. At least he’s been paying child support. But it doesn’t cover everything we need. Not even close.” She paused and gazed again out her window. The rain was drumming louder and louder on the window. “Hence, staying at my parents’ house and my job hunt.”

“Wow,” Jeff murmured, both in response to her words and also to what he was seeing in front of him. Sondra followed his gaze through the windshield and repeated, “Wow!”

Now in view of the bridge, they could see that traffic was almost completely stopped on the icy passage. Cars continued to line up behind them, and soon, they were locked on all sides. Freezing rain pelted the windshield, becoming white noise all around them. Below them the Missouri River raged and rose; above them the sky stretched deep and gray. The final effect was like being trapped within soundproof glass, surrounded by people, yet all alone.

Chapter 8
Telling Stories
Jeff and Sondra's Story

"Well," Jeff said, "Looks like we're not going anywhere for a while." He turned to Sondra. "How about you call the school and tell them you'll be late. Then tell me the rest of that story?"

She nodded, pulling out her phone. "I guess so. But if I tell you my story, then you have to tell me yours."

Jeff pretended to think hard for a moment, then shrugged. "Well, why not. If we die on this bridge then at least one person will know it."

"Funny," she smirked.

Sondra made the call, then pocketed her phone and turned to Jeff.

"Okay. Where should I start? What do you want to know?"

"Well, there is one question I've been wondering." He paused for a moment and turned up the heat. "Your parents always seemed so supportive and provided a good home, didn't they? Unlike mine, for your information." He gave her a meaningful look. "I would have loved to have parents like yours, just so you know. But anyway, you were pretty involved in church growing up, as I recall. Unlike *me*. But then what happened? After you went to college you kind of dropped off the map."

Sondra sighed, looking down at her lap. "Yeah, I did. I guess mostly it was Cory that kept me away from church, but before that . . . well, let me back up."

She cleared her throat and turned to face Jeff. "What you said about my parents is true. They are 'great,' but they're almost too great. I always felt this pressure to be the perfect Christian. I guess I came to resent it. I guess I'm like a pastor's kid who goes off the deep end a little bit."

"Okay," Jeff nodded. "That makes some sense. So, before you met Cory you were not too keen on your parents and you were burned out on church."

"Yeah. I guess I was," Sondra nodded, gaining more clarity as she talked.

"I guess I got sick of playing the 'good Christian,' you know? I mean, I wanted to be a good *person*—and I actually agreed with my parents on things like no drinking, no sex before marriage, because it just made sense. But beyond doing those obvious *smart* things, I just didn't get what the big deal was about being a Christian.

"I still don't see how believing in God or Jesus really helps anyone. I have so many Christian friends whose parents divorced, or cheated on each other, or whose own marriages are falling apart. I have 'Christian' friends who drink and take drugs . . . and they don't seem that different from people who don't go to church."

Jeff crossed his arms and settled back into his seat. "Yeah," he nodded. "I've had the very same thoughts."

"Right?" Sondra commiserated. "And all throughout *my* years in church, *I* never had any big encounter with God." She squinted at him. "I don't know about *you* . . . "

Jeff shook his head. "I wish. Boy, do I wish. But nope. I'm with you. I've kind of been wondering where God is in my life for . . . well, my whole life."

"See? You get this. Anyway, as I went through high school, I started to feel like my parents were so judgmental of others who didn't live the way they did. I just wanted to go out and find my own way of doing things in the world—I was sick of them telling me how to do everything—if that makes sense?"

"It makes perfect sense," Jeff nodded. "I *hate* it when people get on my case. No one should be able to tell another person, no other *adult*, how to live their life."

"Right!" Sondra exclaimed. "So, I went to college, and I deliberately didn't go to a Christian college. I stopped going to church, except when I visited my parents, because honestly, it just felt like a waste of time. And then . . . " she took a deep breath.

" . . . I met Cory, who was this older, cool guy who was really nice and fun, and he wasn't a Christian, but he seemed to have it all together and I thought, 'See? Nice guys aren't always Christians.' So we dated until I graduated, and it just seemed natural to move in together, so we did."

She looked at Jeff gravely. "Well, my parents pretty much flipped out when I did that." She let out a little laugh. "Then I just kinda stayed away. I got a job teaching at an elementary school, and things were going well with Cory . . . And then, a couple years later, we got pregnant . . . " She cleared her throat. "Ahem. Well, I was ready to get married by then—I had been ready since college—and finally Cory agreed. So we had the wedding, and then I told my mom we were expecting after that.

"After the kids, I started to see signs that Cory and I were not the best fit. I kind of wanted to take the girls to church, but he wouldn't have anything to do with it.

"Cory started traveling for work after Autumn was born—and I had quit my job by this time to stay at home—and finally I started accepting my mom's help. We kind of reconciled. I took the girls to visit 'Grandma Liz and Grandpa Tim' a lot when Cory traveled. And I let my parents take the girls to church. But I never went to church *with* them. I just didn't want to deal with all the judgment, you know? I was like a prodigal daughter."

"It's okay, no one's perfect," Jeff said. "I'm certainly no model Christian."

Sondra threw up her hands. "Well, I'm back now. I guess my parents were right when they warned me about Cory, but I didn't listen." She exhaled in disgust. "I'm back to square one. I don't know how church or Jesus can help us—but now I could really use some help."

She choked back tears. "I guess it works for *some* Christians, like my parents, and Zach and Caitlyn. Maybe if I stick around long enough I'll just get some blessings by osmosis? I don't know. That stuff that Gary was presenting last night was pretty interesting because I'm so angry at Cory." She shook her head. "But ugh, I don't even want to think about him."

Jeff looked at her in sympathy. "I can imagine. That must be so hard. I'm sorry."

She dismissed his comment with a wave of her hand. "Oh, it's nothing you have to feel sorry for." She shifted in her seat and motioned to him.

"So, that's enough about me. What about you? *You* seem pretty happy. *Your* life seems to be going well. At least you have a good job. And you're happily married, right?"

He snorted. "Looks can be deceiving."

"What do you mean?"

"Well," he gestured at his surroundings. "I play the hero at work, and I look pretty good at church, but my home life is a mess. *Sheila* sure isn't impressed by me."

Sondra's eyes widened. "Really? You and Sheila seem so happy."

He shook his head. "It's just a front. At home we barely even talk. And if we do, we're usually fighting."

"I can't believe that. I remember your wedding. You guys seemed like such a perfect couple."

Jeff laughed. "Maybe we were . . . back then." He shook his head. "But things change. As you know."

Sondra leaned forward. "So what happened?" She looked outside. They'd barely moved on the bridge. "We have time," she grinned.

"I don't know, really." Jeff furrowed his eyebrows. "I guess it's my anger that's gotten me in trouble most. And Sheila's." He whistled. "That woman has a temper, too. We're like two firecrackers who met in college and didn't realize it until we got married.

Then we started to set each other off all the time."

"Hmmm," Sondra mused. "That's so funny. I would never have guessed that. So, what makes you two angry?" She grinned when she realized what she'd said. "To repeat Gary's question."

"Right," Jeff smiled.

"Well, to start with Sheila, she's this really independent, freethinking woman. She's always had strong opinions about how things should be, and in her home growing up, her dad was this Casanova to her mom. Her parents are a little like yours, I guess. They have a great marriage, they seem to be great Christians, and they raised Sheila to expect to be treated like a princess. Ha," he laughed dryly.

"Then I come along, and I'm in police academy and fighting for justice and looking out for the little guy; meanwhile, she's blossoming into a feminist."

Jeff raised his eyebrows at Sondra. "So, we were both into helping the 'oppressed' in our college days, I guess you could say, and I guess Sheila mistook me for Prince Charming." Jeff smirked. "Well, in the end, I let her down. When all the excitement of fighting crime and injustice fades, I'm not a guy who likes to get close to people." He shrugged. "So sue me, I just don't like to sit around talking about my feelings. Sheila doesn't like that."

His face darkened. "She gets angry because I don't fit her mold of what a perfect husband should look like. I'm not her dad, I'm not her Prince Charming. I'm just a guy trying to do some good in my job and provide for my wife and son and keep the peace."

"Well, what makes *you* angry?" Sondra pressed.

His tone lowered another level. "*I* get angry when Sheila rides me, and nitpicks me, and tries to tell me how to do every detail of my day. It's like she can't see the good stuff I do. All she can see is where I fall short, where I'm not perfect."

Now he turned to look, really look, into Sondra's eyes. "And you wanna know what really burns me up? This goes along with what you were saying before. It's like she's trying to be my judge before God." He huffed a little and shoved his hands in his pockets.

"But Sheila's so worried about appearances. She's always trying to tell me how to act in public—what to say and do. I hate that self-righteous attitude. I hate the belief that a beer will keep me out of heaven. She acts like she's so close to God and just trying to 'help' me be a better Christian, but her attitude actually pushes me away even more." Now his right hand surfaced to gesture along with his words.

"She wants me to open up to her, but I feel like if I were ever open about this stuff, she'd just blast me for what a bad person I am. So I get mad and just say 'to heck with her.' I shut down.

"I'm trying not to let her hypocrisy push me away from God—I mean, Jesus wouldn't be with the goody-goodies. He'd be with the trailer trash. But I get discouraged. I've pretty much plateaued with God." He shoved his hand back into his pocket.

"Wow," Sondra said, letting his words settle for a moment. "You sound pretty angry."

Jeff laughed bitterly.

"Oh, you haven't seen the half of it." He shook his head. "But I've learned to accept that this is what my life looks like. I just try to keep my head down and do the best I can, you know? Get through the bad stuff and enjoy the good stuff."

"What's the good stuff?" Sondra wondered aloud.

"Work," he answered immediately. "Seeing a problem or a bad situation and getting in there, getting my hands dirty, and fixing the problem. Putting bad people behind bars. Saving kittens in trees. A good workout. A good hunt. Coffee and donuts. You know." He grinned, as did she.

"No, really, doing a good job as an officer. It makes me feel good when I know I helped someone. I like going to bed at night exhausted because I worked hard and I accomplished something. And as long as Sheila stays off my back, that carries me through. See, I'm happy when people just keep it simple and let me do my thing."

"Hmmm," Sondra sighed. "I don't know what to say, Jeff. I guess we're both proof that families are not always what they seem on the outside. I'm sorry it's like that with you and Sheila. Have you ever talked of divorcing?"

He shrugged. "Nah. Not seriously. She wouldn't ever want to put our dirty laundry out there. She has an image to uphold." He took a long breath in. "And I don't want to throw Ben's life into turmoil like my parents did to me. Nah. I guess we've gotten this far. I guess we'll stay together for the kid."

Sondra looked at him with pity. "Is that it, then? You've just given up hope that it can get better?"

Jeff shrugged. "What can I do about it? Go crying to some counselor? It's not like I haven't prayed about it and asked God to fix our marriage, fix my anger, take away my depression. I've been doing that for years, but it seems like He's not gonna answer those prayers."

"Well, you're coming to the Bible study on anger. That seems like a step in the right direction."

Jeff shrugged. "Yeah . . . I guess it's a good step. I don't expect anything to come of it, though. When Sheila asked me to go—which she did by having

Zach talk to me, by the way—I only said yes because I like Zach, and I like your parents, and I enjoy a good discussion. And it's interesting."

"Yeah, it is." Sondra shifted with the turn of conversation. "I was really surprised to hear that Zach and Caitlyn's marriage was on the rocks. I wonder what the whole story is?"

"I have a few guesses, being a guy. Anyway, I'm happy for them. It's nice that *some* people have happy marriages. Like your parents."

"Yeah. They *are* happy." Sondra sighed. "I wish I would've taken after them with *my* marriage. And you too." She smoothed the fringe on her coat, looking down at her hands. "And I wish Cory would've found something like that prayer ministry Zach talked about. Straight 2 the Heart, was it?"

Jeff chuckled. "You sound like a typical wife. No offense. It's just that Sheila was throwing that stuff in my face on the ride home last night. I told her she wasn't exactly a peach, either, and maybe *she* should get help—you know, take the plank out of *her* eye first. Ha. Yeah, sitting in a room baring my soul to a group of guys . . . nah. Doesn't sound like something I'd like to do . . . . Hey, traffic is moving again!"

Sondra sat in silence. Jeff had given her an idea.

"So, do you still want me to drop you off at the interview? I can escort you in and tell them I saved you from a horrific car accident; you know, put in a good word!"

"Uh, yes." She pulled out her phone, distracted. She needed to send a message to Caitlyn. Or maybe it would be better to call her later. It would be too much to explain via text. Yes, she'd call her tonight and see if Caitlyn would pray with her.

"Really? Can I come in and pretend I was your hero on the road?" Jeff guffawed.

"What?" Sondra looked up from her phone. "No. I meant yes, take me to the interview—but don't come in. They said we could do it late."

"Aww, shucks."

The car slowed to a stop. They had reached her destination.

"Thanks so much for the ride." Sondra unbuckled her seatbelt. "Or should I say the venting session?" She smiled apologetically. "I'm sorry I took up half your morning." She pulled on her gloves and gathered her purse.

"Hey, don't worry about it! I'm not sorry. It was really nice to talk to you and compare battle scars." He smiled warmly. "And I'm not just saying that. I don't usually share that stuff with other people, but you're really easy to talk to, you know?"

Sondra blushed and smiled back, hand poised on the door handle. "It was nice talking to you, too, Jeff." He held her gaze until she felt a little uncomfortable and looked away.

“I have to go now. Thanks again.” She pushed the door open and stepped out.

“Bye Sondra, good luck with that job interview! See you on Monday night? Bible study?”

She gave him a thumbs-up and then turned up the sidewalk. As she walked, she felt his eyes following her, and that knowledge filled her with pleasure.

Chapter 9
Fruits, Roots, and The Suffering Messiah

A Review of What We've Covered

Monday night came once again, and now it was Sondra, not Elizabeth, who sat waiting expectantly for someone. Everyone was at the Bible study except Jeff and Sheila. Sondra couldn't help but feel a bit disappointed.

What's wrong with you? An inner voice chided. *He's a married man.* She settled into the couch and turned her attention to Zach and Caitlyn, who had just arrived. Sondra had wanted to see them, too. She still couldn't believe how kind they had been to her this past week. After her job interview on Tuesday, Sondra had called Caitlyn to request prayer. Caitlyn had picked her up for lunch on Wednesday, while her car was getting fixed, and texted on Thursday to ask if she needed anything. On Friday, Caitlyn had taken her to pick up her car, and on Friday evening, Sondra had finally been able to drive herself over to Zach and Caitlyn's for a prayer session. The hour-long session had brought tears and vulnerability, but also a closeness to her old friends that she found comforting.

"Hey Sondra," Caitlyn greeted, plopping onto the chair beside her friend. "How're you doing? Have you heard about the job?"

Sondra nodded. "Yeah, I did, just before you guys came over. I didn't get it."

Caitlyn frowned. "Oh, I'm sorry to hear that."

Sondra shrugged. "At least my car's fixed. One thing at a time, I guess."

At the same moment, Sheila entered . . . alone.

"Hi everyone." Sheila waved to the group, then removed her coat. "Jeff's not coming tonight. Police duty called."

"Oh, I'm sorry to hear that," Gary said. Sondra was sorry, too, but busied herself with taking out her Bible and her "homework" from last week.

"It looks like everyone who's coming is here," Gary said in another moment. "So I guess we can begin. I've asked Zach here to start us off tonight with prayer, and then review some key concepts from our first couple studies. Whenever you're ready, Zach."

Zach nodded and smiled. "Let's bow our heads," the young pastor began. "Dear Lord, Thank You for bringing us all back here safely tonight, and please be with Jeff as he carries out his job duties. I ask that You take over in this room, tonight. May we honor You with honesty as we study more about how to let You heal our anger and our wounded hearts. Please speak to each one of us, wherever we are in our journey to becoming all that You would have us be. In Jesus' name, Amen."

Zach looked up. "Well, it's good to see you all again. I know Gary has a lot to cover tonight, so I'll get right to my piece. I'm going to talk a little more about fruit and root, because we weren't all here at the first study—plus, it bears repeating."

The Fruit and Root Principle

He cleared his throat. "So, fruit and root. At the first Bible study, we talked about how anger is a secondary emotion. It's a 'fruit' of a deeper 'root' system. I'd like to suggest that we can heal from anger," Zach said, "if we can understand the *roots* of our anger, and if we can identify with Jesus in our struggles."

Zach cleared his throat again and continued. "So, anger is a fruit—it's the result of a deeper root—something else that happened. For example, think about when you hit your thumb with a hammer. I don't know about you, but I've said some four-letter words when that's happened."

"Me too," Sondra admitted.

"Right. But I don't *want* to swear, just like no one really wants to be angry, or depressed, or fearful, or sad. The swearing, just like a negative feeling, is secondary to something else. A millisecond before you said that four-letter word, what was your thumb feeling?"

"Pain," Caitlyn supplied.

"Right. Intense pain, leading to an expression of anger."

The Source of Our Negative Beliefs

"Another question. Where do our negative beliefs come from? Tim, could you read John 8:44 and Matthew 15:18–19?"

"Sure," Tim said. He opened his Bible and read:

> For you are the children of your father the devil, and you love to do the evil things he does. He was a murderer from the beginning. He has always hated the truth, because there is no truth in him. When he lies, it is consistent with his character; for he is a liar and the father of lies. (John 8:44, NLT)
> But the words you speak come from the heart–that's what defiles you. For from the heart come evil thoughts, murder, adultery, all sexual immorality, theft, lying, and slander. (Matt. 15:18–19, NLT)

Tim looked up. "The Bible says Satan is the father of lies."

"That's right. I like to also say that Satan is the father of negative beliefs, and negative thoughts. So, when does anger come into our lives: *before* Satan attacks us with lies, or *after*?

"Afterwards," Elizabeth said.

"So anger is secondary to the lie. Anger is a *fruit* of the lie, and the lie is the *root*. So based on this, anger is not the most important issue. But Satan sure loves to distract us from the real issues, doesn't he? When we're angry, he loves to have us focus on the person who angered us, and not on ourselves. He doesn't want us to face what our anger says about *us*, or consider the price *we* are paying for holding onto our anger."

Everyone nodded.

"But I better stop there, before I get too far ahead." Zach smiled. "Over to you, Gary."

"Thanks for that introduction, Zach," Gary said, returning the smile. "That's going to play into our study tonight, as David continues in prayer. David is going to transition from his anger into some of his *roots*—or what is causing his anger. So we'll see this fruit and root principle in action." He grabbed his Bible. "But before we move on, I want to quickly review:

- What did we learn about this Psalm,
- What did we learn about David, and
- What did we learn about God and Jesus?"

Review of Psalm 109:1–16

"Well," Tim spoke, "if I remember correctly, this was the most hostile Psalm in the Jewish liturgy."

"That's right, Tim," Gary said. He held up his notes. "In his book *A Sacred Sorrow*, Michael Card says it is 'as dark a place as exists in Scripture outside of Golgotha.' Good. And what makes this Psalm so dark, so harsh? Tell me about David here."

"David has an enemy," Sheila offered. "But it was someone he was close to—someone he loved—and this person wronged him in some way."

"Yes," Elizabeth added. "David says the person lied about him and attacked him."

"Good. What else?"

Sheila continued. "David is basically asking God to curse this guy in every way possible—to have him die and have no mercy on his family, his wife, or his children."

"Or the generations before and after the man's family," Tim added.

"Yes, good," Gary said. He stood and placed his whiteboard on an easel. "Here's our list from last week to help us review what we know about the man, what David wants God to do, and how Jesus identifies with David." *(see summary in the three columns)*

What we know about this man and his family:	What David wants God to do to this man: (and family)	What Jesus has gone through to identify with David *and* us:
1. Wicked, deceitful 2. Making false accusations and lying 3. Betrayal/hatred from someone David trusts and loves 4. Leader/official position with no mercy - seeking to slay/kill David when he is broken hearted	1. Judge him in court 2. Make his prayer sin 3. Man dies–his family become beggars 4. Have no mercy for him or his family–with all the generations before and after him being lost forever	1. Religious leaders lying about Him 2. Judas betraying Jesus 3. Peter denying Jesus 3x, cursing Him the 3rd time 4. *Tempted* to not have mercy on those hurting Him–*Tempted* to curse them (wish ill on them)

"We discovered that David prayed a very thorough prayer. Completely negative, covering all the ways this man could be cursed. But let's pause in this first section of the Psalm for a moment. Last week we said that the content of this Psalm was very bad, but the good thing about it was David's honesty. David is being completely honest with God. He is doing what C.S. Lewis has said we should do: 'We must lay before Him what is in us; not what ought to be in us.'"

"And," Zach added, "Even though his words are horrible, *from a human perspective*, David is not *acting* on his anger."

"That's right, Zach. And I'm coming back to this point for two reasons. The first one we mentioned last week. If we aren't honest about our pain, it just gets worse. In Michael Card's words: 'Without lament these wounds continue to fester. The longer they are denied, the more gangrenous they become.'

"Let's look at the context of that quote, in fact. It gives some good background on the Psalm, and then expands on why it's important for us."

Gary passed around a handful of papers. "Take a moment to read this passage silently. Then we'll discuss it."

> Psalm 109 is as dark a place as exists in Scripture outside of Golgotha. It is never used for worship in Jewish liturgy. David's enemy appears to have been some sort of official to whom he had offered his friendship. Some scholars believe the occasion for writing the psalm was one of the many coups with which David struggled in the latter years of his reign.
>
> In the psalm, David says he has been lied to and attacked, and in return for his friendship, he has been accused.
>
> Then David makes what at first seems an unremarkable statement, until you read the curses that follow… The curse continues, until David exhausts himself–his hurt, his hatred and his anger.
>
> There was nothing else David could do with his hate but take it to God…
>
> We are a people in perpetual denial of the hidden hate we have for our enemies [and those we thought were our friends or loved ones].
>
> Jesus showed us that hatred is a wound that must be healed, that denial is a paralysis only He can heal.
>
> Without lament these wounds continue to fester. The longer they are denied, the more gangrenous they become. These wounds demand that I answer the question: Is there any other way to handle my anger but to bring them to God?
>
> Understand, imprecatory [angry] laments are not some sort of vicious didactic means by which we learn how to curse our enemies.
>
> They represent an invitation to the beginning of a process in which first, we admit that we do have enemies. Then these laments serve to guide us in the process of confessing our darkest hatred towards them with a view toward handing them over to God. [5]

---

[5] Michael Card, *A Sacred Sorrow: Reaching Out to God in the Lost Language of Lament* (Colorado Springs: NavPress, 2005), pp. 76–78.

When it was clear everyone was done reading, Gary said, "Would someone summarize this for us? Especially the last part. How is Card making this Psalm applicable to us?"

Sondra furrowed her brow and studied the quote. "Well," she ventured, still looking at her paper, "Card is saying that Psalm 109 is not a model for how to curse our enemies, or loved ones who betrayed us. He says that laments basically give us permission to admit that we struggle with hatred and anger, so we can start the process of putting it into God's hands."

"Well said, Sondra. Anyone else have any comments about what we've just read? Tim?"

Tim was shaking his head in amusement. "Huh," he said. "The thing that stands out to me is the *relationship* David must have with God, in order to even *say* these things to him."

Elizabeth, sitting next to her husband, nodded in agreement. "This shows a prayer life that is totally unfiltered. This is someone who knows God well and is comfortable letting it all hang out."

Gary cocked his head. "What, Elizabeth? You don't think Christians typically pray like this when they're angry?"

Sheila snorted. "I think maybe Christians *say* these things to themselves, or maybe their spouses . . . " she thought of Jeff and his abusive father, and Jeff's angry rants whenever his dad tried to call. He often said he just wished his dad were dead. "But I doubt too many Christians *pray* these things."

"Interesting." Gary crossed an ankle over a knee and clasped his hands. "So, what kinds of prayers are most, or many, Christians praying, when they are angry, or when they have these big feelings and emotions?"

Zach cleared his throat. "Well, in my experience, and this includes me, too, if I'm not careful, we offer up nice, polite, sanitized prayers to God." He smiled, looking around the group. "Have you ever seen someone rant about another person . . . and then after their rant, they just try to dismiss their anger and say, 'But it doesn't matter. I'm over it. It's nothing.' And you can clearly see they are *not* over it?"

Caitlyn chuckled. "I've done that."

Zach nodded. "We can do the same thing with our prayers. I don't know how many times I've heard a prayer that goes something like this . . . "

Zach clapped his hands together and looked up to the sky, posing in mock prayer: "Dear God," Zach threw his voice into a cheery falsetto and plastered on a smile: "Thank You for being high, holy, and righteous, and loving me and helping me to forgive my [husband, father, mother, wife, grandparent, boss] so I can forget the past, and I never have to think about it again as I move into the wonderful future You have for me. In Jesus' name,

Amen." Zach dropped his hands and dropped his gaze, but kept his fake smile as he looked, wide-eyed, around the group. They laughed in response.

"Point well taken, Zach," Gary smiled. "This leads me to my second point about honesty. When we do not pray honest prayers, we put God in a lose-lose situation. If God answers our nice, polite prayers, God is reinforcing and rewarding our dishonesty with Him. But if God does not answer our nice, polite, less-than-honest prayers, we get mad at God for not answering us."

Putting God in a Lose-Lose Situation

1. If God *does* answer my less-than-honest prayers, He reinforces my dishonesty and a pattern of shallow, superficial praying that creates distance between us, instead of closeness built on trusting Him enough to be completely honest with Him—the same way Jesus was.
2. If God *does not* answer my less-than-honest prayers, I blame God, I get angry at God for not answering my prayers, which creates distance between us, instead of closeness built on trusting Him enough to be completely honest with Him—the same way Jesus was.

"Okay, so we've seen that this was a hostile Psalm and that it is useful to us because David is modeling how to be honest with God through his anger—showing us a God who can be trusted with our deepest, darkest thoughts and feelings. Soon we will see where this leads him in his healing process."

Gary pointed to the white board with the following chart.

David is moving from **ANGER**	Transitioning To…	Transitioning To…

"But before we move on, let's revisit the 'homework' from last week. I wonder, did anyone take a few moments to reflect on where anger is showing up in your life, and who you might be angry at?"

Chapter 10
Sondra's Roots

Connecting Jesus' Story with Sondra's Story

Where Is Anger Showing up in My Life?

Sondra didn't have to think twice. Cory.

Across the room, Sheila smirked. Jeff.

"You don't have to tell me here, of course," Gary assured. "But the reason I ask is to get you to think again about what negative thoughts, or roots, you are having in connection with that anger, and how Jesus can identify with you.

"The second worksheet from last week asked: *How did Jesus deal with His temptations to believe negative thoughts?*"

Now Sondra's mind shifted back to a few nights ago, Friday night. These were similar to the questions Zach and Caitlyn had asked her in their living room after Sondra had called Caitlyn requesting prayer. Her old friend had lost no time inviting her over. "Friends *pray* for each other," Caitlyn had said. And the memory of Caitlyn's words almost brought Sondra to tears again, as she sat surrounded by the group in her parents' living room. She had never had a friend, Christian or non, offer to pray with her about her divorce, or anything else.

"So, talk to us a little about what's going on with you. I know you are dealing with a lot of anger at Cory," Zach had said Friday night.

"Yeah," Sondra muttered. "That's an understatement."

"I wonder, Sondra," he said. "Are any of these negative thoughts familiar to you?"

Her eyes traveled down the list he handed her:

- ❑ I'm rejected
- ❑ I have no hope
- ❑ Poor me/why me?
- ❑ I can't trust others
- ❑ I'm powerless/helpless
- ❑ I'm alone/I'm abandoned
- ❑ I'm not worthy/I'm worthless
- ❑ I have to do more and try harder
- ❑ I never get to have my needs met
- ❑ Something bad is going to happen
- ❑ It's my fault/I'm not good enough
- ❑ I'll never be loved, wanted, valued
- ❑ I can't speak up or share my needs
- ❑ I'm not safe/I have to protect myself
- ❑ I have to be in control/control others
- ❑ I have to look good in front of others
- ❑ I can't trust or rely on anyone but myself
- ❑ I don't have a right to protect myself/exist
- ❑ I'm bad/I should have been better/I hate myself
- ❑ I've got to defend myself and/or control my image
- ❑ I can't be forgiven/accepted—I have to live with guilt

"Ha. It would take less time for me to tell you which ones *aren't* familiar."

Zach waited, pen ready.

Her voice came out in a whisper. "*I'm rejected. Poor me. I can't trust others. I'm alone. I'm abandoned. I can't rely on anyone but myself. Why me?*" She looked up, lip trembling. "I guess I could go on, but that's probably enough." Her head fell heavy into one hand. Her shoulders shuddered a little.

"Yes, of course," Zach assured. "That's fine." He scribbled some notes.

Caitlyn looked at Zach expectantly. He was taking his time writing his notes. She felt horrible that her friend was in such obvious agony, and wondered what her husband was going to do about it.

Zach picked up his Bible and held it up like a weapon. "Now, I'm going to share Jesus' story."

The Suffering of Jesus

Zach looked at Caitlyn, as if reading her mind. "This is the perfect time to share how Jesus suffered like us. Now we know some of Sondra's negative thoughts and roots, so now we can share Jesus in way that will connect her heart to His." He turned back to Sondra.

"Sondra, would you please read Hebrews 2:17–18 and 4:15–16, and tell me what those verses mean to you."

Sondra opened her Bible and read:

> For this reason, He had to be made like them, fully human in every way, in order that He might become a merciful and faithful high priest in service to God, and that He might make atonement for the sins of the people. Because He Himself suffered when He was tempted, He is able to help those who are being tempted. (Heb. 2:17–18, NIV)
>
> For we do not have a high priest who is unable to empathize with our weaknesses, but we have one Who has been tempted in every way, just as we are—yet He did not sin. Let us then approach God's throne of grace with confidence [boldness], so that we may receive mercy and find grace to help us in our time of need. (Heb. 4:15–16, NIV)

She studied the verses silently for a moment, face wrinkling. "Well, it's saying the same thing you said: Jesus suffered like I did—but I guess I don't get it. I'm confused. Jesus was never even married, so how could He understand what I'm going through?"

"I'm glad you asked," Zach said.

He pulled out a brown prayer card and handed one each to Sondra and Caitlyn.

"Jesus struggled to surrender His will in the Garden of Gethsemane," Zach began. "Then He was alone and abandoned when His disciples deserted Him. He was betrayed by Judas, by a kiss, for the price of a slave. He was verbally, mentally, and physically abused when the leaders tortured Him with whips. He was shamed and humiliated as they taunted Him. And He was unfairly treated when He was tried, convicted, and crucified."

Zach took a deep breath as he looked up from the card. "Do any of those experiences relate to what you told me? Can you see a place where Jesus was rejected, or tempted to believe He couldn't speak up? Was He ever treated like He was worthless? Was He ever tempted to numb His pain? Or to get angry at people who had let Him down?"

Sondra swallowed a lump in her throat and nodded.

"Now, remember again about *roots*. When we talk about Jesus identifying with us, it doesn't necessarily mean He faced every *outward* situation we face—even though there are some striking similarities. Where Jesus can't identify with us in our situations—like being married, for instance—He understands pain. And He understands being tempted with negative thoughts."

Zach saw tears pooling in Sondra's eyes, and his voice softened. "Sondra, Jesus went through all these painful experiences so that He could understand every way you have been sinned against, and every form of self-protection you've developed in order to numb pain."

Now both Caitlyn and Sondra dabbed their eyes.

"So, Sondra," Zach coaxed softly. "Where can Jesus identify with you? Can you check off some places on this list where Jesus suffered to identify with you?" He handed her a pen.

Sondra took a shuddery breath and nodded. She read the items aloud as she checked them: "Being abandoned and rejected by those He loves. Being betrayed by a kiss, tempted to be angry when He was taken advantage of by men who should have been protecting Him, and asking God 'why?'" *(see summary in the left and right columns below)*

Sondra's Story of Rejection and Betrayal:	Jesus' Story Connecting with Sondra's Story
Sondra suffered through the pain of being abandoned	Jesus suffered through the pain of being abandoned
Sondra was rejected by someone she loved	Jesus was rejected by those He loved
Sondra was betrayed by a kiss	Jesus was betrayed by a kiss
Sondra is angry at being taken advantage of by the man who should have been protecting her	Jesus was tempted to be angry when He was taken advantage of by the men who should have been protecting Him
Sondra is asking God "Why?"	Jesus hung on the cross asking God "Why?"

Zach nodded solemnly. "Would it be alright with you if we put all of this into a prayer now?"

"Sure," Sondra nodded.

"Okay. Please repeat after me." Zach proceeded to lead Sondra through the following prayer, pausing every few words for Sondra to repeat after him:

> Dear Jesus,
>
> Thank you for choosing to fulfill prophecy by suffering in similar ways I did: being abandoned by those closest to You, rejected by those You loved, betrayed by a kiss, asking Your Father "Why," and being tempted to get angry at the men abusing You.
>
> Thank You for suffering in Your soul in these ways, dying for me, and embracing all the ways I've been wounded in life and all my negative thoughts—including being abandoned and betrayed by Cory, asking "Why God?," being angry at Cory, and the lies that *I can't trust others, I'm alone,* and *I can't rely on anyone but myself.*
>
> Thank You for embracing all of this for me so You could restore me to my true identity as Your daughter. In Your name, Jesus, Amen.

Sondra was crying heavily by the end the prayer. Speaking those deep pains out loud hurt. At the same time, it hurt in a good way she could not explain. Maybe it was like opening a release valve where too much pressure had built up. Maybe it was the fact that someone else was shouldering some of the burden. And not just her friends, Zach and Caitlyn. Jesus Himself had taken on this weight she was carrying . . . long before she'd even prayed this prayer.

How Jesus Responded to Satan's Temptations

"So," Gary asked again. He tapped last week's homework, bringing Sondra back to the present. "How did Jesus deal with His temptations to believe negative thoughts?" Gary pointed at number one.

"Did Jesus push down His temptations to believe negative thoughts in the garden and on the cross?"

"No," Sondra murmured, her prayer session fresh in her mind. She remembered a verse Zach had pointed her to. Jesus in the garden, on his knees, crying out this prayer to God:

> "My soul is overwhelmed with sorrow to the point of death."
> (Matt. 26:38, NIV)

"Did Jesus try to talk Himself out of His temptations to believe negative thoughts in the garden and on the cross?"

Sondra shook her head, another verse from her prayer time filling her mind.

During the days of Jesus' life on earth, He offered up prayers and petitions with fervent cries and tears to the One who could save him from death, and He was heard because of His reverent submission. (Heb. 5:7, NIV)

"Did Jesus try to talk Himself into believing that God loved Him, and that God had not forsaken Him on the cross?"

"My God, My God, why have You forsaken Me?" (Matt. 27:46, NIV)

Sondra shook her head vigorously. Jesus had asked, "Why have You forsaken Me?" showing He was tempted to believe He had been abandoned by God, even though her friends had told her God really had not abandoned Jesus. Yet He experienced the darkness and sense of separation from His Father at Calvary for her.

"Did Jesus talk to God about the negative thoughts Satan was tempting Him with, *immediately, openly, honestly, and continually,* in the garden and again on the cross?"

"Yes, to all of those," Zach nodded.

"Do you all agree?" Gary asked the group.

Everyone nodded.

"That's right. Jesus did **NOT** try to talk Himself out of the negative thoughts coming from Satan, tempting Him not to trust God in the Garden of Gethsemane and at Calvary.

"Jesus did **NOT** try to talk Himself into trusting God.

"Jesus talked **TO** God.

"Jesus shared His feelings and thoughts with God in the Garden of Gethsemane and again on the cross, *openly, honestly, repeatedly, and continually.*

"And Jesus showed His abusers nothing but love because He continued to trust in His Father even when He couldn't see, sense, or feel His Father's presence."

Tim whistled. "Wow."

"Yeah," Sondra reiterated. "Wow." She couldn't imagine showing Cory any love right now.

Jesus did **NOT** try to talk Himself out of negative thoughts.
Jesus did **NOT** try to talk Himself into trusting God.
Jesus talked **TO** God.

"You see," Gary continued, "when we stop talking with God, our only choice is to act out in a human manner, denying our pain and/or defending ourselves in our own strength. This approach tends to sabotage our relationships, leaving us in a prison of fear, pain, and anger.

"But because Jesus suffered through His trials in Gethsemane and His trials at Calvary, He can identify with David through all of David's experiences. Jesus has earned the right to David's trust. Jesus has also earned the right to heal David and set him free. (God is trustworthy, but Rom. 8:6–7 tells us that our sinful minds distrust Him.) He can be that bridge that brings us back to God, back to help, when we're too angry to help ourselves. So, let's move on.

"Let's find David's turning point in this vicious Psalm and see how all this honesty prepared his heart for healing."

Chapter 11
Transition Time

A Study on Psalm 109:17–25

"Let's keep reading in Psalm 109 from where we left off last week, and see if we can find a transition text," Gary continued. "Let's find the verse where David's focus begins to change. In other words, where does David start to move away from thinking about the man and how he wants the man and the man's family to suffer?"

Where Is the Transition Text?

"Let's go the opposite direction from last week." Gary turned to Zach on his right. "Zach, I'd like you to start tonight with verse 17, and let's each read two verses until we get through verse 25 and stop. Tim, that puts us ending at you."

Tim nodded as Bibles opened and pages rustled.

"Sorry Sheila, I guess you're the only one without a verse." Gary smiled apologetically.

"No worries," she quipped. "I'm sure I'll have something to say yet." She winked.

"Okay, here we go," Zach announced. "I'm starting with verse 17."

> 17 As he loved cursing, so let it come to him; as he did not delight in blessing, so let it be far from him.
> 18 As he clothed himself with cursing as with his garment, so let it enter his body like water, and like oil into his bones. (Psalm 109:17–18)

Caitlyn read next:

> 19 Now may his curses return and cling to him like clothing; may they be tied around him like a belt.
> 20 May those curses become the Lord's punishment, for my accusers who speak evil of me.
> (Psalm 109:19–20)

Caitlyn shook her head. "No transition there."

"That's the truth," Sheila concurred. "He still sounds hate-filled and ready for revenge."

Zach nodded his agreement.

"Sondra?" Gary prompted.

Quietly, she read:

> 21 But YOU, O GOD, the Lord, Deal with me for Your name's sake. Because Your mercy is good, deliver me.
> 22 For I am poor and needy, and my heart is wounded within me. (Psalm 109:21–22, emphasis added)

As she read, her voice cracked over the last words: **my heart is wounded within me**. *That's it*, she thought. *That's the transition. I'm hate-filled because I'm hurting.* Her recent prayer session came back to her again, and Zach's discussion on fruit and root.

"There's something beneath the anger," Zach had said, "some negative thought or experience or lie, and it's showing up through anger."

While Sondra pondered this, Elizabeth continued reading:

> 23 I am gone like a shadow when it lengthens; I am shaken off like a locust.
>
> 24 My knees are weak through fasting. And my flesh is feeble from lack of fatness. (Psalm 109:23–24)

Tim finished with the last verse:

> 25 I also have become a reproach to them; When they look at me, they shake their heads. (Psalm 109:25)

"Okay, Guys." Gary smiled. "Does this section end with a different focus than the first section? Sheila, since you didn't get to read, do you want to respond?"

"Sure," Sheila answered. "What jumps out to me by the end of this section is how humble, or humbled, David sounds."

"Humbled," Gary mused. "Good word choice. So, I'll ask it again. Sheila, where's the transition text, and what makes the focus of this verse so different from the first part of David's prayer?"

Why Is Psalm 109:21 a Transition Text?

"There *was* one point where I noticed a definite change . . . " Sheila mused, searching the open Bible on her lap. "Here it is." She placed her finger on one particular spot in her Bible. "Verse 21 is the transition." She looked up.

"I was a good student in English, and there is a clear transition word: *but*. It interrupts the flow, or direction, of where David is going in the prayer."

"Great," Gary said. "And what is the new direction? The new focus?"

"Well," Sheila looked down at her Bible. "The next few words after *but* are '*You O God the Lord*.'" She looked up again. "David is moving away from focusing on his enemy to focusing on God."

As she said those words, Sheila felt a prick in her heart. She could sense where Gary was going in this discussion, and where David was going in the prayer. It wasn't a direction she often traveled with Jeff.

"A-plus work, Sheila," Gary said, eyes twinkling. "Good job."

He now turned to the rest of the group. "Let's open the discussion. David has been venting and being honest with God about his enemy, and now, like Sheila said, he is turning to focus on God." Gary shifted in his chair. "Where else is David focusing?"

Caitlyn placed her finger on verse 21, where Sheila had stopped, and read: "'Deal with **ME**, for Your name's sake; Because Your mercy is good, deliver **ME**.'" She looked up. "David is also focusing on himself now. He's starting to describe himself, and what he needs God to do for him."

"Great, Caitlyn. And what state do we find David in right here, guys? Also, what is he asking God to do for him?"

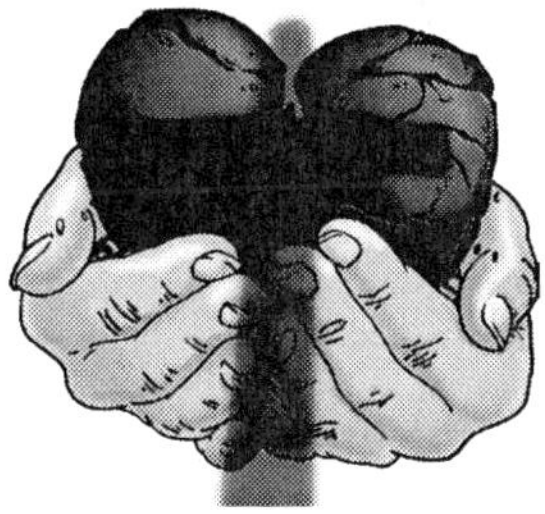

Elizabeth jumped in. "'For I am poor and needy,' verse 22 says, '**And my heart is wounded within me**.'" She looked up. "He's broken. He's hurting. He's admitting he needs help, of all things!" She elbowed Tim. "That's a pretty big step for a man!"

Sheila arched her eyebrows. "You're telling me!"

"No joke!" Caitlyn smiled.

The women all laughed.

"Hey," Tim said, putting up his hands. "I'm starting to feel a little stereotyped here." He winked at Caitlyn.

Gary chuckled. "Well, Tim, are they wrong? You notice how it was the women who jumped all over that transition. Who's typically better at expressing their feelings: men or women?"

"Ha!" Sheila couldn't stop herself. "Men are as dense as a sack of bricks when it comes to feelings. No offense, guys," she nodded to the men in the room.

Zach gave a half smile. "I'll take that criticism. I have to really work hard to sit and listen to Caitlyn when she wants to talk. Unless I make a conscious effort, I can easily tune out and just kind of ignore her."

"You're getting better, though," Caitlyn smiled.

"By God's grace," Zach said, returning the smile.

That's just peachy, Sheila thought. How she wished Jeff were here to hear this. She knew she wasn't perfect either, but it would be so much easier to deal with her husband if he would just take time to put down his work and his distractions and listen to her.

"Well thank God that we men can improve, with His help," Gary said with a wink. "So, to get back to the verses, David has been venting and being honest with God. But now, with this transition, David is trusting God, sharing the pain that is behind his anger, behind his rage, behind his desire for revenge.

"Did you know that being honest with God about our feelings is faith in action? And so is being honest with God about our pain, anger, rage, and desire for revenge.

"Sharing the pain in our wounded hearts with God shows real faith and real trust. It is an admission that we need help, and a vote of confidence in God that He *really* can help us."

Being honest with God about our feelings is **faith in action**.
This includes being honest with God about our
pain, anger, rage, and desire for revenge.

"You know," Zach jumped in, "to go back to an earlier thought, David didn't go out and *do* all those things to his enemy, but I'm sure he could have, being the powerful king and warrior that he was. So it's a really good point, Gary, that David is showing trust and faith in God to handle his enemy. He is asking *God* to deal with it, and not exacting revenge *himself*."

"That's right, Zach," Gary returned. "We can see that David is asking *God* to deal with his enemy, by the fact that he is telling *God* to take revenge—still room for improvement there, of course, because we know revenge belongs to the Lord—but we don't want to miss the good in this prayer.

"And right around the transition, at verse 21, the prayer gets really good. 'Deal with **ME** for **YOUR NAME'S** sake' is a powerful change in focus—to

God's character. No matter what the man has done to David, David is turning to God, because God's mercy is good and he wants God to deliver him."

Elizabeth leaned forward, intrigued. "So David realizes that it's not really his enemy that needs to be dealt with—or not *only* his enemy—it's also himself."

"Exactly, Elizabeth," Gary said. "The more David talks to God, the more David becomes God-focused, and less focused on revenge. Now, instead of focusing only on the man lying about him and his anger, he is shifting his attention to God's name, to his (David's) pain, and his (David's) need to receive God's mercy. David is moving from his external anger to his internal pain."

David is moving from his external **ANGER**	To his Internal **PAIN**	To

"And really, in the long run, what is more important for David to talk to God about: his enemy and what happens to his enemy, or David himself, and how David responds to his pain?"

Sondra exhaled heavily. Again, it was like Gary was speaking directly to her. Out loud she said, "Well, in the long-run, even if this enemy were to get his just deserts, David could still feel wounded inside. Maybe he would feel better right away—for a short time . . . "

She thought of her desire to slash Cory's tires as she said this: " . . . but the outward revenge wouldn't really change his heart, or his pain. So . . . " Sondra shrugged. "I guess it's really more important that David talk to God about himself. David doesn't have to live with this enemy for the rest of his life, but he *does* have to live with *himself*."

Elizabeth watched her daughter, wondering at this mature response. No doubt Sondra was thinking about Cory as she said these words. But where had this new maturity come from?

A few feet away from Sondra and Elizabeth, Sheila pursed her lips. How many times had Jeff told her to stop nagging *him* and take a look at *herself*? She could see where this was a good response in conflict—the "**deal with ME**" part of the Psalm. But if she honored her wedding vows, she *did* have to live with Jeff for the rest of her life—at least, the rest of *his* life—and how could she really focus on herself when he was still there, aggravating her?

"Gary, I get what you're saying here. And good point, Sondra." Sheila nodded to the younger woman to her left. "But Sondra's point also brought another thought to my mind. What if you *don't* get the luxury of being *done* with your enemy? I mean, it's one thing to have a fight with a person, and then go on with your separate lives. I could imagine being able to sit and pray through your pain and anger in a space apart from the *jerk* who hurt you." She winced. She hadn't meant to sound so bitter.

"But when you see that person on a daily basis, and they keep hurting you, how can you really heal from that? How can you stop being angry?"

Gary nodded. "I really appreciate that question, Sheila, and it's such an important one. Many people face that challenge every day.

"Before we answer *how* to overcome that situation, let's answer a more basic question: Is it even *possible* to live with or deal with someone who hurts you, or who exasperates you, and *not be angry*?"

Brows furrowed all around the room.

"Don't answer yet," Gary said. "Let's look at Ephesians 4:26 first. Could you read that for us, Sheila?"

"Sure." She flipped open her Bible and read:

> Be angry and do not sin: do not let the sun go down on your wrath. (Eph. 4:26, NIV)

Sheila exhaled a long, slow breath, thinking it over. "Well, it's not so clear. According to this verse, and the Apostle Paul, you can be angry, but not sin." She paused, deep in thought.

"But then the next part says to not let the sun go down on your wrath. So that implies that we might be angry at someone initially, in the heat of the moment, but that we shouldn't let our anger *last*."

Zach jumped in. "And to answer your question, Gary, the fact that the Apostle Paul is giving this directive implies that it *must* be possible to live with constant irritation, yet not be constantly angry."

Elizabeth spoke now. "What I'm noticing in this verse is the daily marker of time. He says to not let the *sun* go down on our wrath. So he is not telling us not to get angry . . . he seems to allow for the reality that we *are* going to get angry sometimes . . . but then he uses the sunset as a sort of marker of how often we should deal with our anger."

"Good point, Sweetie," Tim said. "That makes me think of the other verse where Paul says 'I die daily.' It seems to me that we could begin every day of our lives angry, but somehow, there is a way that we can turn it over to God by the end of each day."

"This is a great discussion, everyone," Gary beamed. "You are all heading just where I want to go, and that is forgiveness." Gary paused to take in everyone's responses.

Both Sheila and Sondra groaned at that word, *forgiveness*. Zach and Caitlyn looked peaceful, but interested. And Tim and Elizabeth looked earnest and curious.

"By the end of our time tonight, I want to talk about forgiveness, and how forgiveness is a process, even a *daily* process. But first, let's finish discussing our selected verses for tonight. We've already read about David's *emotional* distress, but in the last portion for tonight, verses 23–25, we'll read about the *physical* effects of David's anger. We are going to see, in these verses, why it is *physically* dangerous to hold onto anger, and why it's dangerous when we cannot or *will not choose* to forgive."

Chapter 12
Physical Effects of Anger and Unforgiveness

A Closer Look at Psalm 109:23–25

"So, let's get to our last few verses for tonight, Psalm 109:23–25. As we read, let's think about how David is being affected *physically* by his anger and pain. Does someone want to reread those three verses for us?"

"I'll read," Caitlyn volunteered, lifting her Bible.

> 23 I am gone like a shadow when it lengthens; I am shaken off like a locust.
> 24 My knees are weak through fasting. And my flesh is feeble from lack of fatness.
> 25 I have also become a reproach to them; when they look at me, they shake their heads. (Psalm 109:23–25)

"So, what do you think, guys? How is David doing, physically, at this point?"

"He's weak," Sondra supplied, rechecking the verses. "And feeble."

"That's right, Sondra. David is getting very literal here, sharing the impact of his anger and desire for revenge on his body. Does anyone have another version that gives us other words to describe David's appearance?"

"My version says he's 'skin and bones,'" Elizabeth added. "That's the New Living Translation."

"Mine says, 'My body is thin and gaunt,'" Zach added. "That's the NIV."

David is moving from his external **ANGER**	To his Internal **PAIN** *(and the physical impact on his life)*	To

"I have the Amplified Bible," Sheila said, "And it says David has become 'an object of taunting to others.' I find that interesting," she noted. "David includes the reactions from others, to show that other people are noticing his physical effects. He must really appear pathetic."

"That's a great observation, Sheila," Gary said.

A Real Prayer in Real Time

Zach spoke now. "I like how these verses reinforce the truth that this is a real prayer in real time; it's not just theoretical, because David is describing the effects of his anger on him physically. It sounds like his anger is eating him alive."

"If I may," Gary gestured with his hand, "I want to add one other effect of anger that can *really* sabotage our healing—even if it's not exactly physical."

"What's that?" Zach asked.

"Self-pity." Gary stated, matter-of-factly. "People get hurt, and then they begin to feel sorry for themselves. Now, in Psalm 109, David is naming the harm done to him, and he is naming the harm he wants done to others. He is also naming the harm he is doing to himself. And all of these are critical components in the healing process.

"But," Gary lifted his chin. "This can go too far." He shifted in his chair and continued. "A little bit of self-pity is natural and understandable, but many people end up feeling sorry for themselves in such a way that they sabotage every effort to help them. In fact, I've found that self-pity is the glue that holds much (not all) of our anger together."

Gary squinted and took stock of the group. "Have you experienced this? Have any of you known people who resisted healing because they were so tied up in their self-pity?"

Zach nodded. "Definitely." His mouth twisted into a sheepish smile. "Actually, that would describe me, in my earlier years."

"That's interesting, Zach," Gary mused. "I have a quote here, by John Piper, that compares self-pity to boasting. And he gives a root cause of self-pity." He cleared his throat and read:

> The nature and depth of human pride are illuminated by comparing boasting to self-pity. Both are manifestations of pride. Boasting is the response of pride to success.
>
> Self-pity is the response of pride to suffering. Boasting says, "I deserve admiration because I have achieved so much." Self-pity says, "I deserve admiration because I have suffered so much."
>
> Boasting is the voice of pride in the heart of the strong. Self-pity is the voice of pride in the heart of the weak. Boasting sounds self-sufficient.

> Self-pity sounds self-sacrificing. The reason self-pity does not look like pride is that it appears to be so needy. But the need arises from a wounded ego. It doesn't come from a sense of unworthiness. **It is the response of applauded pride.**[6]

Gary looked up for a response.

Zach's eyes were wide. "Wow."

"So, what do you think, Zach? Does this ring true? Does pride have anything to do with self-pity?"

Zach considered, and chuckled. "Wow. Those are some hard words. But yes," he nodded. "I think there's a lot of truth there."

"And would you also agree," Gary posed, "That this pattern of self-pity sabotages the healing process?"

"Oh, definitely. When we choose to live with a 'poor me' mindset, instead of letting God work through it with us, we end up reliving, repeating, and replaying the pain."

Re-living	Re-playing
Re-peating	Re-sending
Re-winding	Re-minding
Re-creating	Re-senting
Re-inforcing	Re-membering

Cycle of Self-Pity

"Great way to put it, Zach." Gary nodded. "David is being eaten alive by his unresolved anger and rage. While he is modeling complete honesty with God, he is also showing the damage we do to ourselves when we hold onto our anger, rehearsing our wounds over and over again in our minds and/or with our friends."

Gary looked around at the group. "What do you suppose the long-term effects of this unresolved anger could be? Any doctors in the house?"

Elizabeth raised her hand. "I'm not a doctor, but I'm a nurse. I don't know about anger, specifically, but I do know that when people are extremely stressed, they are much more susceptible to body aches and colds, and infections. Also upset stomachs with digestive problems—that's a big one. I see patients who suffer from nausea, and even diarrhea, because of stress."

Sondra wrinkled her nose. "That's disgusting, Mom."

Elizabeth shrugged. "It's the truth, hon."

---

[6] John Piper, The Dangerous Duty of Delight: Daring to Make God Your Greatest Delight (Colorado Springs: Multnomah Books, 2001), p. 34, emphasis added.

"Don't they also say that stress and anxiety can shorten the lifespan?" Tim asked.

"Yes, I believe research bears that out," Elizabeth nodded.

"It does," Sheila said. "In Jeff's profession, police work, the life expectancy for males is about ten years earlier than average. It's largely because the job is so stressful."

"That's terrible." Caitlyn frowned.

"I know." Sheila shrugged. "But what can I do?"

Be nicer to him, a voice whispered inside. She shifted uncomfortably with this reminder. She hadn't thought about how stressful police work was for a long time. She knew Jeff suffered from the stress of his job, but when was the last time she'd asked him how he was doing? When was the last time she'd invited him to talk about his stress at work? She couldn't remember.

"These are great examples of what stress, anger, and anxiety can do to us physically, guys." Gary took the discussion again.

"We know from science that stress increases the levels of cortisol (the fight or flight hormone) in our body. And it's not too different when it comes to anger, because cortisol can make us feel wired and unable to sleep at night." He now held up a piece of paper from the small stack on his lap. "I have some info here on the physical effects of anger from a book called *Forgive to Live: How Forgiveness Can Save Your Life*, and I'll just read one quote for you. This is from a chapter called, 'What You Tell Yourself Can Kill You.'" He began to read:

Physical Effects of Unresolved Anger and Pain

The May 5, 2000, issue of *Circulation* warned, "A person who is most prone to anger is three times more likely to have a heart attack than someone who is least prone to anger."

Other studies have also shown a link between sustained anger and headaches, stomach disorders, joint pain, fatigue, and chronic low back pain. This happens in part because your muscles are wrapped around your spinal cord, the point from which your nerves stimulate and move the muscles, and because the last of the muscles to relax are those closest to the spine. Again, the point should be clear: anger kills.[7]

[7] Dr. Dick Tibbits with Steve Halliday, Forgive To Live: How Forgiveness Can Save Your Life, 2nd ed. (AdventHealth Press, 2016), p. 71.

Gary looked up from his paper. "It has been said that 'bitterness is taking poison and hoping the other person dies.' And we see how anger can result in all the same symptoms Elizabeth talked about with stress—headaches, body aches, and stomachaches—even heart attacks. I've also seen studies that say anger hurts your immune system and your lungs, which confirm truths the Bible was sharing 1,000 years ago. The Harvard Master study showed how adults who have problems with one parent have more health problems than others. And those who have problems with both parents have the highest level of physical health problems.[8]

"And whether we can't eat because our stomach is tied up in knots, which seems to be David's case here in Psalm 109, or whether we overeat under stress, it hurts our physical health and our immune system." [See end of this chapter for more on the physical effects of anger.]

Gary paused, laying the paper on an end table beside him.

"Of course, we know there are genetic and physiological reasons for many of the health problems we experience.

"At the same time," Gary looked around the group meaningfully, "after reading David's prayer, don't you think there's a good possibility that *forgiveness* could help resolve some of these physical problems?"

He turned to Sheila. "Sheila, let's get back to your question now. You asked, essentially, how we can move on when we keep coming in contact with the 'enemy.' I believe you asked *How can we give up our anger?* and *How can we heal?* Would it be appropriate to include the question: *How can we forgive?*"

Sheila nodded. "Definitely. I'd definitely like to know how we can forgive someone who keeps repeating the same offense over and over again."

---

[8] Russek, L. G., S. H. King, S. J. Russek, and H. I. Russek. "The Harvard Mastery of Stress Study 35-Year Follow-Up: Prognostic Significance of Patterns of Psychophysiological Arousal and Adaptation." *Psychosomatic Medicine* 52, no. 3 (1990): 271.

For Further Study: Physical Effects of Anger and Unforgiveness

> In his book *God's Outrageous Claims*, Lee Strobel shared some sobering information about the physical effects of anger, including this statement from *The New York Times*: "Researchers have gathered a wealth of data lately suggesting that chronic anger is so damaging to the body that it ranks with—or even exceeds—cigarette smoking, obesity, and a high-fat diet as a powerful risk factor for early death."
>
> To back these findings, Strobel shared the results of an eighteen-year study of women at the University of Michigan (the study was designed to test who was harboring "long-term suppressed anger"), and a twenty-five-year study of male graduates from the medical school at the University of North Carolina. In the study of women, it was found that "the women with suppressed anger were three times more likely to have died during the study than those who didn't have that kind of bitter hostility." In the study of male medical school graduates, it was found that "physicians with hidden hostilities died at a rate six times greater than those who had more forgiving attitudes."[9]

In his article "What Unforgiveness Does to Your Brain," Charles Stone explains how a series of bio-chemical processes prepares our body to "fight, flee, or freeze" when we are angry, and he lists the following "unhealthy results" of this "state of high alertness":

> *Rumination:* we nurse and rehearse the hurt which reinforces our negative emotions and burns the event and pain even deeper into our neuropathways. When we're not focused on a task, our inner self-talk will often default to rehearsing the painful situation.
>
> *Diminished memory:* when we remain stressed for long periods of time (i.e., we refuse to forgive), cortisol actually causes our brain to atrophy, especially our memory center called the hippocampus.
>
> *Amplified negative emotions:* prolonged stress also amplifies our amygdala's sensitivity, making us even more susceptible to further hurt and pain.

---

[9] Lee Strobel, *God's Outrageous Claims* (Grand Rapids, MI: Zondervan, 2005), p. 16.

> *Schadenfreude*: this concept describes the secret pleasure we feel when we see those who have hurt us experience misfortune themselves. It actually causes our brain to produce the pleasure neurotransmitter dopamine. It actually feels good to see bad things happen to those we don't forgive. It's the opposite of praying for your enemies which Jesus commanded us to do.

Stone concludes his list with these words: "So, unforgiveness not only keeps us chained to our offender but it profoundly affects our bodies and brains."[10]

[10] Charles Stone, "What Unforgiveness Does to Your Brain," *Charlesstone.com* (blog), August 27, 2015, https://charlesstone.com/what-unforgiveness-does-to-your-brain/.

Chapter 13
Objections to Forgiveness

The Process, and Why We Resist

How to Forgive When Someone Keeps Repeating the Same Offense

"Well, first, let me say that forgiveness is a process. I think sometimes teachers and preachers present it as a one-time act, where, after you forgive, the issue is done. It *is* attractive to present healing in that way. But it's not realistic. And Jesus didn't present it that way, when asked the same question you asked, Sheila." He turned to address the group. "How many times did Jesus say we should forgive?"

"Seventy times seven," Tim quipped. [See Matt. 18:22]

"And," Elizabeth added, "based on our discussion of Ephesians 4:26, it sounds like we might need to forgive daily, so that the sun doesn't go down on our anger."

"Great," Sheila and Sondra muttered.

Gary shifted in his chair. "Don't glaze over just yet, ladies. Let me give you what might be a new concept on forgiveness. Did you realize that forgiveness is not something we *do*, but it is a gift we *receive* from God?"

"What does that mean?" Sondra asked wearily.

"In other words, we can't forgive on our own. Jesus Himself said that *He* did nothing in *His* own strength, and *we* can do nothing in *our* own strength [see John 5:19; 6:63; 15:5].

> "The Son can do nothing by Himself." (John 5:19, NIV)
>
> "Apart from Me, you can do nothing." (John 15:5, NIV)
>
> "The flesh counts for nothing. The words I have spoken to You—they are full of Spirit and life." (John 6:63, NIV)
>
> "Forgive as the Lord forgave you." (Col. 3:13, NIV)

1. Jesus did nothing in His own strength
2. We can do nothing in our own strength
3. We are to forgive as Christ forgave

Zach piped up. "I like how Straight 2 the Heart puts it: 'Forgiveness is not something I work to do in my own strength. True forgiveness is the fruit of me receiving healing as my wounded heart is connected with the heart of Jesus Christ, my Wounded Healer.'"

Sheila spoke. "So, if we can't manufacture forgiveness on our own, how do we *receive* this spirit of forgiveness you're talking about?" She couldn't quite hide her skepticism.

"I'm glad you asked." Gary smiled.

"Straight 2 the Heart's ministry also teaches that 'Forgiveness is supernatural—not natural.' So if we've failed at forgiveness in the past, it's because we were trying to forgive in our own strength, trying to do what we are unable to do. That, of course, is an impossible task. So, first, we must stop focusing on our own performance."

Gary exhaled and continued. "As we take the focus off our performance, we focus on Jesus, and how He supernaturally chose to receive His Father's spirit of forgiveness, 2,000 years ago at the cross, for us. And as we focus less on ourselves and our limits, and more on Jesus and His supernatural power, forgiveness becomes possible"

Forgiveness is not something we do.
Forgiveness is a gift we receive from God.

Now Gary lowered his voice and leaned forward. "Every time we get angry, we have a choice to make. We can choose to turn to God and let *Him* deal with it, or we can try to deal with it ourselves. You and I can either try to continue giving mercy and forgiveness when we have not been able to do so. Or we can fall at the feet of Jesus, at the throne of grace, being as honest as David was, acknowledging his need for the mercy of God. Once we receive mercy in our hearts, *then, and only then*, can we offer mercy to those who have hurt us so deeply. Let's sum up two options in separate columns so we can see the approach many have been taught contrasted with one that includes Jesus' words about Satan's lies and His suffering being tempted like us in *all* points." *(see 2 options on the next page)*

Option 1: Powered by Self	Option 2: Powered by Jesus
I choose to write down how I was hurt and how I feel.	I *choose* to write down how I was hurt and how I feel.
I choose to forgive in my own strength and I hope feelings of peace will come – but I often live with anger or fear.	I *choose* to identify all of the negative thoughts in my heart keeping me from *receiving* Jesus' spirit of forgiveness He has already provided 2,000 years ago.
When I have been told that if I do not forgive, God will not forgive me, I may wonder: • *If* God has really forgiven me • *If* I am really saved (*I have met many Christians with this struggle*).	I *choose* to identify where Jesus was tempted with my negative thoughts. I *choose* to pray Jesus' story into my story. I *choose* to receive His spirit of forgiveness He has already provided 2,000 years ago. I *choose* to do this daily as I receive more and more of His supernatural love and peace so I can "forgive from my heart." (Matt. 18:35)

"So what you're saying," Zach jumped in, "Is that forgiveness really doesn't start with us focusing on the person, or on our good intentions to forgive. It starts with us focusing on our feelings, telling God about our brokenness, and allowing God to point out why we are hurting, and why we are angry."

"Right," Gary said. "This is what it means to trust in God's faithfulness to us, to handle our deepest wounds and darkest desires. And this, as you know, Zach, is a process."

"I sure do. I know from personal experience how hard it is to stop focusing on someone who has hurt me deeply and repeatedly."

Objections to Forgiveness

"And why is it so hard to stop focusing on the person who hurt me or sinned against me? Why is it so hard to 'let that person off the hook,' so to speak? What objections might we have to forgiving and letting go of our anger?"

"Well, you said it yourself." Sheila shrugged. "Forgiving others who sin against me lets them off the hook. It seems to me that if I forgive them, they win; they get away with their bad behavior, and there are no consequences for them." Her eyes narrowed as she spoke. "But I, on the other hand, am the one who pays for their bad behavior."

As Sheila said this, she pictured herself becoming a voiceless doormat in her marriage. She pictured Jeff snubbing her again and again, choosing his work and his man cave and his distractions over her all the time. Except when he wanted sex. Was she really supposed to live like that?

That wasn't a marriage. How could she back down from her position and just let Jeff win?

He's living in la-la land, she thought. *It's my job to steer him back, if not for myself, for our son. How can I just let Jeff off the hook? I can't let Ben grow up and become an absentee father like his Dad.*

Gary nodded as Sheila talked. "I hear what you're saying, Sheila. It really feels like forgiving a person means letting him off the hook."

Sondra jumped in. "It definitely feels risky to forgive. I mean, if someone has really abused your trust," she swallowed a lump in her throat, "then if I let down my guard and forgive, isn't that like giving him permission to use and abuse me again and again?" The anguish was apparent in her face.

Sondra tried to picture herself knocking on Cory's door to tell him she'd forgiven him—the home he shared with his new girlfriend—and the thought made her sick to her stomach. What was she supposed to do: prepare a welcome basket for Cory and his new girlfriend, drop it off at their front door, and give them her blessing?

Hi honey, I know we had our differences, and I know you totally destroyed my life and the lives of our daughters, but I've decided not to hold it against you. Here, have some goodies the girls and I made for you. Enjoy your life without us.

Really? Would God ask her to do that? She shook her head in confusion.

Out loud Sondra said, "I could see forgiving the sinner if he apologized and changed his ways." Even now, she thought, if Cory came and knocked on *her* door, asked for *her* forgiveness, and asked to get back together, she would probably do it. How she longed for him to say those words, *I'm sorry,*

I was wrong, and beg for her forgiveness. “But if there is no repentance from the sinner and I forgive him, where’s the justice in that?” she asked, thinking out loud.

“That’s what I mean,” Sheila concurred. “Justice should be served. But if it’s not, doesn’t the victim have a right to protect herself? Isn’t it healthy to set up boundaries so the person can’t keep hurting you? If I tell the person ‘I forgive you,’ how is he going to get the message that I’m not his personal punching bag and doormat all rolled up in one?”

“Wow,” Tim whistled, breaking the silence that had punctuated Sheila’s words. “I think you ladies just turned up the heat in here about 100 degrees. Hell hath no wrath like a woman scorned.”

“No doubt,” Zach chimed in, a slight smile playing at his lips. Then he turned serious. “But these are good questions.”

“You want to address some of this, Zach?” Gary asked. “If I recall, you have a story to share about this process of forgiving an abuser, don’t you?”

“Yes, I do.” His voice quieted. Then his eyes locked on Sondra’s. “It’s mine.”

Suddenly, everyone leaned in.

Chapter 14
The Freedom of Forgiveness
Zach's Testimony

"So," Zach continued, "I told you guys in the first Bible study that I grew up in a dysfunctional home with angry parents. What I didn't tell you was that I was molested by my uncle for five years, from the ages of eight to thirteen—until we moved away from him and moved here."

A collective gasp was heard around the room. Sondra, Tim, and Elizabeth looked stricken.

"I see your reactions," Zach said. "I know my family never looked dysfunctional on the outside."

"Not at all!" Elizabeth exclaimed. "We saw you grow up—well, during your teen years—for goodness sake! Your family always looked like such a nice family."

"That's exactly what I was thinking," Sheila chimed in.

"I know." Zach shook his head. "Mom has always been a successful lawyer and Dad has his IT business. They provided a nice life for me—as far as money and possessions go.

"Unfortunately, they kind of missed some big things as I was growing up. They were never around much, because they were so busy with their careers. I was a latchkey kid from the time I was eight and on. Satan took that opportunity and ran with it. So I would come home after school to an empty house, and my uncle—he lived down the street and ran his own business from home—would come over to 'check on me.'

"Anyway, I won't go into details. But can you imagine what went through my head as I was growing up, going through puberty, trying to morph into a young adult? The kind of lies Satan was telling me?"

"Oh my gosh, Zach, I'm just horrified," Elizabeth said. "I suppose you were feeling like you couldn't tell anyone. Did you ever tell your parents during those five years?"

"You know, it sounds crazy, but I never did, because I was too scared of what might happen. My uncle always told me it was our little secret, and I'd regret it if I told.

"And my Dad loved his brother so much, I felt like I couldn't tell him what was going on. I knew my uncle would be mad if I told, and I thought my dad would be, too. I thought I'd lose their love. So I didn't risk it. The other lies I was hearing from Satan were *I can't trust anyone,* and *I must have done something wrong,* or *I must be bad* to have brought this on myself."

Tim shook his head. "That son-of-a-gun, Satan. I hear this about abuse victims—how they blame themselves—and I just don't get it. *That,* right there, makes me angry. That innocent kids think *they* did something wrong when some sicko starts molesting them."

Satan's Three-Step Dance of Deception

"I know." Zach nodded solemnly. "But it's so common, Tim. And not only for abuse victims. These are lies that Satan whispers to *all of us* at some point in our lives, but often they start very early, after something bad happens to a child, like the abuse in my home. **First, Satan sets us up with lies** "I'm rejected, I'm alone etc.," tempting us to feel unsafe and unloved. Once we assume they are our own thoughts, we have come into agreement with the 'father of lies,' without realizing it. Then Satan comes in for another round of attacks."

"And if I may jump in here," Gary said, "Tim has brought up an important point."

"Please, go ahead," Zach gestured.

"Like you said, Zach, it's common for people who are abused to blame themselves, and even hate themselves, with the same intensity that David hates his enemy."

"Unbelievable." Tim frowned, crossing his arms. "But why? How can abused people even think that it's their fault?"

"Well, in my years of counseling and prayer ministry, I've seen that it's easier for people to blame themselves than it is to admit they are unsafe and unprotected by those closest to them."

"Ugh." Tim exhaled in disgust. "That's so sad."

"Yes," Gary agreed. "It is. But unfortunately, I've also seen it apply over and over again with divorce. Kids tend to blame themselves for their parents' divorce for the same reason: it's easier to turn on themselves than it is to admit that their parents—the ones they depend on for safety, support, and love—have destroyed their security."

Gary nodded in Zach's direction. "I don't want to take any more time away from Zach's testimony, I just wanted to clarify that the principles we are sharing about anger apply whether we are talking about anger at someone else, or anger at self. So no matter whether we are angry at ourselves or someone else, we will have negative thoughts and lies from Satan that we need to process, whether we do it through prayer ministry, counseling, or some other means." Gary motioned back to Zach.

"Thanks Gary. Good points. For my part, I can relate to both sides of the coin: being angry at others, *and* angry at myself, and having the lies spiral into more and more negative thoughts."

Zach shifted in his chair. "Okay, so let me just sum things up here. If I have some negative thoughts, or some lies, from Satan in my heart, then how can Satan attack me even further? If I am feeling unsafe and unloved—because part of the problem here was my uninvolved parents, who I thought "were too busy to help me–I receive thoughts "I have do something to *protect myself,* to *provide for myself.*"

"Makes sense," Sondra agreed, thinking of her own recent attempts to soothe her pain.

"This is **Satan's second set of lies**. After we are hurting, he tells us we have to protect ourselves, or self-medicate. So as a young teen, as I began to realize the dysfunction of what had happened to me, and how detached my parents were, I started getting angry. I used my anger to protect me, and I just carried it inside from that time on, like a sickness in my soul. After awhile, Satan came in with his **third and final set of lies** - in first person language: "I'm no more than my behaviors or sins. I'm so bad that I could never approach God etc.," because he knew these beliefs could steal my hope and separate me from God forever.

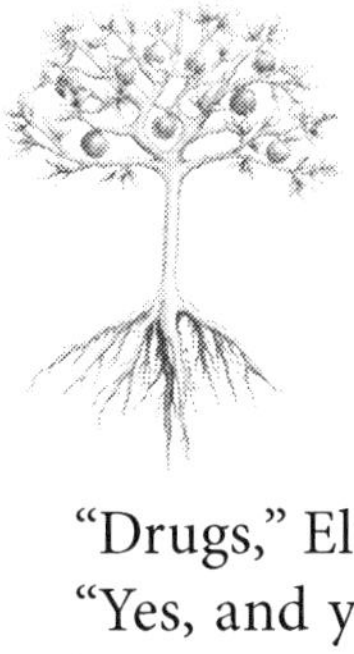

"But let me pause right here and ask you guys, what other things do we do to protect ourselves? What negative fruits do we adopt because we have negative roots, or lies, in our lives?"

"Alcohol," Tim answered.

"Drugs," Elizabeth added.

"Yes, and yes," Zach said. "And I have a praise to give right here that I *didn't* take up those things—because my parents had at least put the fear of God in me over using those substances. I grew up in a Christian home where certain behavior was just not accepted. So I turned to a 'lesser evil.' I got hooked on violent video games. My parents weren't around to see me playing them, and I felt there was no risk to spending half the night, almost every night, in a virtual reality shooting up bad guys.

"Of course," Zach cocked his head, "Those video games didn't really help me with my anger, besides giving me a temporary outlet." He righted his gaze again. "But I don't want to get on a soapbox here. What else? There is another 'tool' of the devil that I used to medicate my pain, and I'll give you a hint: sixty-eight percent of men *in the church* take part in this activity."[11]

"Pornography." The answer, spoken in a flat, expressionless tone, came from Sondra. The unwelcome word unleashed memories of finding lewd websites in Cory's computer history, and then, like darts to her gut, memories of text messages from other women. Finally, these devastating words flashed through her mind: "I just can't commit to one woman for the rest of my life." Every muscle of her body seized up now, fresh hate and anger pouring through her.

"Pornography," Zach repeated. "Bingo. So now you've got a teen guy who is angry, and trying to numb his anger through video games and porn just to survive. I was using all these things to try to feel good . . . because I felt *so bad*. I became a real jerk to live with as a teen, by the way. I never opened up to my parents about my uncle's abuse, and because of that, I became completely bitter toward them. So I would blow up at them all the time. And then they'd get mad, so I'd hole away in my room again to play my games or look at porn. Now, once I engaged in these behaviors, how do you think I felt? Right away, how did I feel?"

"You probably felt good for a little while," Tim said.

"Right. For a little while. But after I blew up at my parents, or after I put down the games or the porn, how do you think I felt?" Zach continued looking at Tim, so Tim answered again.

"You probably felt bad. Guilty." Tim shrugged, as if the answer were obvious.

"Exactly. I regretted my behavior and wished I could take it back."

The Cycle of Sin-and-Forgiveness

Zach leaned forward. "What is going on here? Do you see the cycle? I feel bad, so I blow up, or use video games and porn to feel good, but then I feel bad again. So guess what I do . . . again?"

"The same things over and over." Now Caitlyn spoke.

"Right. And this cycle goes on and on and on. According to Dan Allender, addictions not only serve to medicate ourselves, but also to make us turn against ourselves and that part of us that is trusting and tender—the part that wants love and connection and belonging."

---

[11] See www.conquerseries.com

> Whether the addiction is chemically (alcohol), relationally (sexual), or procedurally (perfectionism) oriented, it serves at least two purposes: (1) to satiate emptiness with intense pleasure that turns into numbness or dissociation; (2) to set up dramas that enable the addict to escape even more painful losses and shame.
>
> It is the drama of sabotage that is the least addressed dimension of addiction.
>
> It is said that every addict is running from something. I fully accept that premise. But I'd say more pointedly: every addict is **trying to ruin something**. After a few hundred experiences of any addictive substance or process, every addict knows the next time is not going to work any better than the last two hundred times. There is a **drive to ruin that subverts the beauty and goodness of the heart**.
>
> Addictions are an effort to defeat any attempt to get close to the deep self-hatred... [or any other negative thoughts like *"I'm not deserving," "I'm not good enough," "I can't be accepted or forgiven," etc.* . . . Dan continues his description of a lady addicted to church work].
>
> She was addicted not only to ministry but to the damage that exhaustion allowed her to experience. The more exhausted she became, the less she felt aware of her body, desires, or inner disgust.[12]

"Now, let me skip ahead a few years, because I want to get to the best part of the story." Zach turned and smiled at Caitlyn. He took her hand. "I met a really great girl, who invited me to her church."

Caitlyn smiled back and blushed.

"What were we, Sweetie, juniors in high school?"

"That's right."

Zach now turned to address the others. "With Caitlyn in my life, I eventually quit porn and was baptized."

"Praise God," Elizabeth said.

"But I didn't know about the porn, at that point," Caitlyn clarified.

"Right," Zach said. "I wasn't going to tell this wonderful girl about my dark secret and risk losing her. Thankfully, having her in my life was motivation enough for me to stop that bad habit. I felt real love for the first time in my life, and I rode that high for years. We had such a great thing going, and I knew I wanted to marry her."

---

[12] Dan Allender, *The Wounded Heart: Hope for Adult Victims of Childhood Sexual Abuse* (Colorado Springs: NavPress, 2008), pp. 132–133, emphasis added.

He took a deep breath before continuing.

"We went to college together, had a great time there, and got married our senior year. I got my pastoral degree, and Caitlyn got her accounting degree. Then, I became an associate pastor and we both got really involved in church. Was I in a better place in my life than I used to be?"

"Of course," Sheila supplied.

Zach nodded. "Yes, I was. But guess what remained in my life?"

"Anger," Tim said.

"That's right. I looked like a great person on the outside, but my negative beliefs remained. Underneath my shiny, Christian exterior, I was still an angry person, and after we were married," Zach gulped, "I got verbally abusive with Caitlyn. Underneath it all, I still had those negative beliefs from Satan, and from my childhood abuse: *I'm worthless, I have to protect myself, something bad is going to happen.*"

He turned to look directly at Sheila. "I also had a bitter spirit of unforgiveness toward my uncle for molesting me, and toward my parents for letting it happen. I carried these beliefs, and that bitterness, right into my marriage. And the longer I harbored this hatred and anger, the more I poisoned my relationship with Caitlyn."

"Amazing," Sheila mused. *Sounds like a marriage I know,* she thought. *Oh, why couldn't Jeff be here to hear this?*

Sondra spoke next. "Guys, I just had no idea!" Until now, she had been reeling in shock. "I thought I knew you both in high school and those early college years, but I guess I didn't know you like I thought I did!"

"Well, we *were* good at hiding it," Caitlyn said. "The other thing was, Zach was *trying* to follow God and do the ministry. Satan, of course, didn't want that. He wanted to sabotage Zach, and God's work. So, he started sending his attacks full force. As Zach got into ministry, praying with and counseling other people with *their* issues, I believe Satan used that to bring up all of *Zach's* old wounds.

"I could see the spiritual battle going on every day. It's like this spirit of oppression came over Zach when he would try to work on his sermons or do church work, or even *get* to church. Our worst fights happened on church mornings. He had so much pent-up anger that he would just explode on me and say all kinds of mean things. I knew he wasn't really angry at *me*, but when he would yell at me, I felt horrible. I told him he needed to make some changes, or I was out."

"That's when I decided to go back to school for my master's," Zach jumped in. "I figured it would do me good to take a break from ministry and go to seminary; I hoped this change might reset things in our marriage. Maybe I could get some help and we could start over."

Straight 2 the Heart's Level 1 and Level 2 Training

Zach exhaled. "I was so fortunate that Straight 2 the Heart came into my life at that time. If you'll remember, during the summer after my first year at Seminary, I went to a men's retreat where I first met Gary. And then, about a year later, in one of my last semesters in school, Straight 2 the Heart's **Leaving a Legacy—Level 1 Training: Praying God's Promises**, came to campus in the form of a class! It was like a divine appointment, because this was a course that hadn't been taught there before!"

"That's great, Zach," Elizabeth said. "So, was the class similar to what we've been learning in this Bible study?"

Zach nodded. "It was. Now, we didn't learn about Psalm 109 during that class, but we laid the foundation for it."

"You're talking about the Hidden Half of the Gospel, right?" Gary interjected. "The information we gave them on the first night of this Bible study?"

"Exactly," Zach said. "Our class meetings were all focused on the sufferings of Jesus, how He suffered in every way we suffer. Since it was a whole semester, we were really able to go in depth with the theology of the message. We spent a lot of time reading and discussing both the Scriptures that *prophesied* Christ's suffering, as well as the Scriptures *showing* Him suffering. We also talked about the fruit and root principle, and how it shows up in the Bible."

Sondra frowned. "Zach, I'm a little confused. Didn't you say you also got personal prayer for your negative thoughts?"

"That's right."

"Well, I guess I'm just wondering then . . . did you guys do that personal prayer thing *in class*? In front of everyone?" As she said this, Sondra remembered again her prayer session with Zach and Caitlyn. She wondered if he had really spilled his guts in front of an entire class. That idea didn't sound safe.

"That's a great question, Sondra. I'm glad you asked." Zach turned to address the group. "So, to answer that question, I have to explain the two levels of Straight 2 the Heart's discipleship training.

"What we learned in class was mostly just the *information* part of Straight 2 the Heart. In class, with the **Level 1 Training**, we learned the *concepts* that we've been discussing here in Bible study. We talked about the three-step

CROSS prayer, which is a template that allows us to connect our stories with Jesus' story. We saw some examples of how we could use the prayer to minister to others. But we didn't have time to share our personal stories in class."

"So when and where *did* you share your personal story?" Sondra asked.

Zach smiled. "I was just getting to that. Our professor set up an optional discipleship group *outside of class time*, using Straight 2 the Heart's **Leaving a Legacy—Level 2 Training: Pure Power—Pure Passion**. *That* is the *application* part of Straight 2 the Heart, where we apply the information in our own lives. And *that's* where I shared my story in a small group and got personal prayer."

Sheila asked the next question. "So, was this a one-time thing? Or was it like an AA group, where you met multiple times with each other?"

Zach laughed, then scratched his head. "Well, I guess it was more like an AA group, in that we met repeatedly for many weeks. But it was *unlike* an AA group in that we didn't keep calling ourselves 'alcoholics,' or sinners. We owned our negative behaviors and we confessed our sins to God—but we did not define ourselves by our behaviors. From the very first meeting, in every prayer, we thanked God that we were receiving our truest, deepest identities as His sons and the victory Jesus had already gained for us."

Tim nodded. "I like that—I like labeling yourself with God's identity for you, and not continuing to label yourself with Satan's identity."

"Bingo," Zach said. "That's the idea. Anyway, having a separate prayer group outside of class worked out great, because the **Level 2 Training** process is typically thirteen weeks, and that's about the length of a school semester."

"Wow," Elizabeth said. "God really worked that out."

"Zach," Gary broke in, "I know we can't go into great detail right now, but maybe you could briefly describe what you did in the level 2 prayer process outside of class, so our friends have an idea of what you mean by *applying the information*?"

Straight 2 the Heart's Discipleship Process

"Sure. Essentially, in Level 2, people pray in small, confidential groups, often even smaller than this group—and usually not a mixed group, like we are." He gestured at the men and women around him.

"Usually, a Level 2 group is all men, or all women.

"There is a trained facilitator who leads each group—in my case, my professor led out—and the facilitator's goal is to teach discipleship through small group prayer sessions."

Zach's Story of Abuse, Anger, and Addiction	Jesus' Story Connecting with Zach's Story
Zach suffered through the pain of being betrayed by his uncle, someone close to him	Jesus suffered through the pain of being betrayed by someone close to Him
Zach was physically violated and shamed by a man in power over him who should have been protecting Him, and remained silent about his abuse	Jesus was physically violated and shamed by the men in power over Him, and remained silent throughout His trials and abuse
Zach learned to believe that he was worthless, he had to protect himself, and something bad was going to happen	Jesus "suffered being tempted" to believe He was worthless, He had to protect Himself in His own strength, and something bad was going to happen
Zach tried to numb his pain through pornography, anger, bitterness, and being critical	Jesus was tempted to numb His pain with alcohol, and tempted to be angry, bitter, and critical

"So," Sondra asked, "Your professor prayed for you out loud in your group? In front of your classmates?"

"Sondra, yes, my professor prayed for me a couple times, modeling how to use the CROSS prayer, or how to connect my story to Jesus' story. *[See cross columns.]* But it wasn't long, maybe two or three prayer sessions, before he moved over and became my coach, training *me* to facilitate prayer with my other classmates in the group."

"Wow," Sheila mused. "That's pretty quick. Weren't you nervous having to lead others through that prayer process?"

"Forget leading others in prayer." Tim raised his eyebrows. "I'd be more nervous getting prayed for—and having to share my story with the group."

"It's true, guys," Zach said. "I *was* a little nervous. All of us were. But the way our professor set up the group, with a contract emphasizing confidentiality, and explaining the ultimate goals of the group, we felt safe to share. We knew we were all there for the same purpose—to get healing for our pain, and training to help others. *And* it was an all-male group, so we felt more comfortable sharing about our unique struggles as men. All of that encouraged us to be honest."

"But Zach," Sheila interrupted, thinking of her husband. "What if someone in your group didn't *want* to share his story? What if he wasn't ready?

What if *you* hadn't wanted to share all these sensitive things you've shared today?"

"Good point, Sheila. That's a question that comes up a lot. And the answer is: no one is ever forced to share something they don't want to share in a discipleship group."

"Sheila," Gary interjected, "If I may add something, the focus in these groups is actually not so much on people's addictions or sensitive, personal information, but on their negative thoughts and beliefs. Was that true in your group, Zach?"

"Oh, definitely. While we were invited to share whatever we wanted, we were told that, in order to participate, all we needed to share was our negative thoughts. Like we've said here, the professor explained that our thoughts are the *roots*, and our behaviors are merely the *fruits*, so it was more important to pray about the roots, or the *causes*, of our issues (issues such as anger) than the issues themselves."

Zach looked at Sheila, who nodded in understanding. He continued. "After my professor had coached me to pray a couple times with different classmates, we rotated; we took turns praying for one another. We would meet for about two hours each week, sitting in a circle like we're doing now, and we usually did two prayer sessions per meeting. Those who didn't facilitate or receive prayer on a given night would silently observe the prayer session, and have a chance to ask questions or add comments at the end. In this way, we were all getting prayer on a regular basis, and we were all getting training in how to pray with one another."

Elizabeth nodded thoughtfully. "That sounds pretty straightforward, and not too intimidating, if you're with the right group of people."

Sheila leaned forward. "So, that leads me to another question: if you only have to list a couple negative thoughts, how is it that the prayer process takes so long? How did these meetings take hours at a time, and how did they last for a whole semester?"

"Another good question." Zach traded a knowing smile with Gary. "Well, besides the fact that we were all getting prayer and being trained, these prayer sessions tended to open up lots of layers, like they always do. People who don't intend to share much often end up sharing more over time as their sense of safety grows. We connect their stories to Jesus' story in a prayer, then pray for blessings or barriers. The person sits quietly and listens for the Holy Spirit (Psalm 46:10), and almost every time, He (the Holy Spirit) brings up more thoughts, or roots, to pray about. So we keep repeating the process. We pray through the CROSS again, we allow wait time for the person to hear from the Holy Spirit, and we pray again about whatever thoughts, or roots, come up. We pray until we run out of time, or until the person ends with peace."

Sheila asked, "But how did you know it was Biblical, and not some kind of New Age meditation or Eastern religion taking place?"

Zach nodded. "That's a good question, and it's important to know that there's a difference between Eastern, or New Age, meditation and Biblical meditation. While we do not have time to get into a long discussion about it now, being still to know God is Biblical. It's also relational. Knowing God is about a personal, interactive relationship with our Creator where we seek His will for our lives. That is very different than emptying our minds in our own strength and chanting phrases, a single word, etc.–what Jesus called "vain repetitions–to get what we want (Matt. 6:7). There's a lot more information on Straight 2 the Heart's website, which shares scripture and science that reveals the difference between the two.[13] Discovering facts from scripture and science allows you to have an intelligent faith, based on God's Word, instead of a living with a fear-based faith.

"Does that answer your question?"

"Yes, I think so," Sheila said. "It makes sense. I can see where we need to do more listening in our relationship with God." "Listening is an important part of *any* relationship," Elizabeth said.

Sheila nodded. "True." *Don't I know it*, she thought.

Zach smiled. "Great. Glad that's clear. So, I hope you're starting to get an idea of the prayer process I went through."

The Seven Phases

"Zach, don't forget the seven phases," Gary interjected. "Those are very Bible-based. And, to return to Sheila's earlier question about why the prayer training takes so long, the phases are quite a process."

"What are the seven phases?" Sondra asked, genuinely curious.

"Well," Zach answered, looking first at Sondra, "AA has twelve steps," then looking at Sheila, "but we have seven phases. We go through a workbook that outlines seven stages of the discipleship process. I guess you could say we are praying the CROSS prayer with a slightly different slant, or focus, in each phase—from phases one and two, where we are honoring our losses, or wounds, and connecting them to Jesus' story, to phase seven, where we are honoring our calling to be in ministry, preparing to go share the gospel with others."

---

[13] Biblical meditation is mentioned many times in the Bible. For instance, see Josh. 1:8; Psalm 1:2; 119:15, 23, 27, 48, 78, 148; 1 Tim. 4:15.

"Zach became a different person over the course of that semester!" Caitlyn spoke up. "As he progressed through the phases, I could see him experiencing more and more freedom from his cycle of sin-and-forgiveness. By the end, he was living a new cycle of forgiveness-and-ministry. It was as if I had a new husband."

Sheila raised her eyebrows. "Wow. Sounds like a magical prayer group. So, what happens in the middle phases anyway? What's the secret to getting to that place of freedom and ministry?" "What's the secret?" Zach mused. "I guess I would say turning things over to God—turning *everything* over to Him. In phases 1 and 2, we turn over our anger, pain, and lies and see where Jesus was tempted in a similar manner. In phases 3, 4, and 5, we deal with our patterns of self-protection, or our patterns of self-sabotage; we pray about our generational patterns, or patterns we've inherited, good or bad; and we pray through our objections to forgiveness. Once we've dealt with all that—" Zach grinned. "Well, for one thing, we've already taken up a couple months."

Sondra's mouth gaped. "No doubt. That sounds like some process. I can see why that would take months." She shook her head. "Actually, I think praying through all that might take my entire lifetime."

Zach laughed. "It definitely could take that long, for some people." More seriously, he added, "Lots of people live their entire lives without taking *any* of that to prayer. Can you imagine?"

Sheila nodded. She *could* imagine that. And it was sad.

"Anyway," Zach continued, "I was saying that, by the end of phase 5, people have typically received a lot of healing for those deep issues. They are feeling renewed, and ready to move into ministry. For me, I was actually excited to share what I had found with others. So then, we enter phases 6 and 7, where we ask God how each person can use their unique life experiences—maybe even their past pain—to minister to others."

Moving into Ministry

"Oh Zach, I just love that," Elizabeth said, eyes glistening a little. "I love how I see you doing exactly what you are describing. You are using your painful story of abuse to minister to us, and, I'm sure, to many others."

Zach blushed, and looked down. "It's the least I can do, when God has done so much for me."

"Oh, Zach," Caitlyn nudged him. "Tell them about your uncle!" She turned to the group. "This story is really proof of Zach's healing, and how far his ministry has reached."

"Oh, yeah." Zach's head snapped back up. "Well, at this point in my life, I hadn't seen my uncle for about fifteen years. But one day, we were grabbing some fast food, and my uncle suddenly appeared in line behind us. I mean, this was a *weird* coincidence: He was passing through the area for some trip, hundreds of miles from home, and he just happened to stop to eat at the same place we did."

"What did you do?" Sondra perched on the edge of her seat.

"Well, first I did a double take! Then, I blinked a bunch of times to make sure it was really him," Zach laughed.

Caitlyn jumped in. "Guys, Zach introduced me to him, and he invited his uncle to come *sit with us!*" Caitlyn shook her head.

Tim blinked. "Wow!"

"Wow," Elizabeth echoed.

"I was shocked," Caitlyn continued. "I knew who this uncle was and what he had done, per what Zach had told me, and I absolutely couldn't believe he was inviting him to sit with us!"

"Were you planning to poison his food?" Sheila smirked.

Zach laughed. "That would seem fitting, wouldn't it?" He shook his head. "But no. I wasn't planning to poison him, or take any revenge, for that matter." His eyes softened. "Believe it or not, I had absolutely no hard feelings against him whatsoever."

All eyes in the group widened.

"You didn't want to poison his food even a little bit?" Sondra joked.

"I really didn't." Zach shook his head. "In my discipleship group, I had already prayed through my anger towards my uncle. I had prayed for weeks about him, giving all my negative thoughts and feelings to Jesus. I had realized that Jesus died for me *and for my uncle*—when we were *both* wicked, ungodly sinners [see Rom. 4:5; 5:6–10; Col. 3:13].

"I knew that God takes sin very seriously—He *does not* excuse it—and my uncle would eventually have to face God for what he had done to me if he did not receive God's gift of repentance. [See Rom. 2:4; Acts 5:31; 11:18.]

Leaving Justice in God's Hands

"The Bible says that the unrepentant sinner:

- Will die in his sins
- Is a slave to his sin
- There is no excuse for his sin
- His guilt remains in him
- Jesus' words will condemn him

[John 8:21, 34; 9:39–41; 12:47–48; 15:22]

"So, when it came time to face my uncle, I didn't feel like I needed to get justice; I knew justice was in God's hands." Zach shrugged. "And frankly, I felt sorry for him. I had learned a little about our family history, and I knew that he had probably been abused as a boy, like I was.

"I realized that my uncle was living in his own prison of pain, and I'm sure he was already suffering under the conviction of the Holy Spirit and the condemnation of Satan. It wasn't my job to make my uncle suffer more. It was my job to hand it off to God, and receive Jesus' spirit of forgiveness for my uncle so I could move on with my life."

"You know, Zach," Gary said, "It strikes me right here that you weren't excusing your uncle by forgiving him. Forgiveness was not a cheap process for you, was it?"

Excusing is just the opposite of forgiving.

"Not at all. I had to name the way I was violated and the pain I experienced. As Lewis Smede has said, 'Excusing is just the opposite of forgiving,'" Zach quoted. "And to me that means that if I had just excused my uncle, I would have tried to push him out of my mind and forget about him. But by wrestling through the process of forgiving him, I did the exact opposite of excusing him."

Answering Some More Objections to Forgiveness

"I had to grapple long and hard with what my uncle had done to me; I had to face the seriousness of his sin. I had to spend many sessions praying with my small group through lies, losses, negative feelings, addictions, and consequences that the abuse had inflicted on me–and the way they spilled over into my marriage with Caitlyn, hurting her as well.

"So, to revisit some questions that were brought up earlier," Zach turned to look at Sheila first, then Sondra, "by forgiving my uncle, I did not just 'let him off the hook.' I named his sin and called it what it was." Zach inhaled deeply. "And I ended up with the blessing of seeing myself based on what God has done *for* me, instead of what my uncle did *to* me."

Sondra trained her gaze on the floor as she listened, brow knitted, lips pursed. Zach couldn't tell what she was thinking. Sheila, too, looked deep in thought.

"Thanks for explaining what forgiveness was like for you, Zach," Gary said. "Your story reminds me of something Desmond Tutu said: 'Forgiveness is taking seriously the awfulness of what has happened when you are treated unfairly.'"

Tim piped up now. "And Zach, just to address another objection, wouldn't you say that forgiving is not the same as trusting a person again?"

"You're right, Tim." Zach nodded solemnly. "Forgiving my uncle did not translate into trusting him. *Trust is earned, distrust is earned, and rebuilding trust is earned.* If he ever takes responsibility for what he did, it will still take me a long time to trust him again."

"That's well said, Zach," Tim returned, crossing his arms. "I think we should also point out that forgiveness doesn't mean letting the abuser continue to mistreat the victim. I'm sure that if you knew your uncle were abusing someone else, you would act to stop it."

"Oh, definitely," Zach said. "Jesus doesn't excuse any sin, *especially* sin against children. He said it would be better for someone to be thrown into the ocean with a millstone around his neck than to hurt one of His little ones [Luke 17:2]. So if we know of some abusive situation going on, then we are sinning if we don't step in and do something to try and stop it. *That* would be a case where we need to report the abuser immediately. But in my case, there was really no action to take against my uncle, besides letting Jesus heal my heart. And that's where Straight 2 the Heart was so helpful."

Zach checked his watch. "There's a lot more I could say, but our time is about up. So, I guess, if you want to know more, speak to Gary or me. And if you want prayer, let us know."

"Thank you so much for sharing your story, Zach," Gary said. "That wasn't easy, but I know it was helpful to our group. I'm hoping it will lead to more of us being honest about our struggles, which we all have."

"Yes, thank you so much Zach," Elizabeth said, shaking her head. "That was really brave." Everyone else nodded and added their own words of thanks.

Making a Choice

"Now," Gary cleared his throat and looked meaningfully around the group. "At this point in the process of reading Psalm 109, I often tell people three things that are not easy to say – but important to say:

1. What happened to you was wrong
2. You have a right to be angry when you have been hurt
3. You have a responsibility to let Jesus heal you and set you free

Gary smiled wryly. "People love #1 and #2.

"Those who choose to live within their prison of anger and rage [see Matt. 18:35] leave at this point in the healing process. They leave the process of healing and freedom because they are not ready to look at:

a. How they have been wounded
b. How they have reacted to being wounded
c. How they have hurt others
d. How they are part of the pattern in all their broken relationships (just like the woman at the well repeated the pattern of being married 5 times and living with someone [see John 4:18]).

"People who embrace #1, #2 *and* #3 move into the process of healing and freedom. And this also opens up possibilities for them to offer the same kind of healing and freedom to others.

"People who reject #3 are rejecting their opportunity and responsibility to let Jesus reveal and release all their anger, bitterness, and desire for revenge, along with all the pain behind their anger. This refusal to let Jesus deal with their pain means they are only reinforcing their anger and bitterness.

"And this also means that they will continue to be the common denominator in all their broken relationships, where they are often living life defensively or 'on-guard.' They are ready to defend themselves against anyone who hurts them. They see life as a battle, where they are often threatened by anyone who does not agree with them.

"Sheila had a concern that forgiving the sinner means we pay the price for his or her sins. I have another way to look at it. What price do *we* pay if we hold onto our anger and if we *don't* forgive? Maybe this is a good question to ponder for your homework."

What is my anger doing to me, to my health? How is my anger hurting my relationship with my spouse? With my children? How is my anger affecting my relationship with God, my ability to witness for Him or be in ministry for Him? My ability to do my job? My ability to parent my child/children?

Am I willing to turn Psalm 109:21–22 into a prayer?

"Dear God, Please reveal to me the negative thoughts, feelings, and behaviors growing out of my wounded heart—and give me the ability to face my pain *with* You, and Your mercy, so that I can receive Your healing and freedom. In Jesus' name, Amen."

After Gary's closing prayer, Sheila eyed him for a few moments, debating. Should she go talk to him? Everything he had said tonight was so relatable to Jeff, and she wanted to ask Gary if he was willing to pray with Jeff about his anger. But Tim and Elizabeth approached him before she even had a chance. "Thanks so much, Gary. Another great Bible study!"

Gary rose, shook Tim's and Elizabeth's hands, and started chatting. Across the room, Sondra, Zach, and Caitlyn looked deep in conversation. Reluctantly, Sheila pulled on her coat. She wasn't in the mood for small talk. Sweeping her purse into the crook of her arm, she bee-lined for the door.

Your Turn: Reviewing Psalm 109:17–25

[17] As he loved cursing, so let it come to him; As he did not delight in blessing, so let it be far from him.
[18] As he clothed himself with cursing as with his garment, so let it enter his body like water, and like oil into his bones.
[19] Let it be to him like the garment which covers him, and for a belt with which he girds himself continually.
[20] *Let* this *be* the Lord's reward to my accusers, and to those who speak evil against my person.
[21] But You, O God the Lord, deal with me for Your name's sake; because Your mercy *is* good, deliver me.
[22] For I *am* poor and needy, and my heart is wounded within me.
[23] I am gone like a shadow when it lengthens; I am shaken off like a locust.
[24] My knees are weak through fasting, and my flesh is feeble from lack of fatness.
[25] I also have become a reproach to them; *When* they look at me, they shake their heads.

For Further Study if You Are Angry

John Ortberg shares his insights about the roots of anger through an incident in which his daughters, ages seven and five years old, were fighting about who invaded whose space after being warned to stop.

> I turned around and began yelling at them with a rage that silenced everyone in the car. I knew the anger was harmful, I knew it was all out of proportion to what they had done, yet I didn't stop. I didn't want to stop. It felt powerful and strong.
>
> But when I finished, I saw a look of fear in those little eyes that haunted me. I wondered where all that anger came from and why I could unleash it on such unsuspecting targets, whom I love so much. I realized that I would rather feel a surge of power from misplaced rage than face the truth about my anxieties and pain about my day, my future.[14]

Dan Allender, in his book *Leading with A Limp*, shares a powerful story illustrating the importance of being honest about the damage done to us by a parent who has violated us, betrayed us, used us.

He was counseling a narcissistic (extremely self-centered) female executive who was controlling and manipulating others under her authority, creating conflict at work. The story illustrates the principle that if we are not honest, the damage *can and will* continue because of the ways we move through life protecting ourselves from our pain: (Please note, her father abusing her was **not** her fault! Taking responsibility for the way she tried to deny her abuse and control others instead of turning to God is part of her journey of faith.)

> God invites the one who rages to collapse in his arms of love. Rest comes when we can no longer sustain our flight, and we find God waiting for us. But rest is not true rest without surrender. For a narcissist, *surrender is equivalent to being young and helpless; it is a return to the original wound of betrayal that gave birth to the fury to be in control.* We must eventually be caught face to face with God and be unnerved by his kindness. Only then will we surrender.

---

[14] John Ortberg, *If You Want to Walk on Water, You Have to Get Out of the Boat* (Grand Rapids, MI: Zondervan, 2001), pp. 106-107.

The female narcissist I mentioned earlier in this chapter finally got caught. It was not by more job conflict, though that continued unabated. She got caught by the death of her father. He had not only sexually abused her, but he had put her on a pedestal and both worshiped her and debased her. He used her wickedly and then rewarded her with glory. As a young child she was not able to see the dark potion of shame and power that he made her drink. *She protected him and diminished any sense of the harm he had done to her.*

Then he repented. On his deathbed and over the span of several weeks, he confessed his harm and tried to enter the harm he had done to his daughter. *It nearly killed her.* She later told me his confession ruined her life far more than the earlier abuse because it *exposed* her shame and heartache and *shattered the role* she played as the highest god to be honored and the greatest whore to be violated. It *tore down the illusion* she had built around their relationship. So she railed against God and against the worm that had eaten her illusion of comfort and control. Her father invited her to enter the agony of her emptiness and … open her arms of faith. [15]

Embracing the truth, she clearly saw her father's sins against her, shattering all the illusions she had built up to protect herself from her pain. Then came the following questions: Had the walls she created really provided the safety and protection she wanted? What price was she paying for the denial and illusions she was living with? Especially when these defense mechanisms resulted in constant conflict on the job, when so much energy was spent trying to control everyone around her?

For Further Study if You Are Depressed

Author Lindsey Gendke shares her story of depression and healing with a Straight 2 the Heart slant in her "brutally honest" book *Ending the Pain: A True Story of Overcoming Depression.* Using her first-hand experiences with Straight 2 the Heart ministry, Lindsey sheds light on the root causes of depression and hopelessness, and how she gained healing by connecting with Christ in His suffering and connecting with others through prayer and discipleship groups—including Straight 2 the Heart's **Pure Power—Pure Passion** group, as discussed in this chapter.

---

[15] Dan Allender, Leading With A Limp: Taking Full Advantage of Your Most Powerful Weakness (Colorado Springs, CO: Waterbook Press, 1996), p, 104.

Chapter 15
Family in Crisis
Sheila's Story

"Sheila, wait a minute." It was Elizabeth. "I couldn't help but notice how engaged you were with our topic this evening. And, Jeff isn't here. I just wondered if there was anything you needed or wanted to talk about."

Sheila scanned the room behind Elizabeth. Gary and Tim were still chatting, and the other three continued in conversation.

Sheila blushed. "I guess I came on kind of strong tonight, didn't I?"

Elizabeth only smiled. "We can step into the kitchen and talk, if you want." She motioned to the kitchen's double doors, and Sheila turned her gaze there, too. For a moment, her body froze as her mind raced. She considered telling Elizabeth about her strained marriage; Jeff's workaholism; her loneliness and anger when he retreated to his "man caves," whatever that meant on a given day.

She waved her hand. "Oh, thanks for the offer, Elizabeth, but I really should get home to Ben." She lowered her voice and leaned in. "I just . . . I just got worked up tonight, I guess, because I was thinking of Jeff, and some of the stuff *he's* been through. I really wish he'd been here to hear what Gary and Zach said. Zach's story reminded me of some stuff Jeff dealt with growing up. I don't know if you know this, but Jeff's Dad was abusive too—physically abusive, not sexually."

Elizabeth's eyes widened. "I didn't know that. I'm sorry to hear it."

"Yeah, it wasn't a good childhood. Anyway, I know Jeff hasn't dealt with his anger and negative thoughts over that. I think he's mostly stuffed the pain over the years, and he's living in denial, trying to cover it up with working too much. . . . " *And anything else that can relieve him of being home*, she fumed inside.

"Anyway," she waved her hand again, trying to keep her tone light. "I just hate to see what it does to him, and I'd love for Jeff to get some healing." She shrugged. "I just wish he would've been here tonight."

Elizabeth's eyebrows crinkled with concern. "I'm really so sorry to hear what Jeff has been through. And Zach. I had no idea about either of their stories." She shook her head. "We all have some pain in our stories, don't we?"

"Um hmm," Sheila concurred, eyeing the front door.

"Well, here's a thought," Elizabeth said. "I know both Gary and Zach offer private prayer sessions with other men." She shrugged, raising her eyebrows. "Maybe we could get Gary or Zach to pray with Jeff . . . if he's willing."

Sheila let out a little laugh. "Ha. *I* would love that. But fat chance getting Jeff to sit and bare his soul to another guy." She smirked. "That's not really his thing."

Elizabeth smiled. "I suppose not. Well, *we* can pray for Jeff . . . and maybe *God* will convict his heart to seek healing." Elizabeth glanced over her shoulder at her daughter. "You never know whose heart God is going to steal next."

"I suppose that's true," Sheila said. "Thanks, Elizabeth. We can pray for that."

But as she said her goodbyes and exited the house, she thought: *There's not a chance in the hot place that Jeff would ever request prayer.* Driving home, she replayed the Bible study in her mind and got angrier and angrier. *Jeff would never let Gary pray with him. He's too closed off to his emotions. And too proud to let anyone in. But why shouldn't Jeff seek help for the family's sake? Doesn't he realize what his anger does to our family? How selfish can he be?*

She thought of their son, Ben, and how she had been finding him holed up in his room with his iPhone more and more. Ben was becoming distant and withdrawn, like his father. His grades were slipping. He rarely seemed happy anymore. And whose fault was that? By the time she pulled into their driveway, she was practically livid. Jeff was going to ruin their son because he wouldn't deal with his own issues!

Sheila entered the kitchen and flipped on the light. She tossed her keys on the counter and peered down a darkened hallway. There were no house lights on at all. Where was Ben?

She grabbed her phone out of her purse. Ben was supposed to text her and tell her where he was in the evenings, and she had silenced her phone for the Bible study.

Sure enough, there was an unread text from Ben. *I'm at Brandon's house*, the message read.

Sheila exhaled. At least Ben was good about letting her know where he was. She shed her coat, unraveled herself from her purse, and trudged into the living room. She collapsed into an armchair, letting her head fall into the cushions. She wondered what Ben was doing at Brandon's.

Zach's story came back to mind. Video games. She would have bet money that Ben and Brandon were playing video games, like they did so often.

But then an ugly thought wracked her body. *It could be more than video games. It could be porn.* She shuddered. Ben was her little boy. But he was also a *teenage* boy.

And she couldn't deny it; her son was showing a lot of the signs Zach had talked about. Withdrawing. Blowing up at her. Was this normal teenage boy behavior, or was it a result of the dysfunction in their home?

Sheila stood and walked down the hallway. She hesitated just a moment outside Ben's door before she nudged it open and walked in. Her eyes swept the room, looking for clues. *What a pigsty!* She felt tempted to be angry at Ben for the state of his room. How many times had she nagged him to keep it clean? Piles of dirty laundry—or maybe it was clean?—covered the floor. Empty dishes and food wrappers littered every surface. The bed was unmade and, like the floor, covered with clothes, magazines, wrappers, and electronics.

Sheila shook her head, thinking of a recent conversation with Ben.

After a few weeks of his clothes piling up, him bringing her three baskets or more at one time, she'd had it. "I won't do your laundry anymore. It's not fair for me to get slammed with two weeks' worth of your laundry at one time; you can learn some responsibility; you can do it."

She'd promptly complained to Jeff about Ben's lack of responsibility, and Jeff had promptly said he'd "take care of it." By "take care of it," she found out, he meant "rescue" Ben. She knew that Jeff now washed Ben's clothes once a week, when he washed his police uniform. Jeff had been washing his own uniform for their entire marriage. It had been one of their first "ground rules": housework was split down the middle, because they both worked. Sheila might wash Jeff's clothes if she was already washing her own; she might cook for him if she needed to eat; but by and large, each partner took care of his or her own needs.

Sheila shook her head. "Disgusting," she muttered, kicking clothes this way and that to get to the bed. "What is he learning, when his dad just rescues him, time and time again? He's learning he can just sit on his keister all Sunday, give no thought to what needs to get done in a day."

She frowned at the thought of Jeff and Ben sitting on the couch on Sundays, watching football. Their sacred tradition. On weeknights when Jeff didn't work, it was movies. She couldn't say her son and husband had a great talking relationship, but she couldn't deny that they *did* have a bond—and she wasn't part of it.

Hmph. She shoved some shirts off the bed and pulled the comforter back to reveal a hard, silver rectangle. Aha. Success!

Sheila sat down on the bed and opened Ben's laptop. She hesitated, just barely, before logging on to the Internet. She'd never spied on her son before, because she never thought she needed to. "He's such a good kid," all his teachers said, and she believed them. She and Jeff had given Ben the talk about appropriate Internet usage when he got the laptop a year ago, and she'd believed him when he'd said, "Got it, Mom. Don't worry." *He really is a pretty good kid,* she thought. *Minus his cleaning habits.* And, of course, the recent attitude.

Google popped up. Sheila's breath quickened just a little as she ran her mouse across the toolbar. It stopped at Computer History. She took a deep breath, and clicked.

Her eyes ran down the list—Facebook, snapchat, sports websites, game websites, some news websites . . . probably for a school assignment, repeat of all the above . . . and then . . .

Sheila gasped. Blinked. Scrolled down farther.

No, no, no! her heart screamed . . . because she had suddenly lost her voice. Raunchy titles and lewd catchphrases suddenly piled one on top of another in the list—a porn binge. Sheila clicked on only one of the sites to confirm the contents before slamming the computer shut. She sat in shock, laptop shaking in her hands.

What does this mean? Sheila's soul cried as her breath came heavy. For a moment, she hunched over the computer, shaking her head in confusion. Soon she was dialing Jeff's number and pacing Ben's room.

Chapter 16
The Ultimatum
Jeff and Sheila's Story

Jeff's phone vibrated on the desk in front of him. Incoming call: Sheila.

His impulse was to ignore it and continue working through the stack of paperwork in front of him—his "police business" for the night—but with each vibration, he felt his stomach clench. *She's probably calling to tell me what I missed at Bible study. She's probably calling to complain that I should have lined up a coworker to cover for me so I could have been there.*

He exhaled and sank back into his chair, eyeing the phone. *She always does this to me. She always breaks into my peace to tell me what I should be doing.*

He looked at the papers in front of him. He *was* conducting police business, but it was business that could have waited. He was doing an extra project for the police chief, hoping to speed up the promotion he wanted. Since home life had gotten really tense in the last year, it had been easy to throw himself into his work. With this and other projects he'd volunteered for, he could easily come up with honest and "valid" excuses to work extra hours.

Tonight, his other motivation for avoiding Bible study had been Sondra. After their car ride last week, he couldn't stop thinking about her, to the point where he had even dreamed about her—several times. Worse, he had almost called his wife by her name, because the names were so similar. *Sheila*, said the incoming call on his phone. But he wished it said *Sondra.*

A pang of guilt tightened his stomach. Reluctantly he reached for his phone.

"Hello?"

"Jeff? We need to talk. It's Ben."

Jeff shot straight up in his chair. "Is Ben alright?"

"I don't know." Sheila's voice came out in a strangled whisper.

Jeff's breath caught in his throat. "Well, is he hurt? Is he dead?" Images of his only child flashed through his mind's eye: Ben trapped in a crushed car, Ben dying in a hospital bed. Because Jeff saw these scenes all the time, it was too easy to imagine Ben in one of them. "Do you need me to go somewhere?" Jeff placed his hands on his wallet and keys, readying for a quick exit.

On the other end of the phone call, for one tender moment, Sheila's heart opened to her husband, the protector-provider—the part of Jeff that Sheila had fallen in love with in college.

"No, no, Ben's not hurt. It's nothing like that."

Jeff exhaled, leaned back in his chair. "Well, what is it, then?"

"Jeff, I found porn in Ben's computer history." Her voice landed flat. Silence followed.

"Oh," Jeff finally said, voice equally flat. But his palms got a little clammy.

"Well?" Sheila prompted.

"Wellllllll . . . " Jeff paused. "He *is* a teenage boy."

"Oh, so are you saying this is *normal*?"

Jeff shrugged. "Kind of."

"He's only thirteen, Jeff!"

"He's hitting puberty, Sheila."

"I can't believe you're taking this so lightly!"

"I can't believe you're so upset!"

"Ugh!" Sheila had to restrain herself from throwing the phone across the living room, where she was now pacing.

She took a deep breath. "Okay, just help me understand this, Jeff. I know, *I know*, that teenage boys have hormones on steroids." She took another deep breath. "But I taught him better than that! *I taught him better than that!*"

Sheila took several paces, huffing with each step. "Haven't I taught him to respect women? *Haven't I modeled that women are more than just bodies?* That we are intelligent and smart and we deserve respect?" She turned on her heel, turning the conversation in the same step. "Haven't I been a good mother? I've tried so hard, Jeff, *so hard* . . . to raise the kind of young man that would champion women, and make me proud." Her voice buckled on these last words.

"Sheila," Jeff halted, touched by his wife's anguish. "Slow down. This isn't about *you*."

"Yes, it is!" she insisted. "I feel like everything my son *does* is about me. Everything reflects on me and what I've taught him. If he fails, *I* fail!"

"Whoa, hold your horses, honey. There you go again, taking the world on your shoulders." He shook his head. Sheila was so intense. She was intensely annoying, it was true. But she was also intensely invested in their son. She put her heart and soul into everything she did, in fact, be it nagging him, or making sure Ben's body and mind were properly fed. This intensity with which she lived life was one thing he admired early on about his wife, and still admired . . . when she wasn't too annoying.

"Trust me, this is *not* all about you."

"How can you be so sure?" Sheila demanded.

"I just know." Jeff bent over in his chair now, trying to still the churning in his stomach.

"What?! Jeff, why do you think you can just dismiss my concerns with those dumb phrases? I'm not some child that you can just brush off with *because I said so*!"

"Okay, okay." Jeff quieted for a moment. When he next spoke, his voice was lower, more serious. "Well, for one thing, Sheila, Ben has *two* parents. He has you, but he also has me. I'd like to think that *I* have some influence on his life, too."

"You're right, *honey*. You *do* have an influence on our son. He's learned a lot from you." Sheila gritted her teeth. "He's learned how to shut down his emotions with media. He's learned how to live in a house with me and barely have one conversation in a whole day. He's learned to retreat to his man cave so he doesn't have to deal with conflict. What has it been, Jeff, eight months since you really *talked* to me? Plus a decade or more of shutting me out? That's a long time for Ben to learn the art of web surfing and channel surfing and texting and getting into all kinds of things he shouldn't be into."

Jeff bolted upright once again, anger freshly ignited. It was one thing for Sheila to belittle him and his habits; it was quite another to accuse him of poisoning their son. He loved Ben with all his heart; couldn't she see that?

"Wait a minute Sheila. Let me just understand what you're saying. Are you accusing me of ushering our son into porn, just because I like my technology? I like my alone time? And yes, I like to avoid conflict with you? Is that what you're saying?"

"I didn't say that."

"But it's what you insinuated."

"I'm just pointing out patterns in our home life, Jeff." Sheila paused, then went on, unable to stop. "There's also the pattern of Jeff, the emotionally absent Dad who spends too much time at work—and Jeff, the husband who tunes out his wife because she tells him things about his character he needs to hear, but things he refuses to deal with. Have you ever thought of getting help for your past abuse, Jeff? Your dad's abandonment? I know you say you're better than your father because you don't hit and kick me and Ben . . . but can you say you're really the father you would have wanted? I know you reside in the same house we do . . . but Jeff, it really feels like you've abandoned us, because you are never there for—well, I won't speak for Ben—but you're never there for *me*."

Jeff gasped for air as if punched in the stomach. The words left him speechless.

These were echoes of his own father's voice when Jeff was a young boy. These, like the words his dad had doled out freely in drunken fits, along with punches, kicks, and knees to the gut—both to Jeff, and to Jeff's mother. Jeff was amazed, looking back, that his mom had stayed with his dad as long as she had, until Jeff was ten. But Dad always said he was going to "get it together." And Mom, for so many years, held out hope that he would.

After enough years of empty promises, his mom finally left his dad when he lost yet another job and their house got repossessed. Jeff remembered spending his preteen and early teen years with family members who extended helping hands until his mom could get on her feet. He remembered rides from policemen and other strangers sometimes when their old beater broke down on the way to or from school; and he remembered finding his mom crying in her room, so many times, in those lonely years without a husband.

As he grew into his college years, he vowed to be better than his father. He wanted to be the protector, provider, his father never had been. For his wife, he wanted to be the safe man that his father had never been for his mother. Beyond that, he never wanted to be out of options or out of resources again. Police work appealed to him not only because it provided a car and a gun, but also a badge—a mark of authority and power—something he'd never before felt he'd possessed.

But, apparently, he'd failed. He punched the stack of papers on his desk. He already knew he was failing as a husband. But now, according to Sheila, he was a failure as a dad, too. The thought that he'd repeated his own father's mistakes anguished him. How could he convey this to Sheila? Much less keep dwelling on a subject so painful? He resorted to the only safe course he knew: anger.

"Ahh, well, in that case, let me point out some patterns, too. When was the last time you were intimate with me, Sheila? When was the last time you made yourself available to me? I know you are more than a body—you are intelligent, you are smart, you are a whole person—but Sheila, part of your person is your body. Part of a marriage is intimacy. And yes, I mean sex. When was the last time I didn't have to beg for sex? When is the last time we were healthy in that department? If you didn't notice, Sheila, it was more than six months ago. Maybe while you are busy looking for the causes of dysfunction in our family, and busy bashing *me*, you should go look in the mirror and size up what *you've* done to contribute to the problem."

Sheila's jaw hung open. "What are you saying? *I* caused the porn problem? It's been six months since we had sex, but it's been years since we were intimate, taking time to talk and listen to each other!"

"Ugh," Jeff muttered in disgust. "It's like talking to a brick wall. You won't ever look at *your* part. But to get back to the porn question, the answer is yes. Yes, Sheila. You *did* cause the porn problem in our family."

"How dare you!" Sheila screamed. "How can you say that?"

"I'll tell you how, Sheila." Jeff's voice got low. "Because *Ben* isn't the one looking at porn."

He heard her gasp. "*You!*"

"Oh, don't act so shocked. You can't deny a man sex and expect him not to seek a replacement."

"Oh, great," she huffed. "I suppose you're having an affair, too."

Jeff's jaw tightened. "No. I'm not. I've never stepped out on you, Sheila." *Even if I've wanted to.*

She made a choking noise. "Whatever, Jeff. You've always put something else in front of me. It might as well be another woman."

Jeff's face wrinkled in pain. "What do you want me to do, Sheila? Yes, I haven't been the model husband. Did it ever occur to you that I *want* to be an awesome husband, but maybe I don't know how? And you don't make it any easier, always criticizing me. What do you *want* from me?"

"Get help." Her voice landed flat. "Get prayer from Zach and Gary." She paused. Then her calm and measured voice broke. "I don't know if I can go on in this marriage, Jeff, unless you get help. Please. If not for me, do it for Ben. You and I may not last, but your son needs you. Right now, I don't want anything to do with you."

At that, the phone went dead.

Jeff held the dead phone to his ear for a moment, frozen. His wife wanted "nothing to do with him."

Why not another woman? He sneered to himself. Those were his wife's own words. Nothing he did made her happy, so why *not* another woman, a woman who actually appreciated him? Before he realized what he was doing, he was texting Sondra.

Chapter 17
Change of Heart

Sondra's Story

Sondra sat propped up in bed, reading Gary's homework questions, while her girls slept in the room next door.

"What is my anger doing to me and my health?" She paused over the question, ignoring her pinging phone for a moment, thoughts blurring through recent days.

For one thing, she was sleeping too much. And she was drinking. She was doing whatever she could not to feel the pain of Cory's rejection, doing whatever she could just to survive. And that was working okay . . . until it came to her relationships. She reread the whole question again:

> What is my anger doing to me, to my health?
> How is my anger impacting my relationship with my spouse? With my children?
> How is my anger impacting my relationship with God, my ability to witness for Him or be in ministry for Him? My ability to do my job? My ability to parent my child/children?

The last part was the real kicker. Her ability to parent her children? She scoffed. She *had* no ability to parent her girls right now. She didn't even have a desire to *engage* with them. And the girls were suffering. She saw the pain in their eyes when she told them, "Not now," or "Mommy's tired. Go find something else to do."

Sondra heaved a heavy, guilty sigh. She *wanted* to do better for her girls. She *wished* she could heed her mom's words and "Get out of bed more often and *be there for the girls.*" But she just couldn't right now.

Sondra shook her head as Jeff's message pinged. She knew tomorrow morning would be no different. She would continue to let her mother pick up the slack, get the girls out of bed and off to school, because there was nothing Sondra wanted to get out of bed for, not even her girls. *Especially* not her girls. She felt like her gloomy presence did more harm than good.

Her phone pinged again, and now Sondra reached for it.

"Hey, how's it going?" the message read. It was from Jeff.

She blinked. Jeff? She checked the time and blinked again. It was 10 p.m.

"Hi," she replied. Then she stared at the phone, trying to guess what a 10 p.m. text from Jeff meant.

"I was just wondering, are you still looking for work?"

"Sadly, yes, I am," Sondra replied, butterflies stirring her stomach.

"I was working late at the office, and I remembered our receptionist is leaving soon. We have a job opening coming up, so I thought of you. You should apply."

He thought of me. "Aww, that was nice of you…thanks! Maybe I will." *Maybe I will*, she thought, butterflies multiplying. She imagined herself manning the front desk, watching Jeff come and go on his rounds, exchanging conversation and winks.

"Would I get free coffee and donuts?" She smiled. It felt good to flirt.

"Sure, as much as you want," Jeff texted back with a winking smiley face. "Hey, I'll be at the office tomorrow between 4 and 9 if you want to stop by and fill out an application. I can introduce you to the chief and put in a good word." Another smiley.

Wow. The text was so forward. Sondra couldn't help but feel like he was asking her out on a date. *Was* he? He was certainly extending himself more than he had to. *I wonder if things are okay with Sheila?*

She paused before replying. This felt like more than just a friendly job lead. And she wasn't sure how she felt about that.

"I'll have to see how my day goes," Sondra answered. *I'll see what my gut says tomorrow*, she thought, laying down her phone. *Or maybe what God says . . .* another voice whispered in the back of her head.

*****

"Thanks for meeting with me Caitlyn," Sondra said to her old friend the next evening. The two women were sitting on worn leather couches in Zach and Caitlyn's living room for an impromptu prayer session—which Sondra had requested that morning. The colors in the room, soft blues and neutrals, calmed her.

"Of course!" Caitlyn assured her. "Zach and I are always happy to pray for you, or just hang out. Whatever you need!"

Sondra smiled gratefully. "Well, I feel like I need a lot of advice, and a lot of prayer right now. Ugh." She shook her head as if to clear her thoughts. "You know, since we talked last night, a lot has happened. I have a lot of thoughts swimming in my head, and I just don't know what to do with them."

"Well, I'm really glad you were willing to ask for prayer a second time, and see healing as a process," Caitlyn smiled. "I think you did the right thing. Prayer is always a good response."

Sondra nodded.

"On that note, let's officially open up our session with prayer."

Sondra bowed her head.

Caitlyn cleared her throat and prayed: "Dear Father, Thank You that You brought Sondra here today to pray with me, so *You* could talk to her about her wounded heart. Thank You that Jesus came to heal the brokenhearted and set the captives free. He came for Sondra, and right now Sondra is a captive to anger, and other negative thoughts and lies, but Jesus can set her free. Please lead and guide our prayer session tonight, and speak to Sondra about what's in her heart and how Jesus suffered like her to heal her. Thanks for being here with us, in Jesus' name, amen."

Sondra looked up, surprised at how much the short prayer had touched her. "Thanks for that."

"Of course." Caitlyn picked up a pen and a notepad. "I hope it's okay if I take some notes. I just like to write down what you tell me so we can pray really specifically about your needs. And all these notes will go home with you."

"Sure." Sondra shrugged.

The Three-Step CROSS Prayer

"Okay, good. So, let's start with what's going on with you today. I know in the last session you were dealing with a lot of anger at Cory."

"Yeah," Sondra muttered. "I still am." She stuffed her hands under her thighs. She thought of how, when she'd last picked up the girls from Cory's, he had been stretched out on the couch, a beer in hand. The girls had been planted in front of the TV. They'd probably been watching TV all day. And the whole weekend, Sondra thought.

She fumed at the memory.

"Well, there's a lot going on with me. How much do you want me to share?"

"Totally up to you," Caitlyn said. "Share whatever you want to, but eventually we want to pray about your negative thoughts and feelings, and, like we talked about in Bible study, what negative effects that anger is having in your life. But let's start with the anger, and see where that leads."

Sondra frowned, a storm settling over her face.

"Okay. Yes, I'm angry. I'm living with my parents, trying to find a job to support myself and my two girls. Meanwhile," her features tangled into a snarl, "*their dad* is off doing whatever he wants to—drinking, dating, you name it. It's like the day he decided to leave me, he decided to give up all responsibility whatsoever."

She thought back to how, when they were married, he rarely drank in her presence, and never in front of the girls. She'd never been a drinker, before he left her, and asked him to keep it out of the house. For the most part, while they were married, he had. But now—and this *really* made her angry—he wasn't even trying to hide his drinking from their girls.

"That's hard," Caitlyn sympathized.

"Yeah, and it really hurts because I really need a break sometimes. I thought that at least I could count on him to be responsible on the weekends I dropped the girls off, but now I don't trust him. I don't know what he'll do in front of the girls—I know he's not trying to hide the fact that he's 'with' someone else." She gulped. "And I know that hurts the girls."

"And you too," Caitlyn said quietly, nudging a box of tissues toward Sondra.

Sondra's lip trembled; she struggled to speak.

"Remember how we talked about there being pain underneath the anger?"

Sondra nodded.

"Can you identify some of those negative thoughts behind your anger and pain?"

Step 1: Identify Negative Thoughts and Feelings

Sondra scrunched up her mouth and knitted her eyebrows. "I don't know. The only thoughts coming to mind right now are that *I have to protect myself. I need to do whatever it takes not to feel the pain.*"

"That makes sense," Caitlyn murmured. "You've had such a loss. I can't imagine."

Sondra dabbed at her eyes. She shrugged. "Yeah, it stinks. So I just try to go numb and not think about it, try not to feel it."

"And get angry?" Caitlyn added, raising her eyebrows.

Sondra smiled a little. "Yeah, I guess. It helps a little to imagine setting fire to Cory's new car."

Caitlyn smiled too. "Your heart is 'wounded within you.' It makes sense that you're angry, and that you want to be numb." A pause.

Step 2: Identify with Jesus

"Sondra, I wonder, can you see any ways that Jesus might have been tempted like you? Last time we identified how He suffered like you, being abandoned and betrayed by a kiss by His closest friends."

Sondra nodded, deep in concentration.

"So, when Jesus was facing His darkest time, with none of His earthly friends there to help Him, no one to stand up for Him, what do you think He was feeling? What temptations was He facing?"

Sondra chewed on her bottom lip. "Well, He must have been tempted to be angry at His so-called 'friends.'" She shook her head. "Boy, they really let Him down."

Caitlyn nodded.

"And I bet He felt tempted to protect Himself, and to escape the pain He was going through." She studied Caitlyn's face. "But He didn't escape. He stayed there and went through His pain—with no support, no painkillers. He was *fully conscious* of the awful things happening to Him, and He just took it." Sondra shook her head again, moved with the awfulness of Jesus' story.

"You're right, Sondra. He really suffered, and He did it for *you*."

Sondra gulped back tears.

"Let's pray again, okay?" The two women bowed their heads as Caitlyn prayed: "Dear Jesus, Thank You that You suffered in every way Sondra has suffered, being abandoned and betrayed by a kiss, and being let down by the ones who should have been protecting You. Thank You that You were tempted to get angry at Your abusers and protect Yourself, but You left vengeance to God, so You could gain victory for Sondra and set her free from her anger and her desire to protect herself in her own strength. Thank You that You rose to give Sondra new life and restore her to her true identity as Your daughter. In Jesus' name, amen."

"Amen," Sondra repeated, heaving a deep exhale.

Step 3: Pray for Blessings or Barriers

Caitlyn looked up at Sondra. "Sondra, I'm going to pray again for you, and this time we're going to ask the Lord to reveal any blessings or barriers related to your anger and negative thoughts. When I finish this time, just keep your head bowed, remain silent for awhile, and listen for the still, small voice of God to speak to you. After a minute, if you have any thoughts, impressions, whatever, and if you are comfortable sharing with me, please let me know."

"Okay." Sondra nodded and bowed her head with Caitlyn, who again prayed:

"Lord, it's not Your will for Sondra to live in her prison of anger and numbness. You know that the enemy is trying to sabotage Sondra through her anger, and separate her from You—the only True Source of healing. So today, Lord, we ask *You* to deal with Cory, and we ask *You* to deal with Sondra's heart.

"Lord, do You have any blessings for Sondra right now, or are there any barriers or negative thoughts keeping Sondra from Your peace?"

Sondra rested her head on clasped hands, listening for the still, small voice she had heard in her first prayer session. After a moment, her head snapped up.

"I am angry at Cory, and that anger is blinding me. I'm focusing on Cory so much because it feels easier than focusing on the pain in my heart." She shook her head. "But that's a barrier," she said matter-of-factly.

"Why?" Caitlyn perched her chin on her fist and leaned forward. "What is bad about your anger at Cory?"

"Because I'm using it as an excuse not to deal with my *own* behavior. I'm using my pain to justify bad behavior. Because Cory is being irresponsible, I'm being kind of irresponsible, too. And now, because of my behavior . . . " Sondra took a shuddery breath. "I am not just hurting myself. I am hurting my daughters." This last part came out in a whisper as silent tears slid down her cheeks.

Caitlyn nodded. "That's so like Satan, isn't it? He just uses our pain to hurt others."

"He's such a jerk," Sondra agreed, trying to smile through her tears.

"Let's pray again," Caitlyn said. "Lord," she bowed. "Where were You tempted to numb Your anger and pain, like Sondra is tempted to numb *her* anger and pain?"

Sondra's Story of Betrayal, Anger, and Pain	Jesus' Story Connecting with Sondra's Story
Sondra suffered the pain of being abandoned by Cory	Jesus suffered the pain of being abandoned
Sondra was rejected by her husband	Jesus was rejected by those He loved
Sondra was betrayed by a kiss	Jesus was betrayed by a kiss
Sondra was angry at being taken advantage of by Cory, who should have been protecting her	Jesus was tempted to be angry when He was taken advantage of by the men who should have been protecting Him
Sondra was trying to numb her anger and pain with alcohol to avoid suffering	Jesus was tempted to numb His pain with alcohol to avoid His suffering
Sandra was struggling with unforgiveness towards Cory	Jesus was tempted not to forgive, but said, "Father, forgive them for they know not what they do."

Sondra closed her eyes, and this time, instead of bowing her head, she lifted it skyward.

"He was tempted to numb His pain with alcohol on the cross," Sondra answered, keeping her eyes closed. "He was also tempted to not forgive those abusing Him . . . and to not go through His suffering on the cross." She opened her eyes.

Caitlyn nodded. "That's true. It's amazing to see how He was tempted to take an easier way out at every step of His journey." She motioned with folded hands to Sondra.

"Sondra, we're going to pray again, and connect your story with Jesus, and this time, would you repeat after me?"

"Sure," Sondra said.

"Great. Let's pray." Caitlyn bowed her head and Sondra followed suit, repeating these words after her friend:

Dear Jesus,
Thank You that You chose to suffer like me, being abandoned and without support, tempted to numb Your pain, and tempted to escape Your responsibilities to Your children. Thank You that in Your time of darkness You refused the drink offered to You, so You could suffer, die, and rise for me, to set me free from all the ways I have tried to numb my pain. Thank You that You gained the victory for me so that I can be strong for my daughters, through *Your* strength—and not turn to false comforts that will only separate me from You. In Your name, amen.

Keeping her eyes closed, Caitlyn continued in prayer. "Lord, Thank You for doing all this and more. Now, what is the next step for Sondra?"

What is my anger doing to my girls? Gary's question came back once again to Sondra as she sat listening, waiting. *And what do I do with it?*

In the silence following Caitlyn's prayer, many thoughts passed through Sondra's mind. Images she had blocked now played in her mind, a movie reel she didn't want to see. She saw herself reacting from the anger, shoving her daughters at her parents while she went out drinking. She saw herself lying in bed, hung-over, letting her parents pick up the slack yet again. She saw herself surfing on the Internet for hours, when she should have been job hunting.

Selfish, selfish, selfish, the word echoed in her brain. Her behavior had been so *selfish*. Since Cory left, she had chased any impulse that made her feel good, anything to numb the pain. But at what cost?

Sondra shuddered. Now she saw dark, shadowy images—God's glimpse of what He had saved her from so far. She saw pictures of herself crashing in a drunk driving accident . . . pictures of some policeman pulling her over for drunk driving . . . pictures of . . . Jeff! her own policeman . . . taking her into his office, pulling her in for a passionate kiss, pulling off her clothes . . . and she . . . falling right into Satan's trap.

Oh!

Sondra buried her head in her hands in silent shame. This last image was the same one that had lulled her to sleep last night, after texting with Jeff . . . but last night, it had been a fantasy. Today, it was a nightmare.

What am I doing? Sondra thought. *How reckless. How selfish. What would this do to Sheila? To Ben? How could I even consider being a home wrecker—destroying another family just like Cory destroyed ours?*

"Is anything coming up?" Caitlyn broke into Sondra's thoughts. "Do you have any images, any next steps from the Lord?"

Sondra inhaled long and looked up, away from her friend. "Oh yes," she nodded painfully.

Caitlyn remained silent.

Sondra sighed. "It's kind of embarrassing."

"Don't worry; you don't have to share anything you don't want to."

"Well, I guess the bottom line is this: The Lord is telling me to deal with *my* anger, because it is threatening to poison my whole life."

Sondra turned to look straight at Caitlyn. "I hear Him telling me that if I don't deal with *my* negative behaviors, then I *can* and *will* hurt a lot of other people." She sat straight up. "I know what I need to do now," she said, feeling peaceful for the first time in a long time.

> The Lord is telling me to trust in His faithfulness to me to heal my anger because it is inside of me and threatening to poison my whole life.

Your Turn: Use the Three-Step CROSS Prayer in Your Own Life

Find a quiet place and use the following prompts to pray into the roots of your own anger, anxiety, depression, etc. etc., *using the prayer on page 51 for Step 3 as well.* Be sure to allow some "wait time" to allow God to speak to you. Don't rush! When you have prayed these steps, you may repeat them as time allows. Pray until you can end on a blessing, or if possible, until you sense more of God's peace. (Psalm 46:10; Isaiah 26:3)

Step 1: Identify Negative Thoughts and Feelings Pray: Dear Jesus, What are the negative thoughts behind my anger and pain? (*See examples below*)	**Step 2: Identify with Jesus** Pray: Dear Jesus, How can You identify with me? How were You mistreated and tempted in a similar manner? (*See examples below*)
❑ I'm alone ❑ I'm rejected ❑ I have no hope ❑ Poor me–why me? ❑ I'm can't trust others ❑ I did it–I need to fix it ❑ I'm powerless/helpless ❑ I'm not worthy/I'm worthless ❑ I need my anger to protect me ❑ I have to do more and try harder ❑ It's my fault/I'm not good enough ❑ I never get to have my needs met ❑ I'm bad/I should have been better ❑ I'll never be loved, wanted, valued ❑ I can't speak up or share my needs ❑ I'm not safe/I have to protect myself ❑ I don't have a right to protect myself ❑ I have to be in control/control others ❑ I have to look good in front of others ❑ I've got to defend myself (image control) ❑ I can't trust or rely on anyone but myself ❑ I can't be forgiven/I have to punish myself with guilt, shame and regret ❑ I don't have a right to exist/be alive ❑ Other____________________ ❑ Other____________________	❑ Being born to an unwed mother (Luke 2:7) ❑ Being a refugee in Egypt ❑ Being tempted in the wilderness to trust in His own strength ❑ Being rejected by those He loves ❑ Sweating blood as He was struggling to surrender His will to His Father ❑ Being alone and abandoned, without support ❑ Being betrayed for the price of a slave ❑ Being denied by and cursed by Peter ❑ **Choosing to be powerless as He was being:** ❑ Being stripped naked ❑ Being physically violated with a whip ❑ Being verbally, mentally, emotionally abuse ❑ Being shamed, humiliated, embarrassed by authority figures in power over Him (religious and political racism) ❑ Tempted by Satan to numb His pain and agony ❑ Crying out, "Why?" to His Father when He was rejected, forsaken, and abandoned ❑ Being unable to breathe ❑ Being unsafe, unfairly, treated ❑ Falsely accused, tried, convicted, and crucified for our sins ❑ Being a Man of "grief and sorrows" ❑ Other____________________ ❑ Other____________________

Chapter 18
Personal Responsibility
Sondra's Choice

Sondra checked her watch while waiting in the police station lobby—8:30 p.m. Holding a Bible in one hand and her purse in the other, she exchanged a polite smile with the receptionist, who eyed her from behind the glass. The attention made her uncomfortable. *Was I wrong to come? The Bible says to avoid even the appearance of evil.* She looked longingly at the exit, wishing for escape. But Jeff had already been buzzed; he would be here any moment.

Maybe she wouldn't have come to talk to Jeff in person if Zach and Caitlyn didn't live within blocks of the station, or if Sheila hadn't left her Bible in the living room after Bible study last night. Anyway, she was here. And she was nervous.

Sondra clutched the Bible to her heart, trying to quell the doubts brewing within her. *You're okay, Sondra. It's okay to be here. This is a public place, and Jeff is a public servant, and I am not here to do anything wrong. I am here to return his wife's Bible. And to clear up any mixed signals I might have given Jeff . . . if he shows interest in me today.*

She felt uncomfortable imagining the coming conversation, but holding the Bible steadied her nerves, strengthened her resolve. And suddenly, the idea occurred to her: *I could pray right now, instead of worrying.* Hadn't Zach and Caitlyn been teaching her how to put every thought into prayer?

She bowed her head right there in the waiting room and silently prayed:

God, I know I have not always followed Your lead, but I am giving it my best shot from now on. I want to live to Your glory; please don't let me do or say anything to bring dishonor to Your name. I just want to get myself and my life straightened out for my girls' sake, and I don't want to hurt anyone else in the process.

Thank You for hearing my prayer, and thank You for being with me on this dreaded errand. Please bless the conversation I have with Jeff, and please bless his family; please bring healing to Jeff and Sheila's marriage.

While she was still praying, a door adjacent to the receptionist's desk opened; Jeff walked out. Sondra looked up, and their eyes locked.

"Sondra!" His whole face lit up. "You *did* come."

She smiled feebly. "I did."

"Well hey! It's nice to see you." In no time, Jeff had crossed the distance between them and was taking her elbow—the one that enfolded his wife's Bible. "Why don't you come back to my office and we'll talk about your employment." He flashed a smile that looked purely friendly, but his close proximity suggested otherwise.

"Oh," Sondra piped up, as if remembering something. She straightened the arm with the Bible and grabbed it with her other hand, gracefully shedding Jeff's hand in the process.

"Before I forget," she held up the Good Book, then thrust it at Jeff's chest. "Here's Sheila's Bible. She left it at our house last night."

"Oh!" Jeff stumbled for a moment before receiving the Bible. "Well, thanks."

"After you," Sondra said, motioning to the inner door and stepping a careful distance behind Jeff's six-plus feet of muscles.

"Boy, all business!" Jeff remarked, as he led her through the door and down a short, dark hallway.

"It's a school night," Sondra replied with a smile. "I know my girls will be in bed when I get home, but I have to get to bed early, too, so I can get up with them in the morning. I haven't been involved with them much, lately, and I want to change that."

Jeff led her into a small office and motioned to the only chair available, besides the one behind his desk. "Have a seat." She did, while he deposited the Bible on a bookshelf behind him, and then plopped into his own chair. Sondra was glad the desk separated them.

"So, you're working on being a better mom. That's great, although I'm sure you're already a great mom." Jeff leaned back in his chair, gripping the leather arms.

"Oh." Sondra blushed. "Not so great since Cory left. But that's going to change. I've realized that Cory is not the only one at fault. I have my own problems, too. I'm trying to get help with my own hurts before I do further damage to the girls."

A pensive look settled over Jeff's face.

"Wow," he remarked, rocking back and forth in the chair, drumming his fingers together. "You're singing a different tune from the first time we talked. Last time you were all about Cory's faults, and your parents' faults; now you're talking about your own. That's pretty big of you."

Sondra raised her eyebrows. "Well, don't think too highly of me. Actually, this situation with Cory has brought out everything *bad* in me." Against her will, Sondra began to tear up a little. "The only *good* I can do is to take it to Jesus. And as I do that, He's starting to straighten me out." She smiled bravely while Jeff winced.

"Am I getting too religious for you?" she joked, seeing his face.

"No, no." He shook his head. "I just don't understand. Last time you said you'd never really encountered God or Jesus on a deep level—but to hear you talk now . . . wow. It just seems like something has changed, even within the last week."

Sondra blushed and looked down. *Thank You, God,* her soul sang. *Jeff sees the change. And I believe it is disarming him. Thank You that You are changing my heart! Please do the same with his.*

"Something *has* changed in the past week." Sondra sat up straighter now; she looked Jeff in the eye. "I've been praying with Zach and Caitlyn, and . . . I mean . . . I can't describe it, but for the first time, I really *feel* God's presence when I pray . . . He feels more real to me."

Jeff remained silent, unsmiling, but not unreceptive. She went on.

"Praying to a Jesus who understands what I've gone through—because He was abandoned and betrayed and temped to numb His pain, too—just makes such a difference. It brings Him close to me. It softens my heart." She shrugged.

"And the way Zach and Caitlyn have been praying . . . it's teaching me to listen for God's still, small voice. And I'm finally hearing it! I was praying with Caitlyn right before I came here, in fact. And I heard God tell me to deal with my anger at Cory."

Sondra suddenly felt shy; she looked down at her fidgeting hands. "God is telling me to stop numbing my pain with sinful things—stop looking for a quick substitute for Cory—and wait on God to supply my needs in *His* time, according to *His* ways."

She looked back up at Jeff. "Does that make sense?"

"Hmmm." Jeff's mouth twitched, but his face remained expressionless.

"So, I'm not going to apply for the desk position here, Jeff. I really appreciate your concern, but I don't think me working here would be best for my family. Or yours."

For a brief moment Sondra caught Jeff's eye, then she broke his gaze and stood. "And now, I should be going."

"I think I get you." Jeff stood, too. "Thanks for telling me clearly where you stand." He moved around the desk, leaving obvious space between them. He opened the door.

"Well, thanks for stopping by."

"Of course," Sondra said, stepping into the hallway. "I'll see myself out."

She started toward the waiting room, then half turned. "Say hi to Sheila for me, and don't forget to give her that Bible."

Jeff twitched a little at the mention of Sheila, and her Bible. "Ah. That's right." He half smiled. "I'll definitely return it to her." *And maybe I'll read it a little before I do*, a still, small voice whispered to him.

Chapter 19
Road to Resolution
The Final Bible Study

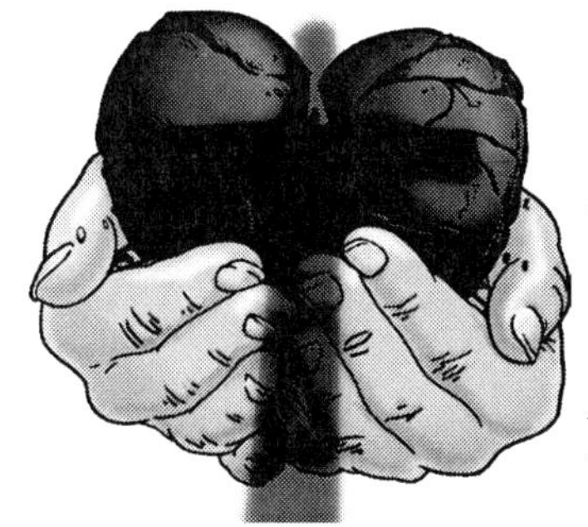

One more Monday night rolled around, the last night of Gary's Bible study. Elizabeth and Sondra bustled in the kitchen, Elizabeth heating water in the kettle and Sondra pulling chocolate chip cookies from the oven. Tim was setting up chairs in the living room. Autumn and Alice stood back a few feet from the oven, salivating over the cookies.

"Mommy, can I have one?"

"I want a cookie too!"

Sondra laughed. "Be patient girls! And please take another step back. These are hot!" She wrested the pan of cookies from the oven, maneuvering away from her girls, and laid it on the counter. Despite their mom's words, the girls rushed the counter, faces upturned to smell the steaming cookies.

"Hey, hey!" Sondra bent down to their level. "I need you to wait, okay? If you eat a cookie now," she clapped her hands over her mouth and writhed as if in pain, "Ow, owwww!"

"What, Mommy?" Alice asked, wide-eyed. Autumn grabbed Sondra's face and stroked it with a soothing motion.

"HOT COOKIES!" Sondra exclaimed, widening her own eyes. "They'll hurt you if you eat them too soon!" She hugged her girls and kissed them. "Love you, munchkins, but I gotta keep you safe!" She pulled back. "Here, let's get you some juice and get your movie set up, and then the cookies should be cool. Can you sit at the table?"

Obediently the girls took their seats, and Sondra opened her laptop, her babysitter tonight during Bible study.

Elizabeth looked up from what she was doing and smiled. "I really like how you've been interacting with the girls these last few days. You seem so much happier than when you first came to stay with us. If I didn't know better, I'd say you were on something."

"Ha," Sondra laughed, raising her eyebrows. "Not unless prayer counts for a drug." She had told her mom about her prayer sessions with Zach and Caitlyn, and it was true: she felt better these days. Lighter. Like she wasn't carrying the weight of the world anymore.

Elizabeth held Sondra's gaze for a few moments. *Thank You so much,*

God, she prayed silently. *Thank You that my daughter is coming back to herself. Thank You that she's finding You in the midst of all of this. And thank You that she is letting me be a part of it.*

She still could hardly believe how much Sondra was opening up to her lately. In the last week, Sondra had even apologized to her for being a "snotty teen" and for not listening to her advice about dating Cory. Elizabeth shook her head. *What a wonderful God I serve*, she thought. *Thank You, Lord, for the Bible study coming at just the right time, and for Zach and Caitlyn being able to pray with Sondra. Just, thank You for everything.*

*****

In the living room Sheila was just settling into her seat when Elizabeth walked in with a plate of cookies. She checked the clock. Fifteen minutes to start time.

Elizabeth greeted Sheila as her eyes swept the room, hesitating in front of the chair that would be Jeff's. "Will your hubby be making it tonight?"

Sheila looked up blankly. "Hi Elizabeth." She shrugged. "I don't really know. I haven't spoken to Jeff today."

Elizabeth nodded. "Oh, I see." She set the cookies on the coffee table and sat in Jeff's chair. "I know how work schedules can make it hard for couples to talk during the day."

"Yeah." Sheila averted her attention to her handbag. She ran her hands over the leather straps for several moments. Then she took a deep breath and looked up. "The truth is, we haven't really spoken all week, Elizabeth. But I've been praying all week that Jeff would come."

Elizabeth nodded, reflecting the pain she saw in Sheila's eyes. She remained silent, sensing Sheila had more to say.

"We've been going through some hard things for awhile, but they kind of came to a head after last week's Bible study." Sheila shook her head. Her lower lip trembled. "I just don't know what to do, except pray that God will work a change."

What Sheila didn't say out loud was that she had been praying about whether or not to leave Jeff. And this morning she had asked God to give her a sign: if Jeff showed up tonight, then she would give him another chance. If he didn't, she would separate from him, sending a clear signal that she was serious about Jeff changing his ways. She had not reminded Jeff about tonight's Bible study once in the past week. And now she waited, sick to her stomach, to see whether he would show.

Elizabeth placed one hand on Sheila's shoulder and motioned with her other hand. "Let's pray right now, Sheila. Would you allow me?"

"Of course." Sheila nodded.

The two women bowed their heads.

"Dear Lord," Elizabeth prayed, "Thank You for bringing Sheila to Bible study tonight to learn more about You and to experience Your love through this body of believers. Lord, I pray right now for Jeff, who isn't here . . . yet. I know You want to draw Jeff close to your heart and draw Jeff and Sheila closer together. Thank You that You know exactly how to do that. You know how to fix what needs fixing in their relationship, and You know how to restore it and make it beautiful—in Your time.

"Help Sheila to wait on You for Your timing and Your answers, and please give her Your peace in the meantime. And please bless Jeff, wherever he is, whatever he's doing right now, and speak to his heart whatever he needs to hear tonight. Bless this room tonight and the people in it, and the families represented here. Strengthen us during this study tonight that we might be a light to those around us, and may lead others to You. In Jesus' name, Amen."

*****

Fifteen minutes later, Gary looked around at the group members who had gathered in the living room, minus Jeff. "Before we start anything new, would a couple of you briefly summarize the first two sections of Psalm 109 for us? What did we learn about David in the previous Bible studies?"

A Review of Psalm 109:1–25

"Sure," Caitlyn offered. "In our first study of Psalm 109, we learned that David was betrayed by someone close to him, so he's really angry, and he wants God to curse the guy in every way possible."

"Yes. Exactly. And what was good about this prayer?"

Elizabeth spoke. "Well, David is being honest with God. And he is allowing God to be the One to deal with his enemy, as opposed to carrying out revenge himself."

"Really good, Elizabeth. David is being completely honest with God, as Jesus was, during a very painful time in his life. Remember, we learned that Jesus did **not** try to talk Himself out of the negative thoughts coming from Satan at Gethsemane and Calvary.

"Jesus did **not** try to talk Himself into trusting God.

"Jesus talked **to** God, sharing His feelings and thoughts openly, honestly, repeatedly, and continually—and Jesus could definitely connect HIS-story with David's story."

"As we're reviewing, we can take one more look at what we know about

David's enemy, about Jesus' ability to identify with King David, and how God led him from anger to pain to praise through prayer." (*see columns below*)

What we know about this man and his family:	What David wants God to do to this man: (and family)	What Jesus has suffered to identify with David and us:
1. Wicked, deceitful	1. Judge him in court	1. Religious leaders lying about Him
2. Making false accusations and lying	2. Make his Prayer sin	2. Judas betraying Jesus
3. Betrayal/hatred from someone David trusts and loves	3. Man dies – his family become beggars	3. Peter denying Jesus 3x, cursing Him the 3rd time
4. Leader/official position with no mercy – seeking to slay/kill David when he is broken hearted	4. Have no mercy for him or his family– with all the generations *before and after* him being lost forever	4. *Tempted* to not have mercy on those hurting Him–*Tempted* to curse them (wish ill on them)

"Now, as David expresses his anger, the prayer takes a turn. Could someone summarize how the prayer changes right around the middle of the Psalm?"

"Sure," Sondra said. "After David gets out his anger, he goes into his pain. The focus of his prayer changes. Now, instead of asking God to deal with his enemy, he is asking God to deal with *him*. He realizes that *he* needs to change, because his anger is eating him alive and affecting every part of his life, even causing him physical pain."

"Good, Sondra. So, this prayer begins with David's anger, but then moves to David's pain. Today we are going to see that this process eventually leads David into a much better place than where he began, but before we move on, I want to reemphasize that the principles we are learning can apply to any strong emotion, feeling, thought, or behavior.

"No matter whether we have anger, anxiety, guilt, shame, depression, whatever, we have a God who wants us to talk to Him openly and honestly. He wants us to take every thought and feeling captive to Him. (2 Cor. 10:5)

"Let's look at another quote before we move on tonight, because I believe it recaps our main points from earlier studies on how Christians can struggle with being honest, but how it's necessary to our healing."

Gary cleared his throat and read:

> What must be done to lift the shroud of shame and contempt [anger, anxiety, depression, guilt, etc.]? The answer involves a strategy that seems to intensify the problem: peer deeply into the wounded heart. The first great enemy to lasting change is the propensity to turn our eyes away from the wound and pretend things are fine. The work of restoration cannot begin until a problem is fully faced . . .
>
> It is unpleasant to face the consequences of sin—our own and others'. . . . My fear is that many stop at the point of deep initial relief without delving further into the damage. The initial washing of the wound will not be sufficient if the infection is not treated by even stronger medicine. **The hunger for a quick cure is as deep as the desire for heaven**. The tragedy is that many take the cheap cure and miss the path to a lasting taste of heaven . . .
>
> The journey involves bringing our wounded heart before God, a heart that is full of rage, overwhelmed with doubt, bloodied but unbroken, rebellious, stained and lonely. It does not seem possible that anyone can handle, let alone embrace, our wounded and sinful heart. But the path involves the risk of putting into words the condition of our inner being and placing those words before God for His response.[16]

Zach raised his hand. "I think, when we are starting this process of honesty, that we have to remember the reality of spiritual warfare. Changing to this brutally honest approach to prayer isn't easy for Christians, because we're not used to seeing it in the church. But it's also hard because we have a spiritual enemy, Satan. And Satan is not only threatened when we start to get honest and call out his lies; but he is also threatened when we start to experience freedom in Christ for two key reasons:

---

[16] Dan Allender, *The Wounded Heart* (Colorado Springs: NavPress, 2008), pp. 14, 17, 19, emphasis added.

1. "We begin to have real hope that the gospel is real and it has power to make a difference—causing him to lose more and more influence in our lives.
2. "We begin to have real hope for the lives of those around us, that the gospel is real and makes a difference for *them*, threatening the loss of his influence in their lives as well."

"Right, Zach. I think you and I have both seen that when people start to surrender to Christ through a prayer process like David's, and Straight 2 the Heart's, Satan will step up his attacks. He doesn't want us to succeed in finding healing. But I believe Psalm 109 gives us many reasons to journey through this heart-wrenching process.

As we talk to God about our struggles, He reveals the *source* of those struggles, and He also reveals Himself as the *solution* to those struggles. Tonight, in fact, we are going to see some of the healing benefits of honest, angry prayer. But first, let's pray."

Chapter 20
Moving into Praise

A Study on Psalm 109:26–31

Gary bowed his head, as did the others. Sheila closed her eyes and clasped her hands, as if bracing herself for some conflict.

"Jesus, Thank You that You are here with us tonight, and that You are very present in our struggles, whatever those may be. Thank You that You know every story in this room, and can identify with every person, and every situation they are facing. Lord, thank You also for this honest prayer from David that shows us what to do with our anger and our pain. You want us to take our deepest, darkest emotions, thoughts, and feelings to You, instead of trying to cope with them on our own.

"Lord, You know that we stumble when we try to fight off the enemy in our own strength—we often try to bury our pain with things that ultimately end up hurting us, and hurting our relationships. I thank You that You never sinned, like we do, but You *were* tempted in every way we are tempted. Thank You that we can heal from our hurts as we receive *Your* victory over suffering and sin.

"Now please lead us as we finish our study on Psalm 109. May You guide us into truth as You guided David, and no matter what situations we may be facing in this room, may You bring healing, as You brought healing to David. In Your name Jesus, amen."

After praying, Gary looked up. Sheila took her time unfolding her body and her hands. Then she took a deep breath and looked expectantly at Gary.

"We have just six more verses tonight, and I have four points to make."

Gary turned to his left. "Let's start with Sheila tonight. Sheila, would you please read the first two verses, starting in verse 26, then we'll stop and discuss."

"Sure." Sheila found her place in her Bible and read:

> [26] Help me, O Lord my God! Oh, save me according to Your mercy,
> [27] That they may know that this *is* Your hand—*That* You, Lord, have done it! (Psalm 109:26–27)

"Okay, pause there. Point number 1, and this is a bit of a review. Who is David trusting in here: God or himself?"

Point 1: Dependence on God vs. Dependence on Self

Tim tapped his finger on the verses. "It says, 'Help me *O Lord my God.*'" He looked up. "He's asking *God* to help him."

"Right, Tim. David is putting his trust in God, not himself. But what specific language does David use in these verses to tell us he is not trusting in self-help? How do we know he is not just trying harder to do what he is already unable to do?"

"Well," ventured Sheila, "The language is totally centered on God. 'Save me according to *Your* mercy. That they may know it is *Your* hand. That *You,* Lord, have done it.' All the pronouns are *You* and *Your.* David is asking *God* to be the acting force in his salvation."

"Very good, Sheila. David is asking *God* to act—and specifically, he is asking for God's *mercy* to save him. Verse 26 is actually the fourth time David mentions mercy in this prayer [see also verses 12, 16, and 21]. So David is depending on God's *mercy,* not his ability, not his self-will, to forgive."

"I really appreciate this part of the prayer," Zach jumped in, "because David has totally put God in the driver's seat. This really shows a surrender; and the fact that he wants everyone to know that this was God's doing, not his, shows real maturity."

"You know," Caitlyn added thoughtfully, "I'm struck with how different this approach is from the world's approach. In the secular world, when we have difficulty, we are always told to reach 'within ourselves.' We are told to 'dig deeper,' or 'pull ourselves up by the bootstraps,' or to 'find the strength within.' While that sounds nice, it totally goes against what the Bible says. The Bible says we can do *nothing* good by ourselves, and our righteousness is like filthy rags. I like how David gets that—and keeps laying it all on God's shoulders."

"Well said," Gary affirmed. "David has realized he needs God's mercy, because he has none of his own. He is choosing to turn to God, instead of passively hoping things will get better. Tim, would you continue on with the next two verses for us?"

"Sure." Tim found his place and read:

> [28] Let them curse, but You bless; when they arise, let them be ashamed, but let Your servant rejoice.
> [29] Let my accusers be clothed with shame, and let them cover themselves with their own disgrace as with a mantle. (Psalm 109:28–29)

"Hmmm." Tim ended with a puzzled look.

"Okay, what do we make of this?" Gary asked the group. "We were just praising David for turning everything over to God. How do you feel he's doing at this point? Has he reached perfection as a Christian—is he totally Christlike—or does he still have some growing to do?"

Tim raised his eyebrows. "He is wanting to bless even when they curse him, and rejoice regardless of what they do to him . . . so in many ways, he is no longer being defined by them. But I'd say he's still a work in progress."

"Why, Tim? How do you know David is not entirely out of the woods yet? And by the way," Gary grinned, "that's my second point. David has made progress, wanting to bless instead of curse, and live with joy, but he hasn't reached perfection yet."

Point 2: Progress – NOT Perfection

"Well," Tim eyed the verses, "David still sounds vindictive. I know he was just asking God to change his *own* heart, but clearly he still wants some consequences for the other guy, too."

"I agree," Gary said. "David's not ready to let his enemy off the hook." A smile played at his lips. "But let's explore this."

Gary stood and taped a sheet of paper on his white board. The paper contained two columns, one for verses 5–16, the other for verses 26–28.

Contrasting the Difference in David's Desires for His Enemy

In verses 5–16	**In verses 28–29**
1. He will be judged in court	1. He will be ashamed
2. His prayers will become sin	2. He will be "clothed with dishonor"
3. He will die	3. He will cover himself with his own shame "as with a robe"
4. His family will become beggars	
5. God will not let anyone have mercy on him	
6. Generations before and after him will be lost forever	

"What does David want for his enemy in verses 28 and 29, in contrast to what he wanted for him in verses 5–16? Take a moment to read the chart before you answer."

The group did so, then Elizabeth spoke up. "In the earlier verses, David wants all kinds of bad things to happen to him *and his family*—I mean, physically bad things, like death and starvation."

"He even wants eternal consequences," Sheila piped up. "He wants the man's family to be kept out of heaven."

"Right," Elizabeth agreed. "But in verses 28 and 29, David wants his enemy to be dishonored and ashamed . . . or humiliated, if you will. It seems like David just wants his enemy to realize what he has done and pay the price that comes with lying and turning others against David (since he is using the words 'they,' 'them,' and 'accusers,' showing how others have joined this officer). The intensity has diminished quite a bit, compared to what David wanted earlier."

The group members nodded their agreement.

"Very good, Elizabeth," Gary said. "Do you all notice another shift in focus in these verses? At the beginning of the prayer, David is set on taking revenge in a *physical* way. But now that he realizes the sinfulness of his own heart, he doesn't ask for *physical* revenge . . . " Gary trailed off. "Any comments on that?"

"Yes," Sheila said quietly, looking down at her hands. "I don't read David as being very vengeful here. I think he just wants truth and goodness to win out. He realizes the pain that comes from sin, and he wants this man to realize it, too. He wants the guy to feel remorse so that he will change."

Elizabeth noted pain in Sheila's eyes as she spoke.

"Huh," Tim mused, folding his arms and leaning back. "I didn't read it that way. But Sheila makes a good point. I think David still wants justice, but maybe for different reasons than I thought. I guess we can't know for certain what David's motives are here in asking for the guy to suffer. But he has definitely toned down his prayer request. In the first part of his prayer, on a scale of 1–10, David's hostility registers a 12; but in verses 28–29, it's on a scale of 3 or 4. These later verses represent a much lower level of his anger and desire for revenge."

"Yeah," Zach concurred. "Now the prayer is about the man receiving the *natural consequences* of his sins . . . and when I think of my uncle, for instance, I would say it's almost a reasonable request."

"That's interesting, Zach," Gary said. "Could you expand on that a little, the part about your uncle?"

"Sure. I can identify with David in this part of the prayer, because I no longer want my uncle to suffer endlessly for abusing me, and I don't have standing resentment for him. But I *do* hope, and I *have* prayed, that he will feel ashamed of what he did. I hope that his conscience has troubled him over what he did, so that he will turn to God in a deep way, and never do something like that again."

Zach shrugged. "Also, I hope he will receive God's gift of repentance [Rom. 2:4; Acts 5:31; 11:18; 26:18], and be saved. I hope I *will* see him in heaven. But that process of repentance, if it is true repentance, is certain to bring some feelings of shame and regret for what he did. It will also bear the 'fruit' of taking responsibility and seeking to make amends for what he did."

Brows furrowed as Zach talked. Sondra especially appeared deep in thought.

"Zach, you've forgiven your uncle, right?" Gary asked.

"Yes." Zach nodded solemnly.

"And yet you have prayed for your uncle to recognize his sins and make a change."

"Sure."

"That's interesting. Did your prayers sound like David's prayer here, asking that your uncle be 'ashamed,' or 'disgraced'?"

"Maybe a little," Zach admitted.

"So . . . " Gary's eyes twinkled. "Do we think David has forgiven this man yet?"

Sondra squinted, thinking it over. Sheila inhaled long, then exhaled.

"Hmm," Tim mused.

"Before you answer," Gary said, "Let's finish off the last two verses, and see what those tell us. "Elizabeth?"

"Uh huh." Elizabeth bent over her Bible and read:

> [30] I will greatly praise the Lord with my mouth; Yes, I will praise Him among the multitude.
> [31] For He shall stand at the right hand of the poor, to save *him* from those who condemn him. (Psalm 109:30–31)

"Hmmm." Elizabeth looked up at Gary.

"So, that's the end of the Psalm," Gary said. "What do you think? Happy ending? All things forgiven?"

"Well," Elizabeth ventured, "David doesn't say anything about forgiveness, but he seems to be in a healthier place than where he began."

Gary nodded. "What is David doing by the end?"

"Praising," Sondra said. "David is praising God."

"Why?" Gary prompted.

"Because," Sheila read, "God has helped David in his time of need."

"Bingo," Gary said. "That's point three: David is praising God, because God has helped him."

Point 3: David Praises God

"Now, David says God has helped him. But what kind of help? Has God helped David by answering his prayers to hurt the other guy?" Gary asked with a smile.

Sondra shook her head, and Gary caught her eye.

"Sondra, how would you say God helped David?"

"Well, I don't think God answered David's prayers to torture the guy and his family." She smiled slightly. "But it really seems like God is answering David's prayers about his own heart. David said his heart was 'wounded,' and he said he was physically sick from his pain. But now he is praising God. We don't know if David is totally over it yet—I think we agreed he's not—but he seems hopeful; he seems on the road to recovery."

"Yes, Sondra. I agree. David is clearly moving through a *process* of healing." Gary stood once again and began to write on the whiteboard. "Now we can fill in the third and final column in this powerful prayer.

"David has moved from **Anger to Pain to Praise . . . through Prayer**."

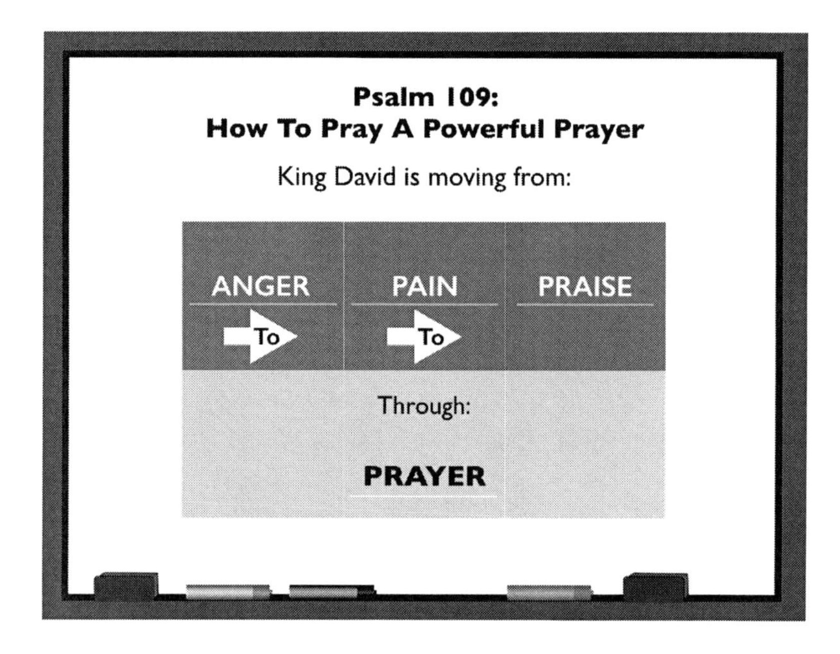

Gary continued. "As he 'places his wounded heart before God,' to quote Dan Allender, his desires are changing. He is no longer praying for God to settle the score, or to hurt the man who hurt him. He is no longer rehearsing the injustices against him."

Gary paused. "So, Sondra said that God did not necessarily punish David's enemy. For all we know, at the time of this prayer, David's enemy is still the same sleazy guy, committing the same sins—including influencing others to betray their king. But," Gary raised his eyebrows, "Does David's freedom from anger, anxiety, depression, etc., depend on what the other guy does?"

Key Question: Does my Freedom Depend on the Behavior of Others?

"Not at all." Caitlyn shook her head.

"No," Zach concurred. "David is fixing his mind on God now, and this new focus is freeing him to praise God, regardless of whether or not his enemy changes."

"So, what you're saying, Zach," Gary clarified, "is that David's freedom from anger does not depend on this man changing his behavior. Is that right?"

"That's what I'm saying," Zach nodded.

"And you've found that to be the case in your own life, as it relates to your uncle, correct?"

"Yes."

Elizabeth shook her head. "Zach, I am just so touched by how you have been able to forgive your uncle—and probably your parents, too—and lead a happy and inspiring life."

"No kidding." Sheila shook her head. *I wish I could say the same*, she thought.

"It's really been a miracle of God," Zach said. "I like the saying from Straight 2 the Heart: *Forgiveness is supernatural, not natural.* It's not something I could have done on my own. 'The life I now live I live *by faith **of** the Son of God*, Who loved me and gave Himself for me' (Gal. 2:20; Rev. 14:12, KJV). It's *His* forgiveness flowing *through* me that has allowed me to forgive my uncle, and it's *His* strength within me that allows me to live a life that is not ruled by anger."

Point 4: Forgiveness is Supernatural, not Natural

"That's so great, Zach," Gary said. "Actually, you just illustrated point 4: Forgiveness is supernatural, not natural." He looked around at the group and cocked his head.

"Many Christians tell me that they have forgiven the person who hurt them, and that the past is in the past. But when they run into that person or think about what he or she did to them, they still have pain in their hearts—they still harbor hard feelings—and this pain creates problems in their significant relationships."

Sheila looked down as Gary talked, fidgeting with the hem of her blouse. Across the room, Sondra studied him curiously as he spoke.

"Many Christians have sincerely said the words 'I forgive you.' And yet they often find out that their sincerity is not enough. Jesus' own disciples were sincere when they said they would fight for Him, go to prison for Him, and even die for Him. But they were sincerely, publicly, and spectacularly wrong [Matt. 26:35]. Sincerity is not a substitute for allowing God to be God. Sincerity is not a substitute for letting God reveal the wounds and negative thoughts in our hearts . . . or as David says in another psalm:

> Dear God, You search my heart and try my anxious thoughts.
> (Psalm 139:23–24)

Sondra nodded along with Gary as he spoke.

"We've said that we can't make another person change his or her heart. We **are** powerless over another person's choice.

But we **are not** powerless over our choice to let God into *our* hearts so He can work out His will in *our* lives. And one major purpose for us—actually, His *main* purpose for us—is that we love others."

Gary raised his eyebrows in challenge to the group. "This includes loving our enemies, and *genuinely* forgiving them when they hurt us. As Jesus said:

> "Love your enemies! Pray for those who persecute you! In that way, you will be acting as true children of your Father in heaven.... If you love only those who love you, what reward is there for that? Even corrupt tax collectors do that much... Even pagans do that." (Matt. 5:43–47, NLT)
>
> "Forgive...from your HEART." (Matt. 18:35, NIV, emphasis added)
>
> "By this everyone will know that you are My disciples, if you love one another." (John 13:35, NIV)
>
> "Humanly speaking, it is impossible. But...everything is possible with God." (Mark 10:27, NLT)

Sondra drew in a long inhale, clearly deep in thought. Sheila, also deep in thought, trained her eyes on the floor.

"Now, we've said that forgiveness is impossible in our own strength. Forgiveness is *supernatural, not natural.* We've seen how David is giving his heart and his thoughts to God through his honest prayer. But now," Gary smiled a little and cocked his head.

"Let's get back to the heart of the Bible, and the core of Straight 2 the Heart. What did *Jesus* say about forgiveness? And more importantly, was *Jesus* ever tempted not to forgive *His* abusers? And what did He do?" Gary leaned back, waiting as the group mulled over the questions.

Chapter 21
For They Know Not What They Do

Jesus' Story of Forgiveness

"The Bible says 'Forgive as Christ forgave you,'" Elizabeth quoted. [Col. 3:13].

"Yes," Gary said. "And how does He forgive us?"

"Well," Tim said, "Jesus forgives us all the time. The Bible says all over the place that Jesus forgives us when we confess our sins." [*See especially Romans 5:8 and 1 John 1:9.*] "And there are numerous examples in the Gospels of Jesus offering forgiveness to sinners, even when they didn't ask for it."

"Ah," Gary smiled and nodded, eyes gleaming. "Jesus offered forgiveness *when they didn't ask for it*. That's exactly right, Tim. And I can think of one very striking place in Scripture where sinners were not asking for forgiveness, but Jesus *pleaded* with God for their forgiveness."

Gary leaned forward, allowing the thought to settle. "You know what I'm referring to, of course . . . "

"The Cross," Sondra breathed.

"The Cross," Gary echoed. "The Cross, where Jesus was shedding His blood for us; where He was writhing in pain, nerves on fire from the nails; lips parched from thirst, body aching from abuse. It was on the Cross where Jesus uttered some very instructive words for us. Can someone remember what those words were?"

"'Father, forgive them for they know not what they do,'" Sheila said quietly.

> "Father forgive them, for they know **NOT** what they do."
> (Luke 23:34, emphasis added)

"Yes," Gary nodded. "This is incredible, isn't it? The fact that Jesus is asking God to forgive those who are literally killing Him!"

"Wow," Sheila blinked. Sondra shook her head.

"How is this possible?" Gary posed, crossing one leg over the other.

Heads shook around the room.

"I don't know," several voices chimed.

Zach smiled. "I know."

Everyone turned to him.

"Jesus forgave the only way *we* can forgive: by surrendering to God and letting Him change our hearts and minds. As the Bible says:

"The Son ***can do nothing* by** Himself." (John 5:19)
"The flesh ***counts for nothing***." (John 6:63)
"Apart from Me you ***can do nothing***." (John 15:5)
Forgive as Christ forgave. (Col. 3:13)
[All emphases added]

Zach shrugged. "Jesus let *God* do the work. And that's what we have to do."

Gary nodded. "Exactly. Jesus was able to forgive by trusting in His Father's supernatural love, and that's the only way *we* can forgive. Take, for example, Marrieta Jaeger.

"Marrieta lost her youngest daughter to a man who kidnapped her and killed her. Here is her response to those who say forgiveness is for wimps: 'Well, I say then, that they must have never tried it. Forgiveness is hard work… it doesn't mean we forget, we condone, or we absolve responsibility … that we try to separate the loss and cost from the recompense or punishment we deem is due,'[17] and she is right. We *choose* to name the sins against us. We *choose* to name our pain and anger. We *choose* to let God reveal anything in our lives that we have turned to for false comforts, the ways we have turned against Him, doubting His love and care, and/or turning against ourselves. We *choose* to receive His healing. We *choose* to receive His spirit of forgiveness. And we *choose* to acknowledge that this is a process that takes place over time, thanking Him for His grace and truth at every step of the journey. In other words, forgiveness is an active process with God, not nebulous or passive, just hoping that somehow it happens in a way that bypasses our anger, pain, and patterns of protection that are really patterns of self-sabotage."

Gary looked around for reactions. "Sheila, I see you're shaking your head. Care to share any thoughts?"

"Not really," she smiled. "I just see that I'm still a work in progress. It's so hard to let go and let God take over."

Gary mirrored her smile. "It seems hard, doesn't it? Surrendering to God is definitely a muscle we have to exercise. One thing that might help, though, is to look more carefully at Jesus' words."

---

[17] *Exploring Forgiveness*, edited by Robert Enright and Joanna North, (University of Wisconsin P, 2008) p. 12.

Gary uncrossed his legs and leaned forward.

"Jesus said 'forgive,' which means there is a sin to be forgiven. So again, forgiveness includes choosing to acknowledge what was done **to** me.

Looking carefully at Jesus' words in Luke 23:34		
Forgive	=	There is a sin to be forgiven
KNOW Not	=	The sinner does not realize all of the spiritual, physical, financial, and relational losses and consequences for his/her sins against me

"Then," Gary raised his index finger for emphasis, "Jesus goes on: 'For they **know not** what they do.' Jesus knows human hearts, and He knew that His murderers had no idea Who they were killing. They didn't realize that He was the Savior of the world. And later some of them would come to regret what they'd done." He paused to size up the group. Sondra was squinting, deep in thought. Everyone else was listening with deep interest.

"Is it possible that when people sin against us and we get so offended, that they don't realize *fully* what they are doing to us?" Gary scratched his chin thoughtfully.

"Of course, a murderer knows he's killing; a molester knows he is trying to hide what he is doing when he manipulates the child into being sexually violated and threatens the child into silence and a cheating spouse knows he is having an affair." Gary paused for effect.

"But in the moment of the sin, do those people know, or consider, all the effects of their actions?

"Do murderers or abusers, addicts or adulterers consider all the ripple effects their actions will have after the fact? Do they think about all the losses they are creating for others in the years to come? Do they consider, or even *realize*, all the pain they will cause others, and even themselves?"

Caitlyn shook her head and sat up a little straighter. "No, they don't. It's been my experience that when a person sins against another person, they are not even *thinking* of the other person. They are thinking of themselves."

Gary leaned his chin on his fist. "Interesting. Can you explain that, Caitlyn?"

"Yes. I'm sure you've all heard that saying, 'Hurt people hurt people.' Well, it's true. For most of us, when we hurt others, it means we, ourselves, are hurting; we just want some pain to stop. And when we are *really* hurting, we get blinded by our pain, to the point that we don't even *think* of the pain we are causing others. And then, when we focus on ourselves too much, and not on God's commands to love others, we end up sinning against them."

"Well said, Caitlyn," Gary said. "Sin happens when we have our focus in the wrong place; and the men who killed Jesus definitely had their focus in the wrong place. Because they took their eyes off Jesus, the Suffering Messiah foretold in the Scriptures, Satan was able to set them up to sin in a huge way. And it's the same with us.

"When we take our eyes off God, Satan sets us up for sin, too. We could be too focused on ourselves and our pain, or too focused on others and *their* flaws—or really anything. The point is, being separated from God gets us in trouble. And then Satan can easily use us to bring trouble on others.

"Our sins always have ripple effects on those closest to us. Sometimes our sins have far-reaching effects. And it is these ripple effects that Jesus is talking about when He says 'Forgive them, for they *know not what they do.*' For example, we could study a number of stories in the Bible where God's best friends made sinful choices that still affect us today."

Ripple Effects of Sin in the Bible... and God's Far-Reaching Forgiveness

Did Adam and Eve know that Cain would kill Abel when they took the forbidden fruit? *No.* But it still happened.

Adam and Eve Were Forgiven:

❑ *Only* for their sinful behavior?

❑ For everything they did and did not know about their losses and consequences they created for themselves – and for us?

Did Abraham and Sarah know they were starting a 4,000-year war between Ishmael and Isaac's descendants when they used Hagar to have a son, without talking to God first? *No.* But it still happened, impacting billions of people today, with the consequences still taking place.

Abraham and Sarah Were Forgiven:

❑ *Only* for their sinful behavior?

❑ For everything they did and did not know about their losses and consequences they created for themselves – and for us?

Did King David know that he would kill Bathsheba's husband, Uriah, when he first started lusting after her? *No.* But he still had Uriah killed and the baby still died.

David Was Forgiven:

- ❑ *Only* for his sinful behavior?
- ❑ For everything he did and did not know about the losses and consequences he created for himself, Uriah, Bathsheba, the baby, Israel – and for us?

"I'm curious," Gary mused, looking around the group. "Does anyone relate to this personally? Is there a situation in your lives where some sin was committed, by yourself or others, and the effects of it went way beyond what you, or the sinner, ever imagined?

"Did you ever do something that ended up hurting someone else, and you *didn't know* that it was going to hurt them so much?

"Or did someone ever sin against you, in a big or small way, and it led to your suffering—but is it possible that they *don't know* the extent of what they did to you?"

Across the room from Gary, Sondra knitted her brow and chewed her lower lip. To his left, Sheila fought back tears. Gary hoped someone would answer the question out loud—he knew that Bible discussions were so much more powerful when people shared their personal stories—but he never pushed people where they didn't want to go. Like Jesus, he tried to lead people to healing, but he would never force them.

"Don't feel like you have to answer those questions out loud," Gary said, looking with compassion at the pained faces before him.

"Before we close tonight, I *will* ask you to be brave and share some testimonies of what studying Psalm 109 has meant to you. But first, before we leave this point about forgiveness, I want to invite you to think about someone who has hurt you, perhaps someone you are struggling to forgive. And when you go home tonight, I invite you pray like Jesus did: 'Father, forgive him [or her], because he [or she] doesn't know all that they have done to hurt me.'

"And a few more principles on forgiveness. When people struggle to forgive, we want to focus on the 'roots' behind their struggles instead of telling them to try harder. So we pray, 'Dear Jesus, Please reveal all the negative thoughts and objections I have that are keeping me from receiving Your spirit of forgiveness. And thank You also for revealing where You were tempted with the same negative beliefs and objections I am struggling with.

David's Story of Betrayal, Anger, and Pain	Jesus' Story Connecting with David's Story
David suffered through the pain of being lied about by someone close to him	Jesus suffered through the pain of being lied about by his close friends, Judas and Peter
David was angry and bitter, wanting revenge and payback, cursing instead of offering forgiveness	Jesus was *tempted to* be angry and bitter, *to* seek revenge and payback, *to* curse instead of praying "Father, forgive them for they know not what they do."
David had a wounded heart, filled with pain behind his anger, because of the way he was lied about	Jesus had a wounded heart, filled with pain and *tempted to* become angry because of the way He was lied about

"Then we pray, integrating Jesus' story into our story, so we are casting 'all' of our burdens upon the Lord, not some of them [1 Peter 5:7]. And we thank Him that we are receiving His victory over Satan, the 'father of lies,' as we receive our truest, deepest identities as His sons and daughters, with His spirit of forgiveness for what the person did and did not know, instead of trying to forgive in our own strength.

"Now, that may not resolve all the pain and anger in your heart—and you will need to keep praying *daily* through your negative thoughts and connecting them to Jesus until you find peace. You may even need to talk with a physician to identify any medical problems.

"But," Gary raised his eyebrows and lightened his tone of voice, "many people I've prayed with have found *this* forgiveness prayer—from the lips of Jesus—to bring a breakthrough." And here is what Dr. Tibbit discovered from his forgiveness workshops:

"During interviews at the end of each forgiveness training program, I invited participants to describe what they found most helpful in our weeks together. Each time I expected them to say something like 'I feel good about being able to reduce my anger' or 'I was delighted to lower my blood pressure,' answers that would reflect the two major emphases of the program. But you know what I heard most often? It may surprise you.

'I had a spiritual awakening in my life,' the participants said. '*I feel that my life now has direction and purpose.* I feel like I'm getting on track with where my life should have always been.'

Even though I had focused on the mental and physical benefits of practicing forgiveness and had discovered that forgiveness does indeed positively impact both, the majority of the people I worked with were most thankful for the *spiritual* benefits that forgiveness gave them.

In short what I had demonstrated in real life and supported by hard statistics was the *forgiveness has the power to bring healing to the whole person: body, mind, and spirit.*" (Forgive To Live: How Forgiveness Can Save Your Life, Dr. Tibbit with Steve Hallady, pp. 77–78, 10th anniversary edition, 2016, emphasis mine)

Gary let his words settle for a moment while he cleared his throat and reshuffled the papers on his lap. He knew, without looking, that both Sheila and Sondra were pondering his words, and that made him glad.

From talking with other group members, he knew bits and pieces of what they were going through, and he could tell that both of them had been tracking with him tonight, as he had spoken to their struggles and needs.

When it appeared that no one intended to speak, Gary looked up. "If there are no more comments on forgiveness, let's move on to closing thoughts on Psalm 109."

Just then, Sondra raised her hand, lip quivering. "Hold on. I have something to share about forgiveness."

"Go ahead," Gary motioned. "The floor is yours."

Chapter 22
Testimonies

Reactions to Psalm 109

"Umm," Sondra began. "This is kind of awkward. I've never shared something so personal in a group before, and I didn't plan to do this tonight." She cleared her throat and glanced at Caitlyn, who nodded her encouragement.

"But I just had to share, because I felt like someone else might need to hear this."

Sondra gestured at Gary and Zach. "As you guys were speaking about forgiveness tonight, God was speaking to my heart."

Sondra brushed her hair over one shoulder. "Let me back up. I've been praying with Caitlyn here, and Zach, because, well," Sondra looked at Sheila and Gary sheepishly. "I'm sure you all know what's going on with me. How my husband dumped me for another woman and how I'm living with my parents and, basically, trying to piece my life back together again. Ahem."

Sheila nodded sympathetically. Gary looked on with kind eyes.

"Well, the prayers with Zach and Caitlyn have really been helping me. The first time I prayed with them, I was able to express my anger and my hurt feelings, and they helped me understand how Jesus understands, and how He suffered like I suffer. That was really comforting, and I began to connect with Jesus like never before. I started to learn to listen for how He was speaking to me.

"The next time I prayed with Caitlyn, I realized God was telling me to deal with the pain in my own heart, and stop focusing on Cory. Well, I've been doing that. I've been asking the Lord to show me where I was sinning and hurting others because of the pain I was in. And believe me, He showed me!"

Several people laughed.

"And God has been helping me to change. In the last week, I stopped running from my responsibilities, and I started being a mom to my girls again. And I started looking seriously for a job again."

"How is that going, by the way?" Sheila asked.

"Oh, yeah." Sondra smiled. "I didn't tell you all that I found something, at least temporarily. An administrative assistant at my girls' school is going on maternity leave soon, and I've been hired to take her place until the end of the school year. They said it's no guarantee, but if it goes well, they could probably find a spot for me next year."

"Oh, wonderful!" Caitlyn enthused.

"Yeah, it's an answer to prayer," Sondra said. "And it's just been lots of little things like that, showing me that God is taking care of me as I surrender to Him."

Sondra inhaled deeply. "But before tonight, there was one area I just couldn't trust God with." She looked down at her hands. "I just couldn't imagine forgiving Cory."

"And now?" Gary prompted softly.

"Well, I'm still a work in progress, as my dad said." Sondra smiled at Tim, who placed a reassuring hand on her shoulder.

"But I hear God whispering to me to forgive Cory, because he doesn't know what he's doing."

Sondra shook her head. "You know, part of all this honesty I've been learning has been facing the truth about *myself*." She looked painfully at Elizabeth.

"My mom warned me about Cory when we first got together, because Cory wasn't a Christian. And I was stubborn, and I didn't listen."

Elizabeth put an arm around her girl.

"Well, Mom was right. Cory wasn't a Christian when we met, and he has never become a follower of Jesus since then." Sondra heaved a sigh.

"So Cory made some really selfish choices, some really *hurtful* choices . . . " she blinked back tears. "But I believe he doesn't feel remorse because he doesn't follow Jesus; and he doesn't follow God's laws. He follows the world—a world that says, 'Do what feels good,' 'Do what makes you happy in the moment.' And because Cory is listening to Satan, he doesn't realize that he is not living with real peace, or that he's just medicating his own pain, and shirking the responsibilities he has before God."

Sheila nodded in sympathy.

"In the last few weeks, because of my prayer sessions, I was doing better not thinking about Cory. But anytime I *would* think of him, I would get *so angry* at his selfish choices."

Sondra shrugged. "But then, during this study tonight, when you all were talking about forgiveness, and sin, and Jesus on the cross, I started to see it differently. Some of you said, basically, that sin is a consequence of separation from God, and when people don't have a sense of their sin, it is because they are not connected to God. And that resonated when I thought of Cory.

"Cory is not connected to God—he has his focus in all the wrong places—so Satan was able to use him to really hurt me and the girls. But," Sondra looked up and smiled, "I've learned here that my happiness doesn't depend on what Cory did, or does. It still hurts, but I have hope, now, because I know how Jesus suffered like me and for me, to give me a new life. I know He is going to restore what I lost, in time."

Elizabeth hugged Sondra tighter. Caitlyn smiled bravely at her friend.

"And secondly, I feel like I can eventually get to a point of forgiving Cory, because I'm starting to see that he really doesn't know what he's doing," Sondra shook her head.

"I'm even starting to feel a little sad for Cory, because he doesn't see how great a sin he is committing, not just against me, but against God. Cory hasn't just rejected me, he's rejected God—and when all is said and done in this life, *Cory* will be the big loser if he doesn't turn it around.

"Like I said, it still hurts to think of him, but I'm going to start praying for him, that he will change, for his own sake, and for my girls. He *is* still their dad, even if he's not my husband." Sondra looked directly at Gary with glassy eyes. "Thank you, Gary, for showing me how I can pray to receive Jesus' spirit of forgiveness for Cory. I know that using Jesus' words will be helpful, because I already feel more peaceful about it."

"You're welcome," Gary said. "And thank *you* for sharing all of that with the group. It was brave of you, and it's really encouraging to hear how God is working on your heart, even as we speak."

Sondra nodded, heart racing. It had felt good to speak all of that out loud, even if it had been a little scary.

Gary's eyes swept the group. "I wonder, does anyone else want to share any reactions to Psalm 109? Is there anything that stood out to you, or anything new you've learned about prayer, God, or yourself?"

Elizabeth nodded. "Yes. I was really struck by the whole theme of honesty. I think especially for the older generation like Tim and me—" she elbowed Tim, "Being open with each other, and being brutally honest with God, is a foreign concept."

"Ow," Tim feigned, then saw the serious look on Elizabeth's face. "She's right," Tim agreed, straightening up.

Elizabeth continued. "Growing up, we were taught to keep quiet, and keep our business to ourselves. We learned that you don't show your ugly sides in public, especially not at church. We were *never* taught to pray like David did in this Psalm. And we *never* heard anything like this prayer modeled by any of the preachers or teachers in church. Right, Tim? Did you?"

"Never did. That's true," Tim concurred.

"So digging into this prayer and the benefits of honesty was really eye-opening for me. Also," Elizabeth turned to Zach. "Hearing Zach share his story of abuse was really touching, too. Especially because of what my daughter is going through.

"Zach and Caitlyn, I just want to thank you for taking Sondra under your wing and praying with her when she really needed that support. And thank you for letting your painful story become a blessing to others, sharing it in such a way that the healing you've found has been passed on to my daughter. It really means so much." Elizabeth's voice cracked over these last words.

Tim put his arm around Elizabeth, who still embraced Sondra. "I agree. I know it's not easy for us guys to share our soft sides, but I can see how the church really needs small groups like this to support each other. It would be great if every church offered some small group like this—whether it's a Bible study, prayer group, or discipleship group—where people could go when they are struggling with things like abuse, or divorce, or any of that hard stuff."

Tim cleared his throat. "Enough mush, though." He retracted his arm from Elizabeth. "What I really wanted to comment on with Psalm 109 was how David shows us that he is a work in progress. I think we need more church people to admit that they have problems, that they are not out of the woods yet, even though they are 'good Christians' serving at church. For me, this would be living with a bold faith. I like the permission not to be 'perfect.' I think we could attract more people to church, in fact, if we didn't appear so 'perfect.' Newcomers wouldn't be so intimidated if we just showed our warts a little more and tried to work through our problems together. I'm just saying," Tim shrugged.

Zach nodded. "I agree, Tim. I think you're spot-on. *Theology without community leaves people empty—and hungry for real healing and freedom—* because they don't have anyone to help them move from information to application in a way that offers transformation.

"The apostle Paul said that he loved the Thessalonians so much that he could not share the gospel story without sharing their lives, their own stories, because they had become so dear to him (1 Thess. 2:8)."

Tim nodded. "That's a good example of what I'm talking about."

Zach tapped his Bible. "And there are other examples we could find of Biblical community in here, beginning with Jesus inviting His disciples to live life and do ministry with Him."

Zach cleared his throat and shifted in his chair. "But my specific comment, in response to Psalm 109, is that I like how David is learning to depend on God more and more, and on himself less and less. This is a lesson we guys really need, because we want to be so independent. It's not natural for us to ask for help, or to admit that we can't do something in our own strength. But that's exactly what David does in this prayer. He admits that he is 'poor and needy,' and he needs God to help him.

"I'm still trying to learn this in my prayer life, but I keep practicing. And the more I admit that I can't do it on my own, and give my brokenness to God, the more I allow Him to work powerfully in my life."

"I agree," Caitlyn said. "Zach and I are *both* learning more about this. We've had some rough patches in our marriage, as you know, but the *best* times have been when we are both surrendering to God, trusting Him first to focus on our individual part in the problem, and then surrendering to each other and honestly admitting that we need help—from God, and from each other.

"So, what I take from this Psalm is a humble attitude. A humble attitude will get us far in our prayer lives, because then we are ready to hear what God has to say. And a humble attitude will help in our relationships, because it means we are thinking of others and not just ourselves." Caitlyn nodded to Gary to show that she was done.

"Thank you, Caitlyn, and all of you. Those are great takeaways." He looked around the circle once again. "Is there anything else? Sheila?"

Sheila smiled weakly. "It's been a great study. I've learned so much . . . everything everyone else said, and more. Zach and Sondra," she turned to face both of them. "Thank you so much for sharing your personal stories, especially how you have forgiven, or are starting to forgive, your 'enemies.'"

She shook her head. "Honestly, I'm not there yet. There is someone I am really struggling to forgive . . . " *And struggling to live with,* she thought. "My 'enemy' is still very much a part of my life." Her lower lip trembled. "And it's getting hard to deal with." *He didn't show up*, she thought. *And I prayed, in good faith, that God would have Jeff show up if He wanted me to stay with him.*

"We appreciate you sharing, Sheila," Elizabeth empathized. "God knows your heart and your pain, and He knows it takes time. And I'm sure the rest of us could all share about people we're still struggling to forgive."

Caitlyn nodded sympathetically.

"Yep," said Tim, with a quick nod of his head.

Sheila swallowed a lump in her throat and looked at Elizabeth. "I *want* to forgive my enemy, but I might need some distance to be able to do that." She looked down at her hands. *I guess maybe it's God's will that we separate. Then I can deal with my anger, and work at forgiveness . . . from a distance. But I cannot see how I can go on living with Jeff in an environment that's toxic for me and my son.*

Sheila shrugged, looking once more at the group. "While I'm still a work in progress, though, I'm really glad for David's focus on praise. I'm going to work on praising God more—focusing on God more—instead of on my hurt feelings and my enemy." She smiled and nodded at Gary to indicate she was done speaking.

"Thanks, Sheila," Gary said. "I appreciate the honesty, from everyone." He looked around the group gratefully.

"And now, our study is about done, so I can give you my last piece of advice, the one I always close my Psalm 109 studies with. Remember: when it comes to prayer, *honesty is the best policy.* Give God any and all of your anger, rage, hurt feelings, fears, worries, et cetera. He can handle it, and He will help you deal with it. That said, remember that Psalm 109 is a model for how to pray to *God*—not a model for how to talk to other *people.*" Gary raised his eyebrows.

"God is more forgiving than people are, so while you *should* be honest with others when they hurt you, DON'T blast them like David does. That is *not* a model for how to win in your relationships." Gary smiled and the group chuckled a little.

"Let's close with prayer, and then you'll be free to leave if you need to, or stay and chat if you want."

"Or eat some cookies." Elizabeth smiled and gestured to the full plate of cookies on the coffee table.

Gary nodded in thanks to Elizabeth, then bowed, and the rest of the group followed suit.

"God, Thank You again for this honest prayer from King David, showing us where to start when we are angry, or overwhelmed with any negative thoughts or feelings. May we continue to meditate on what we've learned and apply it to our lives and relationships—so we can move from anger (or any strong emotion), to our pain, to praise. Bless us now as we go from here, and thank You, for Your Son, Jesus, who makes all things possible. In Jesus' name, amen."

At those closing words, Sondra turned to chat with Zach and Caitlyn, while Sheila sank limply into her chair. *It's over. He didn't come.*

Elizabeth marked the look of defeat on Sheila's face, rose, and walked to the younger woman, who promptly, and blankly, looked up.

"He didn't come," Sheila simply said.

Elizabeth sank into the empty chair beside her. "I know, honey. I'm sorry."

"I guess this means we're separating." Sheila spoke the words numbly.

Elizabeth refrained from commenting, but rather focused on being present with Sheila in her pain. She had learned the lesson from parenting Sondra that too many words, too much advice, often went unheard and unappreciated when a person was in pain. As Sondra had said to her this last week, *When people are hurting, sometimes it's just best to shut up and listen.*

Sheila shook her head. "I mean, all I wanted, all I needed, was to see a little bit of effort on his part. Some indication that he wants to *try*." She grabbed a cookie from the coffee table and bit into it. "But in the last week, I've seen nothing," she said through a mouthful of cookie. "I guess he just doesn't care."

Elizabeth nodded with sympathy. "That's so frustrating." She took a cookie, too, and lifted it to her mouth, but then paused and lowered her hand. "Sheila, you said you haven't seen much of Jeff in the past week. I just wonder . . . " Elizabeth tilted her head. "Could it be possible—well, I'm just thinking of how Tim is, and how men generally are. Could it be possible that Jeff is not indifferent to your feelings, but he's just processing his *own* feelings—in his *own* way?"

Sheila frowned and Elizabeth continued. "I can't speak for Jeff, obviously, but it seems to me that you can't really speak for him either, until you've at least talked to him. It may be that he wants out of the marriage—but it may also be that he would be willing to work at it, if given an invitation to join you in growing together."

Elizabeth paused, then went on: "I've learned a lot from trials in my own marriage and The Empowered Wife,[18] a book that focuses on my life and what I can do, very similar to the 'deal with me' principle we've been studying about. It helps us to receive the sense of connection we want in positive ways and it is based on talking with wives who have been successfully married for at least fifteen years, with stories of marriages coming back from the brink of divorce. Including it with prayer could be a powerful combination."

Since Sheila said nothing, Elizabeth went on. "Forgive me for being so forward, but have you made Jeff feel welcome, and wanted, in your marriage lately? I'm not saying you haven't, I just know that men thrive on feeling needed and wanted, and we independent women can tend to forget that. We can also tend to be a bit proud. And our men tend to hear our words and assume we mean what we say, instead of understanding what we want them to hear and do. If I am angry or sad and tell Tim to leave me alone, he hears my words in a literal way, even though I want him to know I am hurt and I

---

[18] Elizabeth Doyle, *The Empowered Wife: Six Secrets for Attracting Your Husband's Time, Attention, and Affection* (Dallas, TX: Benbella Books, 2007).

want him to pursue me, to reassure me that I am important to him."

Sheila chewed her cookie and stared at Elizabeth, surprised at the pointedness of her remarks. *I should probably read that book,* she thought.

Elizabeth waved her hand and chuckled a little. "Oh, communication between a husband and wife can be so hard. But it can be so worth it," she said, looking over at Tim, who was happily chatting with their daughter and Zach and Caitlyn.

Sheila followed Elizabeth's gaze. She couldn't believe how at peace Sondra looked, given her recent history.

There is power in prayer, Sondra had said during her testimony. And *Honesty is the best policy*, Gary had said. But he meant when it came to talking to God, not necessarily with people. Blunt honesty, with unfiltered criticism, was NOT necessarily the best policy when talking to other people.

Now a few of Jeff's words came back to Sheila, from their fight after the first Bible study: *How about you, Sheila? I don't know if you've taken your negative thoughts and feelings to God, but you certainly bring your garbage to me. Maybe you should try talking to God first, Sheila, and get the heck off my back.*

Sheila shuddered. Jeff was right. Gary was right. And Elizabeth was right. Jeff had done his share of damage to their marriage with his silence and violence and unresolved anger, but so had she, with her nagging and criticizing and lack of affection.

She always said that Jeff didn't listen to *her*, but had she listened to *him*?

She always said she was starving for intimacy, but hadn't Jeff told her the same thing exactly one week ago? Why hadn't she listened?

Because I was blinded by my own pain, she thought. *Oh God, deal with me*, she prayed in her heart. She didn't really want her marriage to end. But was it too late?

Sheila looked up at Elizabeth. "So, you think I should go talk to Jeff?"

The older woman nodded. "Yes, I do. Talk to him one more time before you make any big decisions."

From a few feet away where he was gathering his belongings, Gary leaned over. "Excuse me, ladies, but I couldn't help but overhear your conversation." He scooted his chair closer and turned to face Sheila.

"Now, normally it wouldn't be any of my business, Sheila, but I have good reason to agree with Elizabeth. Go talk to Jeff."

Sheila stared at Gary. "But what if he doesn't want to see me? I'm so tired of fighting with him."

"Trust me," Gary said. "He wants to see you. And he's tired of fighting with you, too. And, to speak to what Elizabeth said, I'm pretty sure he wants to make the marriage work. He just needs the right invitation from you."

Sheila squinted and frowned. "How do you know?"

Gary just smiled.

Sheila cocked her head. "Have you . . . talked to him?"

"I might have."

Sheila froze. Something like hope caught in her chest.

"Have you . . . prayed with him?"

Gary's eyes twinkled. "Well, it's kind of like a doctor/patient relationship. I'm not supposed to disclose what was spoken about . . . or prayed about . . . during our appointment. But you can certainly pump Jeff for the details . . . when you talk to him."

Sheila sat back, breathless. Had Jeff sought out Gary like she had asked him to? Was it really possible her guarded, closed husband had opened up to this man who wanted to help, and was it possible Jeff had even requested prayer?

She grabbed her purse and stood. "Thank you, Gary. Thank you, Elizabeth, for all you've said to me tonight. But now I have to go. I have someone I need to talk to."

Chapter 23
Marriage on the Mend

Jeff and Sheila's Story

Jeff was bent over Sheila's Bible when he heard his office door creak open. "Sheila?"

"Hi Jeff." She closed the door behind her quietly. He, in turn, closed the Bible in front of him.

"Hey." Sheila did a double take. "Is that my Bible?"

"Oh." Jeff colored a little. "Yes, it is." He picked it up and held it out to her. She took it.

Jeff cleared his throat. "Yeah, I guess you left it at Bible study last week. Sondra brought it by when she was in the neighborhood. I meant to return it to you . . . "

"But we haven't really seen each other," Sheila finished.

Jeff nodded.

"Mind if I sit down?"

"Please."

She sat. Silence filled the office while they sized each other up. Then, at the same moment, both spoke:

"Sheila, I . . . "

"Jeff, did you..."

They laughed.

"You first," he said.

She inhaled. "First of all, I want to say sorry about our phone conversation last week. Giving you an ultimatum was premature of me. I realize I didn't give you a fair hearing. Please understand, when you told me about the pornography, I was angry, and I was hurt. I wondered why I wasn't good enough. So I responded rashly."

"Oh." Jeff was taken off guard. "I appreciate that. Thank you." He cleared his throat. "I need to apologize for a few things, too." He looked down and fiddled with some papers on his desk. "It's hard for me to admit that I am wrong—and even harder to ask for help. But I want to be clear with you." Jeff inhaled and met her eyes. "Looking at pornography was a sinful choice I made, instead of making healthy choices to work through our problems."

"Wow, Jeff. I'm just . . . astounded. I didn't expect to hear you say that."

Sheila held his gaze for a moment, then looked down at her Bible. "I appreciate you taking personal responsibility for your actions, and I have to do the same."

After a moment, she looked up. "I'm sorry for all the negativity I've brought to our marriage. I know I've criticized you a lot, and pushed you away, even when that's the last thing I wanted to do."

Sheila took a shuddery breath. "And I understand why you retreat from me like you do. It's because I'm not very pleasant to live with. I haven't listened to you, or affirmed you. Or the . . . you-know-what." She smiled lamely.

"Umm, I guess what I'm really here to say is . . . I didn't mean what I said. I *do* want to be married to you, and I want to work on what's broken." She forced herself to hold his gaze. "That includes the verbal side of our marriage, so that the physical side can also be included in a way that is meaningful."

Sheila inhaled. "Jeff, I think if we were sharing feelings with each other, really listening to each other, I would feel more connected to you and want more physical intimacy with you. So . . . I came to tell you I'm willing to work on my part, and I hope that you would be willing to work on yours."

Jeff sat frozen, hardly able to believe what he was hearing. It had been so long since Sheila had apologized. And this time, she really sounded sincere.

Sheila searched his face but couldn't read it. "I was hoping to tell you this at Bible study tonight, but I understand why you wouldn't want to be near me." She squirmed in her chair, as if preparing to leave.

"Sheila . . . " Jeff pleaded, and something in his voice made her pause. "I didn't come to Bible study because I thought *you* didn't want anything to do with *me*. And that's why I've kept out of your way this last week. Please stay, Sheila. We need to talk."

Sheila's breath caught in her throat. She froze where she was.

"Sheila, it's true, you drive me crazy sometimes, but I know I drive you crazy, too. We both have lots to work on. But you came here tonight, and I was praying you would come. I prayed that if we were supposed to stay together, you would call me, or come see me."

"Really?"

"Really."

Sheila leaned back in her chair, breathless. "Jeff, I was praying the same thing. Only I was praying you would come to Bible study."

"But I didn't come. So why did *you* come here?"

"Well," she shrugged. "Gary gave me reason to believe that you had met with him for prayer." She looked up shyly. "I just wanted to see that you were serious about working on our marriage. Knowing you had sought out Gary was good enough for me."

"Ahhh." Jeff leaned back. "You found me out. Yes, I went and had prayer with him a few days ago."

Sheila shook her head. "Amazing. God answered my prayer even before I prayed it."

Now she leaned forward. "I just have one question. What made you finally pray with Gary?"

"Well, a couple things. First, I guess it was our conversation last week, about the porn habit. That bothered me." He averted his eyes.

"What else?" Sheila pressed.

"When Sondra returned your Bible, she told me a little about her prayer sessions with Zach and Caitlyn, and I could really see a change in her. She seemed peaceful, despite her horrible situation with her ex. And I wanted the peace that she had."

"Oh," Sheila nodded. "I know what you're talking about. Sondra shared some of her testimony tonight, and I want that, too." She fidgeted with the zipper on her coat for a moment, then she looked up.

"Hey, Jeff, as long as we're getting things out on the table, I have one other question."

"Shoot."

"Um, I don't say this to nag you about the porn . . . but I'm just wondering: why were you looking at it on Ben's laptop?"

Jeff's head shot up. "What?"

Sheila put up her hands. "Hey, I'm not nagging you. I just want to protect Ben from accidentally seeing it. Don't you agree that you shouldn't look at it on Ben's laptop?"

Jeff tilted his head, a strange look on his face. "Of course I agree." He shook his head, an amused smile playing on his lips. "Sheila, I would *not* look at pornography on our teenage son's laptop."

"So it really *was* Ben!"

Jeff nodded. "I cannot tell that lie anymore. I can't have you thinking I'm *that* stupid."

They both laughed at the misunderstanding.

"Well, that's a relief," Sheila said. Then she furrowed her brow. "But also, it's not." She pressed her lips together. "Jeff, that means our son has a porn habit. What are we going to do about it?"

"Relax, I'm already handling it."

"What does that mean?"

Jeff put his hands behind his head and his feet up on the desk. "It means I'm handling it."

"Now, hold it right there, Officer," Sheila said sternly, but not unkindly.

"Jeff, I'd really appreciate if you would try not to be the Lone Ranger anymore. I'm not saying you're doing it wrong with Ben on this issue—in fact, I'm glad to let you handle this one."

She uncrossed her arms and softened her voice. "It's just that we're a team, and we should be talking to each other about this kind of stuff. I just want us to communicate more. Be open and honest with each other."

Jeff rocked back a little in his chair. "Fair enough. You're right. We should address these things together." He placed his feet back on the floor and slapped his hands on the desk, businesslike.

"So, I've already talked to Ben about it. Told him I was disappointed in him, and it was wrong, and it was disrespectful to women, and that I've struggled in the same area of life." He inclined his head to his wife as he said this. She nodded her approval. "And I told him I wouldn't tell you about it if he would stop, and . . . " Jeff grinned, leaning forward.

"What?" Sheila asked.

"And I made him clean the toilets in the police station last week, because I told him if he wanted to put his mind in the gutter, he might as well put his hands in, too, and at least be productive."

Sheila clapped her hands in glee. "Oh, that was perfect, Jeff!" She giggled. "What did Ben say to *that*?"

Jeff smiled. "Well, he rolled his eyes at the toilets, but after I told him that I had put a tap on his computer, and the whole police force could check his computer activity, he looked real scared and said, 'I got it, Dad. I won't do it again.'"

Sheila doubled over, laughing. "Oh, Jeff, that's priceless!"

Jeff practically glowed. It felt so good to finally do something *right* in his wife's eyes, and to be *told* about it.

"So, on a more serious note, Sheila, it actually bothered me a lot when you told me that our son was looking at porn. It was a wakeup call to me to pay more attention to my family and my own addiction. I figured I'd been neglecting Ben, and maybe if I were more involved, he wouldn't be looking at that trash. And . . . " he looked meaningfully at his wife. "As the week went on, I figured I had been neglecting you, too, and you had a right to be angry with me."

Sheila nodded. "Well, maybe I had a right to be angry. But I've learned that I also have a responsibility to let Jesus heal me and set me free."

She looked deeply into Jeff's eyes. He looked back.

He smiled. "I have that same responsibility." Jeff reached across the table and took her hand in his. "That's why I'm joining a men's group with Zach. And he recommended a book, 'Unwanted: *How Sexual Brokenness Reveals Our Way to Healing*.' It helps to reveal the problems and the Godly desires that have been highjacked by pornography. I don't want to just put band-aids on the problem anymore. I want to gain freedom in a way that will allow me to help other men . . . including my son. I know that it will take time to rebuild trust. I know there will be speed bumps in the journey. But that's a call of duty I want to answer."

Tears filled Sheila's eyes. *Praise You, God,* she prayed. *I didn't expect this in my wildest dreams. My husband is actually willing to seek You and make our marriage work. It's a chance Sondra is not getting, and a chance Jeff and I almost passed up. But thank You, God, for teaching us about brutal honesty just when we needed it. Thank You that each of us took the chance . . . and now You are healing us. Amen.*

A note to the reader:

Jeff and Sheila's story gives us a shortened view of a long-term process that is just beginning for them. It allows us to see individuals who are both learning to take responsibility for their part in the relationship, *without* blaming their spouse for his or her negative, sinful choices, anger, bitterness and addictions.

Please see pages 194 and 202 for a description of our: "Betrayal and Responsibility Packet"

King David's powerful prayer gives each of us, individually, a choice to:

❑ **Receive** God's invitation to trust *His faithfulness* to heal our wounded hearts, choosing:	❑ **Reject** God's invitation to trust *His faithfulness* to heal our wounded hearts, choosing:
To pray Psalm 109:21–22 *daily* **To** receive healing whether our offender chooses to change or not **To** avoid letting Satan build his 'foothold' of anger in our hearts	**To** not pray Psalm 109:21–22 *daily* **To** wait for our offender to receive healing or take responsibility first **To** avoid facing our pain/letting Satan build his 'foothold' of anger in our hearts

Please see Appendix A, page 202, to receive information on worksheets:

- Assessing your offender's willingness to take responsibility for the betrayal, abuse etc.
- Assessing the degree of Biblical or unbiblical counsel being received
- Assessing 2 key dangers in the process of healing and freedom for the person who was betrayed or abused

Your Turn: Review Psalm 109:26–31

[26] Help me, O Lord my God! Oh, save me according to Your mercy,
[27] That they may know that this *is* Your hand—*That* You, Lord, have done it!
[28] Let them curse, but You bless; when they arise, let them be ashamed, but let Your servant rejoice.
[29] Let my accusers be clothed with shame, and let them cover themselves with their own disgrace as with a mantle.
[30] I will greatly praise the Lord with my mouth; yes, I will praise Him among the multitude.
[31] For He shall stand at the right hand of the poor, to save *him* from those who condemn him.

AFTERWORD by Paul Coneff

I first started sharing Psalm 109 in 1990. Then I presented it at the National Association for Christian Recovery convention in 1992. Walking people through David's words in Psalm 109, in my office, time after time, has given them permission to be completely honest with God. For many, this is the first time in their lives that they have understood the truth that God is compassionate enough and strong enough to be trusted with their deepest wounds and darkest desires. Psalm 109 has also opened their eyes to the importance of sharing with God all their anger and pain. Whenever I pray with people who are angry, I share the same three principles:

1. What happened to you was wrong.
2. You have a right to be angry, hurt, fearful, etc.
3. You have a responsibility to choose to let Jesus heal your anger, fear, hurt, etc. - so it does not become an emotional cancer in your heart.

Principle number three is the one that makes the difference between those who receive healing and those who remain prisoners in their own hearts, their own minds, and their own lives.

Acknowledging Anger Is OK—As Long as We Take It to God

People can be as angry as they want—as long as they commit to telling God *after* they tell me. Otherwise their angry words go out of their mouths and into their ears, and they reinforce the negativity in their lives, without letting God begin the process of releasing it, step-by-step, over time, building anchors of hope along the way.

On the other hand, when we stop talking to God, Satan is only too happy to step in and offer a variety of other "solutions," ranging from denying our pain, to defending ourselves in our own strength, to turning against ourselves to avoid being vulnerable again (food, video games, pornography, work, self-righteousness/needing to be right and/or correct others etc.). But these

approaches sabotage our relationships. And when we push our loved ones away like this, blaming them and never looking at our part, we are left to live within a prison of fear, pain, anger, shame, and a pattern of broken relationships.

The Pricc We Pay When We Don't Talk to God

Here are a few examples of the price I pay (and the price others pay) if I turn away from God to lesser gods/idols to avoid facing my anger and pain:

Turning Against Others

- Believing negative thoughts such as: "I can never be safe," "I can never trust anyone with the negative parts of my life," "I will never be loved or protected"
- Blaming everyone else, leading me to push everyone away with my anger
- Putting myself in a prison of isolation and solitary confinement where I can never see or own my part in the patterns of my relationships (blaming, judging, shutting down emotionally, losing jobs, relationships, etc.)

Turning Against Myself

- Believing negative thoughts such as: "It was my fault," "I caused it"
- Blaming myself for the way I was abused or betrayed, instead of seeing the other person's responsibility in the damage that was done
- Trying to destroy something inside of myself like my tenderness, loyalty, faithfulness, and trust in others, in an effort to reinforce and repeat negative patterns, to avoid being vulnerable, etc.

My Passport to Freedom Depends on My Focus

At Straight 2 the Heart, we share Christ's suffering, death, and resurrection in a way that is personal and practical. Then we invite people to respond to the goodness of God (Rom. 2:4).

Some people choose to receive healing and freedom in Christ, while others choose to hang onto their patterns of self-protection, whether it is anger, worry, food, pornography, being critical, feeling sorry for themselves, blaming others, etc.

So, we invest time with those who are ready to receive freedom and victory in their lives. And we continue praying that God will ripen the hearts of those who are not yet ready to let go of their patterns of self-protection, addictions, false comforts, and false idols.

Our hope at Straight 2 the Heart is that each of us will read this story and ask God what He wants us to focus on, as we pray like King David: "God, deal with *me:* reveal *my* negative thoughts, *my* part in *my* pattern of relationships, and anything that would keep *me* from walking in Your freedom or living in community with *my* family and friends" (Psalm 109:21–22; 133:1; 139:23–24; 1 Thess. 2:8). As we pray this way, we hope to move from isolation and shame to the freedom described by Dr. John Townsend:

> Their flaws are like a sword hanging over their heads by a thread. They are terrified of inevitability. It's a foregone conclusion to them that at some point the thread will finally snap and their exposed weaknesses will heap shame, rejection and isolation from God and people upon their uncovered heads…
>
> The purpose of confession is to bring the unloved, hated, bad parts of ourselves into both the light of God's grace and the clear direction and instruction of His truth.
>
> It brings the parts that need forgiveness into relationship. The toxic nature of the badness is disinfected. Therefore, it can't contaminate the rest of us.
>
> ---
>
> [19] John Townsend, *Hiding From Love: How To Change the Withdrawal Patterns That Isolate and Imprison You* (Colorado Springs, CO, Navigators, 1991)

Avoiding the Physical Consequences of Anger

We also hope that by praying like King David, we can avoid or reverse the negative consequences of anger, bitterness, and unforgiveness, such as shortened lifespan, high blood pressure, rumination, diminished memory, and amplified negative emotions, to name a few (see chapters 12 and 22, as well as our end notes for more info on the physical consequences of anger).

My Freedom DOES NOT Depend on the Other Person Changing

The Bible does not guarantee that the people hurting us will change (for example, the people in David's life seem to continue lying about him). Zach's uncle and Sondra's ex-husband are examples of those who will not change, who will not speak the language of personal responsibility. At the same time, Jesus reveals how we can find healing by focusing on what He has done for us, whether or not our offenders or abusers change. In the ideal situation, both people will change and turn to God at the same time—they will seek help from others as they mend their relationship, finding peace with God and one another—as Jeff and Sheila begin doing at the end of this story. But in the end, our freedom *does not* depend on the offender changing, it depends on each us choosing to let God heal our hearts.

Honesty, Plus the Cross, Equals Healing

Whether we have been rejected, abused, or betrayed (etc.) by others, our own healing starts with honesty about our pain. The cross, with all of Christ's suffering, validates our painful experiences, allowing and inviting us to bring all of our negative thoughts and feelings to God. We can breathe a sigh of relief, because we don't have to pretend that the pain is not there, or that "every day with Jesus is better than the day before." We don't have to try and be more than who we are. We don't have to keep our pain, anger and negative thoughts inside of us.

Because Jesus suffered through His trials in Gethsemane and at Calvary, He can identify with David, and with all of us, through our suffering, He has earned the right:

- To win David's trust, and ours…*and*
- To heal David and set him free…*and*
- To heal us and set us free…*and*
- To heal those who have sinned against us and set them free *as* they choose to receive His gift of repentance
- To define us by what God has done *for us* instead of what was done to us

Why? Because God gave Jesus the power and strength and love to go through all of His suffering, betrayal, abuse, rejection and temptation for us, so we can trust God with our deepest wounds and darkest desires.

Please Note: If you are currently in an abusive situation or don't know if you are, please see Appendix A, "Getting Help for Abuse" on the next page.

—Paul Coneff, President of Straight 2 the Heart

Appendix A

Getting Help for Abuse

At times, the conflict in which you find yourself may require outside mediation. Please seek professional help when you need it and/or you don't know or understand:

- What an abusive relationship is – if someone is blaming you for his or her behaviors all the time and never taking responsibility for his or her part, making threats or using physical violence, abusing or stealing from elderly people…you are probably in an abusive, controlling relationships –
- What codependent behavior is– if someone has patterns of lying, stealing money, addictions like gambling, pornography, affairs etc. and you are not requiring that person to get help in ways that promotes long-lasting change… you are helping the person reinforce his or her negative patterns or behaviors (see Nancy Groom's book, *From Bondage to Bonding: Escaping Codependency, Embracing Biblical Love*, page 95 where she wrote: "If you are a codependent, you please other people because you believe that no one would choose to be with you unless you are serving them. You constantly feel you must earn their love, and you neglect your own needs because you do not feel that you are worthy enough to deserve to have your own needs met."
- What choices God wants you, yourself, to make, instead of trying to change the other person
- How to make healthy choices through the power of God's grace and truth
- How to receive support to follow through with healthy choices for long-term change
- How to trust in a healthy way and how to make sure that trust is earned after trust has been broken

Resources To Consider:

Domestic Violence Hotline: (800) 799–SAFE / (800) 799–7133
http://hopeandsafety.org/learn-more/the-cycle-of-domestic-violence/
Sandy's story in "The Hidden Half of Gospel: How His Suffering Can Heal Yours" (pp. 155–160)

Getting the Right Kind of Help

Sadly, not all "Christian" counselors, pastors, or church members give Biblical counsel when it comes to abuse or manipulation. Telling abuse victims to return to their abusive parents or partners to "just be more submissive and it will all work out" is NOT what Bible writers had in mind when they talked about submission.

Why Do Some Religious Leaders Protect Abusers?[19]

It is unfortunate but true that some religious leaders are more interested in protecting the reputation, power structure, and pocketbook of their churches than protecting their flocks. George Crabbe put it this way: "Deceivers are the most dangerous members of society. They trifle with the best affections of our nature, and violate the most sacred obligations." When pastors deceive, they indeed violate sacred obligations.

Playing politics with the safety of the children entrusted to their care, pastors and religious leaders end up sacrificing them on the altar of their own self-preservation (or church organization, avoiding conflict, protecting the system, etc.). At times, this can even include blaming the victims they are supposed to be protecting. According to Jesus, they will face the consequences for all their sinful decisions when they stand before His judgment seat. (Matt. 18:6–7; Ezek. 34:1–10; Jude 1:12).

Understanding Biblical Freedom and Submission

Biblical Freedom **does not** mean becoming a doormat or someone else's punching bag. Biblical freedom includes setting healthy boundaries in situations where there is lying; gambling; and/or physical, verbal, or mental abuse/manipulation.

Biblical freedom will lead you to give the other person choices to grow, to own his or her part, and to get the help he or she needs. If the person seeks help like Zach, Sondra, Jeff, and Sheila, praise the Lord.

---

[19] For a good resource on this topic, see the book Battered into Submission, which challenges the church to protect women and children from being victims.

On the other hand, if the person chooses to continue in his or her negative behavior (demanding, abusing, manipulating, blaming, etc.), then we apply **Ephesians 5:11**, which tells us to "take no part in the worthless deeds of evil and darkness; instead, *expose them*." Please note that **verse 11 comes *before* verse 21**, which tells us to "**submit to each other** in the fear of God." Verses 11 and 21 also come *before* verse 22, which tells wives to submit to their husbands, and husbands who are to love their wives "just as Christ loved the church and gave Himself for her."

Unless we are willing to submit to God first—which includes exposing evil doers and leaving their abusive deeds—then we are dishonoring Biblical "submission," we are *not* honoring it.

God Himself gives choices and then sets healthy boundaries when sinful choices are made, just as He did with one-third of the angels in heaven (Rev. 12:34), just as He did with Adam and Eve in Eden, just as He did with Israel and its kings, just as the king in Matthew 18 set a boundary with the wicked servant (Matt. 18:6, 32–34), and just as He does with us.

For those with a partner who is choosing to blame you for everything, instead of looking at his or her part in the patterns of his or her life, instead of speaking the language of personal responsibility, we also encourage you to seek a counselor or life coach who specializes in physical, mental, and/or emotional abuse/manipulation. This is especially true if the person moves from being the offender into the role of being or playing the victim when you name the problem. Godly freedom and forgiveness will never, ever, ever lead a person to become a doormat without choices. Instead:

- Godly freedom and forgiveness will include choices and healthy boundaries. (Matt. 18:6, 21-35; Eph. 5:11, 21–22)
- Godly freedom will make sure that trust is earned based on a consistent pattern of choices and behaviors, including owning his/her problem and getting support to face it and change over time, instead of the victim hoping against hope the person will become trustworthy and/or accepting a "quick-fix" approach and promises to change without investing in support to change. Trust is based *on* performance revealing change, *not on* a promise to change, especially when that promise reveals an unwillingness to receive support that promotes and reinforces healthy change.

Straight 2 the Heart's *top priority* is focused on having both people receive healing and freedom at every step of their individual journeys.

Unfortunately, counsel that by-passes the need for deep healing in the heart of the one who has been betrayed or abused does not work, because:

- Jesus said we need to "forgive from the heart" – and Christ-centered forgiveness is impossible apart from God's redemptive power (Matt. 18:35; 19:26)
- Jesus said that negative thoughts flow from our hearts (Matt. 15:18–19)
- King David cried out to God, "Deal with me – with my wounded heart." (Psalm 109:21–22), **trusting God's faithfulness** to him, instead of trying to trust someone who has betrayed him (Isaiah 49:15; 1 Thess. 5:23–24)
- God's Word tell us to "take every thought captive to the obedience of Christ," to avoid *increasing* our anger, fear and distrust that grows into bitterness (2 Cor. 10:5; Eph. 4:26–32)
- We *decrease* our ability to receive Godly discernment to set healthy boundaries or rebuild trust when we do not allow God to replace our anger, pain, fear and distrust with His supernatural peace (Luke 4:18; Phil. 4:7)
- It fails to address the need to offer redemptive responsibility, accountability and long-term change on the part of the person causing the harm

Please go to www.hiddenhalf.org/contact and request the **"Betrayal – Responsibility Packet"** if you would like worksheets assessing whether or not:

- You are receiving Biblically balanced, holistic counsel prioritizing God's redemptive power in your life
- You are willing to invest in the *process* of long-term growth in a way that focuses on God healing your own hearts in *every* phase of your journey
- The offender is willing to take responsibility for his or her choice to keep secrets, lie, betray trust etc.
- The one who has been betrayed is falling into one of the two key danger zones that makes his or her situation worse

Appendix B

Selected Resources on Forgiveness

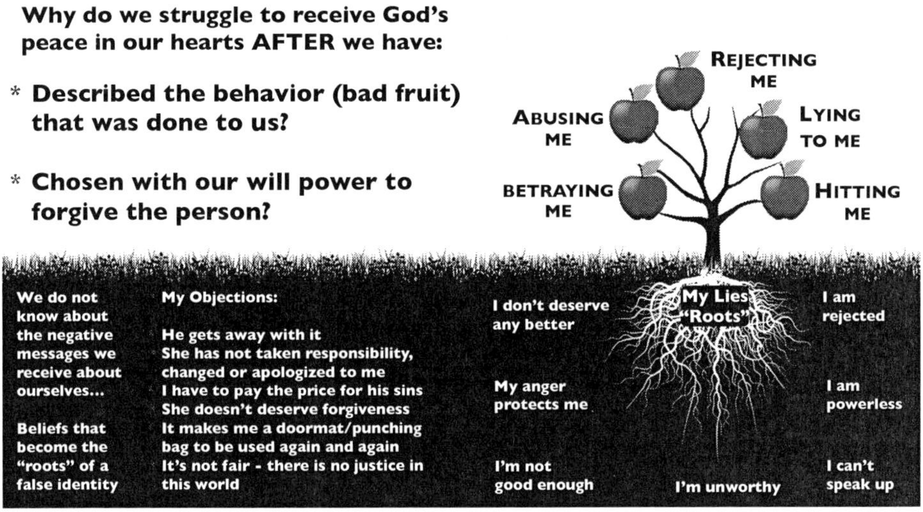

Why do we struggle to receive God's peace in our hearts AFTER we have:

* **Described the behavior (bad fruit) that was done to us?**

* **Chosen with our will power to forgive the person?**

REJECTING ME

ABUSING ME

LYING TO ME

BETRAYING ME

HITTING ME

We do not know about the negative messages we receive about ourselves...

Beliefs that become the "roots" of a false identity

My Objections:

He gets away with it
She has not taken responsibility, changed or apologized to me
I have to pay the price for his sins
She doesn't deserve forgiveness
It makes me a doormat/punching bag to be used again and again
It's not fair - there is no justice in this world

I don't deserve any better

My anger protects me

I'm not good enough

My Lies "Roots"

I'm unworthy

I am rejected

I am powerless

I can't speak up

The stupid neither forgive or forget;
the naïve forgive and forget;
the wise forgive but do not forget.
~ Thomas Szasz

Forgiving does not erase the bitter past.
A healed memory is not a deleted memory.
Instead, forgiving what we cannot forget
creates a new way to remember.
We change the memory of our past into a
hope for our future.
~ Lewis B. Smedes

He who is devoid of the power to forgive
is devoid of the power to love.
~ Dr. Martin Luther King, Jr.

What Does True Biblical Forgiveness Include?

Forgiveness includes admitting what was done TO me.

Forgiveness includes asking God what I have learned to believe about myself and the other person because of the way I was hurt, along with all of the losses I have experienced (physical, emotional, mental, financial, spiritual, relational, etc.).

Forgiveness includes asking God how I have learned to protect myself in my own strength, instead of trusting God—and asking Him to release me from my negative thoughts and patterns of self-protection, which are really patterns of self-sabotage.

Forgiveness includes receiving Jesus' words about forgiveness as He was hanging on the cross (Luke 23:34)—and asking God to forgive me for everything I did know and everything I did NOT know about my experiences (*including all the unknown, unplanned, and unintended consequences of my anger and pain*).

Forgiveness includes receiving Jesus' spirit of forgiveness for everything the person did and did not know about his or her sins against me, without minimizing or excusing the harm I have experienced.

A Sample Forgiveness Prayer, Based on Psalm 109*

Dear God, Thank You for not *minimizing, justifying, excusing or denying what was done* ***TO*** *You or to me.* Thank You for also revealing to me:

1. All the ways You have brought healing to my heart and/or all the ways You *want* to bring healing to my heart
2. All of my negative thoughts, feelings, and objections to forgiveness
3. All the losses and consequences I have experienced
4. All the ways my offender has hurt himself (or herself)
5. All the ways You have connected his (or her) story with Jesus' story, paying the price for his (or her) sins against me
6. Everything he (or she) did know and did not know about harming me or sinning against me.

In Jesus' name, Amen

*Please note: in this prayer, we have included the very specific words "not minimizing, justifying, excusing, or denying what was done" to make sure that forgiving others does not avoid, excuse, or minimize the way they have hurt you or sinned against you.

Note, also, that this prayer will not work if it is used as a "formula," or if you simply say the words in the prayer without personalizing them. For best results, we encourage you adapt this prayer with your own words and personal details, and enter into the process of discipleship. The more you personalize the prayer, the more meaningful, the more "real," it will become.

Selected Bibliography

Allender, Dan. *Leading with a Limp: Take Full Advantage of Your Most Powerful Weakness.* Colorado Springs: Waterbrook Press, 2008.

---. *The Healing Path: How Hurts in Your Past Can Lead You to a More Abundant Life.* Colorado Springs: Waterbrook Press, 1999.

---. *The Wounded Heart: Hope for Adult Victims of Childhood Sexual Abuse.* Colorado Springs: NavPress, 2008.

Card, Michael. *A Sacred Sorrow: Reaching Out to God in the Lost Language of Lament.* Colorado Springs: NavPress, 2005.

Coneff, Paul with Lindsey Gendke. *The Hidden Half of the Gospel: How His Suffering Can Heal Yours,* 3rd ed. Mill City Press, 2016.

Gendke, Lindsey. *Ending the Pain: A True Story of Overcoming Depression.* Pacific Press, 2016.

Levy, David. *Gray Matter: A Neurosurgeon Discovers the Power of Prayer . . . One Patient at a Time.* Tyndale, 2011.

Ortberg, John. *If You Want to Walk on Water, You Have to Get Out of the Boat.* Grand Rapids, MI: Zondervan, 2001.

Piper, John. *The Dangerous Duty of Delight.* Colorado Springs: Multnomah Books, 2001.

Stroble, Lee. *God's Outrageous Claims.* Grand Rapids, MI: Zondervan, 2005.

Tibbits, Dick with Steve Halliday. *Forgive to Live: How Forgiveness Can Save Your Life*, 2nd. ed. Altamonte Springs, Florida: Florida Hospital Publishing, 2016.

Townsend, John. *Hiding from Love: How to Change the Withdrawal Patterns that Isolate and Imprison You.* Colorado Springs: NavPress, 1991.

Discussion Questions

Roots of Anger *(see Chapter 1)*

1. Why do we choose to use anger to protect ourselves? How does anger make anything better? How does it make us *feel* better?
2. What's *good* about anger? Is there a good kind of anger and a bad kind of anger? Is there a type of anger that can actually, *legitimately*, protect us?
3. How do we know the difference between good and bad anger? And how do we heal from the bad kind of anger?
4. What do you tend to do with your anger: explode, stuff it, or something in between?

The Hidden Half of the Gospel *(see Chapter 2)*

1. What is meant by "The Hidden Half of the Gospel"?
2. In what ways did Jesus suffer throughout His life and ministry?
3. How can Jesus identify with *you*?

A Study on Psalm 109:1–16 *(see Chapter 4)*

1. Why is David asking God not to be silent?
2. If David loves these people, are they his friends, or are they his foes? And what difference does it make?
3. Would I want King David praying for me?
4. Does God want us to pray like King David does in Psalm 109 when we're angry – being completely honest with Him? Or does He want us to tell Him what we *think* He wants us to say?
5. If David's prayer is inspired by the Holy Spirit, what do I do with my anger?
6. David's words are not good. So what *is* good about his prayer? Why is it written in Scripture for us?
7. If David actually prayed this prayer, and if God thought it was worth showcasing in the Bible, what might that say about God's character?
8. When we're angry or hurting, why is honesty important?
9. Who is the perfect person to share our pain and anger with? Who understands like no one else can?

10. How can Jesus identify with David being lied about and betrayed in Psalm 109? Can He identify with the temptation to wish harm on others who have hurt Him?

Fruits, Roots, and the Suffering Messiah *(see chapter 8)*

1. How would you explain the fruit/root principle?
2. Is anger "fruit" or a "root?" How do you know the difference?
3. Where do our negative beliefs come from? (See John 8:44; Matt. 15:18–19)
4. Where is anger showing up in your life? Who are you angry at (God, yourself, others)?
5. Where was Jesus tempted with the same kinds of thoughts you have, that have grown out of your feelings of anger? Where has Jesus been tempted with your negative experiences?
6. How did Jesus respond to His temptations?

A Study on Psalm 109:17-25 *(see chapters 9-13)*

1. Where is anger showing up in my life? Who am I angry at (God, myself, others)?
2. Is anger a way to protect myself from feeling my pain (or fear, worry, powerlessness, hopelessness, weakness, vulnerability, etc.)?
3. Where is the transition text, where David's focus begins to move away from the man and how he wants the man and the man's family to suffer? What makes the focus of this verse so, so different from the first part of David's prayer?
4. Reread Psalm 109:22. Where is the source of David's pain?
5. What part of David's anatomy is being referred to here? And what is important in David's description of it?
6. What are the objections we have to dealing with our part and forgiving when the other person is at fault and seems to be moving on with life?
7. How can we forgive someone when they keep repeating the same offense over and over again? (see Eph. 4:26)
8. If we don't forgive, what price do we pay? In other words, what is our anger doing to me and my health? How is anger impacting my relationships with my spouse, children, or others? How is my anger impacting my relationship with God, and my ability to witness for Him, be in ministry for Him?

9. What difference does it make to know that "turning everything over to God" includes being honest about:
   - Our objetions to forgiving the person
   - Our negative thoughts and feelings about the other person
   - Our negative thoughts and feelings about ourselves—and the way they have hurt others close to us (like Zach's anger and pornography hurting his wife, Caitlyn)?
10. How does it help us to know that:
   - Jesus did nothing in His own strength
   - Jesus said that we can do nothing in our own strength
   - We are to "forgive as Jesus forgave" (Col. 3:13)
   - We can receive His love, His forgiveness, and His victory over all of our objections, fears, and negative thoughts—instead of trying harder to do what we are already unable to do?

A Study on Psalm 109:26–31 *(see chapter 18)*

1. Who is David trusting in here: God or himself?
2. What specific language does David use in these verses to tell us he is not trusting in self-help? How do we know he is not just trying harder to do what he is already unable to do?
3. In the last few verses of Psalm 109, how is David's approach to handling his pain different from the world's approach?
4. In the final verses of Psalm 109, how do we know David is not entirely out of the woods yet?
5. What does David want for his enemy in verses 28 and 29, in contrast to what he wanted for him in verses 5–16?
6. Does it seem like David has forgiven his enemy yet?
7. What is David doing by the end of Psalm 109, and why?
8. David says God has helped him. But what kind of help?
9. Does our freedom from anger, anxiety, depression, etc., depend on the behavior of others?

A Study on Jesus and Forgiveness *(see chapter 19)*

1. What did Jesus say about forgiveness?
2. Was Jesus ever tempted not to forgive His abusers? And what did He do? Who was His source of strength and love?

3. What did Jesus mean when He said His abusers "know not what they do"?
4. In the moment of a sin, do people know, or consider, all the effects of their actions—including effects that will take place 10, 20, 30, 100, or 1,000 years from now?
5. Is there a situation in your life where some sin was committed, by yourself or others, and the effects of it went way beyond what you, or the sinner, ever imagined?
6. Has someone ever sinned against you, in a big or small way, and it led to your suffering—but is it possible that they *don't know* the extent of what they did to you? Are they still accountable to God?

Reacting to Psalm 109 *(see chapter 20)*

1. Where do you tend to share your negative thoughts and feelings, if you share them at all? How might your answer be affecting your relationships with God and others?
2. Do you feel like your current church (if you have one) provides a safe place to share your deepest wounds and darkest desires? Or do you feel like, at church, you are not supposed to "show your warts," so to speak?
3. What objections do you have to dealing with your part and forgiving when the other person is at fault and seems to be moving on with life?
4. Zach says, in this chapter, that theology without community leaves people empty, and hungry for real healing and freedom. Do you agree? What has been your experience with "theology and community" in your local church?
5. Do you feel that praise comes easily to you in your prayer life, or is it something you need to work on? How could you make praise a habit in your life?

About the Authors

Paul Coneff is the founder and director of Straight 2 the Heart, a nonprofit prayer and discipleship ministry that provides training on how to move from brokenness to freedom. A licensed marriage and family therapist, Coneff has more than twenty-five years of experience in pastoral ministry and has spent more than fifteen thousand hours counseling and training in many countries. For more information on his ministry, or to check out his first book, co-written with Lindsey Gendke, *The Hidden Half of the Gospel: How His Suffering Can Heal Yours,* visit www.hiddenhalf.org.

Lindsey Gendke is a wife, mother, writer, and teacher who loves sharing what God has done for her and encourages others to do the same. In addition to publishing her testimony of overcoming depression, *Ending the Pain: A True Story of Overcoming Depression*, Lindsey has shared her story at various women's retreats and on television. A former high school teacher, Lindsey holds bachelor's and master's degrees in English and cowrote *The Hidden Half of the Gospel* with Paul Coneff. Currently Lindsey stays busy teaching college students, parenting her two little boys, pursuing her doctorate, and blogging when she can find a spare moment. Connect with Lindsey on her Facebook Writer Page or read her ongoing story at www.lindseygendke.com.

About Steve Siler

Steve Siler wrote the foreword. He is the founder and director of Music for the Soul, a multi-award-winning ministry using songs and stories to bring the healing and hope of Christ to people struggling with life's most painful issues. An accomplished songwriter and music producer, Siler has had over 500 of his songs recorded in the Christian, pop, and country markets. Siler is also the author of two books, *The Praise & Worship Devotional* and *Music for the Soul, Healing for the Heart: Lessons from a Life in Song.* For more information, visit www.musicforthesoul.org.